HER TURNING POINT:
Her Divine, Glorious, Happy Divorce

Loosely based on a true story!

Nelly Cotto

Publishing Details:

Title: Her Turning Point: Her Divine, Glorious, Happy Divorce!

Author: Nelly Cotto

Estimated Publication Date: November 2014 - January 2015

Copyright: November 2013

ISBN# ISBN-10:099601750X

ISBN-13:978-0-9960175-0-3

First Run Will Be in E-Book and Softcover

Prices: Softcover - $15.99
        EBook - $11.99

Publisher: Her LifeZest Institute
                  456 San Benito Avenue
                  Los Gatos, CA 95030
                  (650) 492-3702

"Love is what we were born with. Fear is what we have learned here."

Marianne Williamson, Author and Spiritual Teacher

"We shall not cease from exploration, and the end of all our exploring will be to arrive where we started and know the place for the first time."

TS Elliott

For Kelly

I refer to you as the Angel who dared to venture deep into the depths of hell to save me. I may never eradicate the smell of smoke, but at least I'm no longer burning.

Prologue

I should be dead by now. I certainly had arrived at that particular doorstep. But then I got saved. Then I got saved again and again. Then divorce came. Then I woke up.

I am still smiling today, all these years later. And I'll admit, it's easy for me to smile now that I'm free from the crippling clutches of a horrific marriage. I'm divorced now, and oh so happy—so gloriously happy. I have plenty of divorced girlfriends who can't seem to find a solid wisp of ground to step on, so I especially feel lucky when I catch myself smiling and smiling. And I must add here: I now get that my divorce was unlike most others. Considering the awfulness of my marriage, divorce was a breeze, practically pain-free.

I liken my divorce to the woman who gives birth to a nine-pound baby after ten grueling hours of labor. Afterwards, she can't understand what all the birthing brouhaha had been about, nor can she recall the whole dreadful affair—only the miracle of it all.

Wait, what do you mean by "was it difficult?" Oh, no, no, I loved the whole experience including the delivery. My baby was a darling from day one!

That was my divorce.

What do you mean by "was it bitter?" Explain "vicious"... Huh, "vindictive"? How exactly? Oh, I see. Oh no, not mine. My divorce was a breeze; easier than going from first to second grade.

My divorce was so easy that I became a self-proclaimed ambassador of divorce, floating higher and higher into the realm of impossibility. I was determined to straighten out the world, starting with the topic of divorce, and most definitely starting with women. One day I excitedly shared with my therapist my intention to write about my happy life after divorce. I told her all about my plan to teach divorcing women how to experience an easy friendly divorce and how to live a happy life ever after. I was practically bouncing talking to her.

Then, in her usual quiet soft way, my therapist nodded and said, *"Yeah, and don't forget to go back to the beginning and take a close look at all the pieces that led to the final divorce. You might find it wasn't one big, happy event. Make sure you assemble the whole story."*

That was when it hit me. My life that I now refer to as "my divine, glorious, happy life" was once hell—the real deal with dragon-breath fire, scorching heat and agonizing torture. I was so deeply grounded in a happy divorced life that I had very cleverly blocked out my painful experience pre-divorce; and certainly pre-marriage. It seemed that as soon as I allowed myself to think about the hell, the memories immediately gushed out of hiding.

The first memory was what my ex-husband, Harry Fielding, had said when I first told him I wanted a divorce. *"Ha! You're fucked! How are you going to support yourself when you haven't worked in twelve years!"*

Oh yeah, this was the sort of thing my therapist meant. But then a few short weeks later older memories began arising—dating from well before my marriage to Harry Fielding—some as early as floating in my mother's womb. These memories from my near fifty-year life bobbed in my consciousness no longer restrained in any way whatsoever. I then found myself day after day, week after week sifting through the entirety of what contributed to arriving at death's door again and again. That day my therapist pointed out the obvious, I had no clue she was referring to my entire life. And like the woman whose birthing experience was supposedly, brilliantly pain-free, I'd left out the weeks and months of unrelenting morning sickness, sleepless nights and unsightly swollen ankles. When I finally realized the improbability of experiencing a divine, glorious, happy divorce without the hell, I understood what my therapist had hinted at. Only after the pain can one experience the full extent of appreciation for the relief, or the joy, or the freedom.

I'll get to how I ended up with a divine, glorious, happy ~~divorce~~ *life* because that is what I enjoy today. But first, let me layout the many preceding decades of hell…starting from the beginning.

Part One

Her Beginning

ONE

My name is Isabel Gomez. I'm one of twelve kids—five boys and seven girls. Our names are, from the oldest to youngest: Sandalio, Celestina, Teresa, Pedro, Maribel, Lourdes, Lupe, Isabel, Sarita, Juan, Pablo and Manuel. The names of the oldest four were chosen by my paternal grandmother (which explains why Sandalio, our oldest, carries our paternal grandfather's name). Later, when my parents arrived in the United States, my aunt, who had moved to the U.S. before my parents, chose the next five names. After my aunt remarried and moved back to our home country with her two daughters and new husband, my mother named the last three siblings. I'd like to tell you that our names represent sacred saints. But not one saint lives among us.

I'm sibling number eight. Being born so far from either end of the youngest or oldest spectrum afforded me an inordinate amount of indifference from just about everyone. But I was born incredibly wise—which was how I could figure things out at a very young age, and which was why it didn't take me long to figure out that being cursed and missing blessings altogether wasn't anyone's fault. It was fate. What was anyone supposed to do about that?

It was my great wisdom that led me to become invisible. Before I could speak one word, I instinctively understood how shrinking myself down to the tiniest speck of dust could keep me safe from the impending danger that seemed to linger wherever I roamed. You may feel compelled to label this ability as a "blessing," but I figured that having to escape as a way of making it from one day to the next was indeed a curse. For some unearthly and inexplicable reason, the natural evolution of man had skipped me entirely leaving me stuck in the Stone Age, running and fighting for survival—starting from day one on earth. This was why invisibility became a part of me before my clever feet could maneuver my tiny frail body about. It became the part of me that got me through the days.

By the time I could talk, I already understood that if I wanted attention I would have to become sickly. Or, I would have to miraculously generate gobs of money as a mere toddler. Looking back, I recognize my knack for enterprise at an unlikely early age. But as a toddler, being sickly or rich weren't options for me, even though I kept keen eyes open for any prospects. Instead, "most ugly" was what I ended up with, which was fine with me.

Folks never figured that their dumbfounded stares at my over-sized mouth that was chock full of misarranged teeth registered with me, perhaps because I grew increasingly blurred before their blinking eyes—which must have been why they would shake their heads so hard. I remember one time when I was around eleven or twelve years old, a few of us girls along with a couple of family friends were hanging out in my family's kitchen. One friend, Maria, blurted out in Spanish, *"Isabel's the ugliest of you girls."* I figured no one could see I was standing right there, because the conversation progressed from her assertion to everyone's agreement, and then to my sister Lupe securing the "prettiest" title—or was it Lourdes? I can't recall since I seemed to have vanished, and I was suddenly sitting crisscrossed on the picnic table in our backyard where my brother Pedro sat. My brother Pedro was the number four sibling, and he had been my ally from the moment I was born. He was also one of the few who could always see me.

"What's bothering you?" Pedro asked me.

"They all just voted me ugliest," and I started to mope about it, but my brother didn't care for that nonsense.

"What? Who did?"

"The girls, and Maria and Evelyn."

"And you believed them? Are you kidding me? Listen, don't tell them I told you this secret, but they're just jealous because they know you're the prettiest. Of course they're going to say that when they're so jealous."

Pedro then smiled and waited for me to give him a sign that I had shifted to his way of thinking. But I was already wise beyond my years and I knew exactly what my brother was doing. I rolled my eyes at him and refused to play along. There was no doubt in my mind that I was born "ugliest" and that this status was with me for good. I'd say it felt fine one minute and awful the next.

Like the time in 8th grade when my brilliant teacher, Mr. Moran (Moron!), decided that holding up everyone's individual school photo in front of a bunch of pernicious, hormone-crazed thirteen-year-olds was a good thing. There was, as you would expect, an inordinate amount of laughter and jeering. The decibel level in that classroom had increased by hundreds possibly thousands, rendering Mr. Moran powerless in the midst of sheer chaos. That was, until he presented my photo. The instant my face was in full view for all to ravage, the laughter, the jeering, the commotion ceased completely. To go from ear-splitting pandemonium to absolute quiet in one infinitesimal speck of time was one of the most jolting moments of my relatively brief and somewhat uneventful life. We all seemed to stop breathing and the room rapidly grew void of air. I thought I would faint. I willed myself to disappear like I so often could do, but all the side glances told me everyone could still see me. I looked to the door, measuring if the distance was close enough for me to make an undetected escape. But then finally, finally our venerable class clown piped up and said, *"God, she looks like a frog!"* And with those blessed words the jeering and laughing immediately returned to its pre-Isabel photo level, and all was back to normal. I was saved! I could breathe again.

But it wasn't just being "most ugly" that deeply informed my psyche. Coming from a poor family and always being the kid wearing "cheapers" and ill-fitting, worn-out hand-me-downs, nor ever having the "cool" foods for lunch, clearly conveyed my family's economic status. This combination, which I later learned precipitated so much that went wrong in my life, served to force my head down and hunch my shoulders. It didn't help that especially throughout my pre- and teenage years, I rarely thought it was necessary to groom myself beyond bathing once or twice a week. This made my greased-down hair and smelly armpits even more prominent features than my unruly teeth and rumpled clothes. I figured since no one could really see me, what did it matter? And even though I eventually figured out that others could see me, I was certain I remained undetectable at home.

Part One: Her Beginning

Growing up, my family of fourteen lived in a 1,200 square-foot apartment with six bedrooms. My parents had one room, my two oldest sisters each had their own room, my two oldest brothers shared a fourth room, and my three youngest brothers shared a fifth, which left the sixth and second-smallest room to the remaining five girls. I got to sleep in that tiny room on a twin-sized bed with my sister, Sarita, the youngest of all seven girls (and who, until she was about twenty years old, we used to call "Coochie," because in the first days I began talking, it was what I had started calling her)—spooning left to right, right to left all night year after year. Sarita not only could see me just fine, but she could read my mind. She'd get right in my face and say, *"What was that you said?"* And I would stare at her and use my brain to answer her.

My family was too poor and too large to rent a regular apartment in a regular house. So we lived in subsidized housing in the projects. Our city of Bridgeport in Connecticut was peppered with these housing projects. The one my family lived in was named Father Panik Village. It was far from resembling any village, especially any of the ones my parents left behind in Puerto Rico where palm trees, rolling green hills and rich vegetation abounded. Father Panik Village was a swath of concrete with 50 three-story brick and concrete buildings set in perfectly aligned rows. They resembled the interior of a prison, where, in cell after cell, misery-festered broken souls resided.

A family our size didn't phase my parents even a tiny bit, because for us Puerto Rican Catholics, putting food on the table was what really mattered—not school, not friends, not an army of kids, not most anything. My mom would go about her daily chores measuring, then doling out twelve of everything whether it was our meals, chores, clothes or her famous deep red spankings. She did a great job making sure she got the job done and it was left up to us kids to figure out how to either get in on the other side of a good thing or run and hide from a devastating one. Often, she'd call out a good seven or eight of us before she settled on the one she had originally meant to call. I imagined her not only getting our names all jumbled up in her head, but our features and characteristics as well. She must have seen bits of each of us in all her kids.

Most days, my dad was off working at the local factory, and then living a rather carefree life afterwards, drinking and having a jolly time with his friends. He didn't seem to understand that all that money spent on his friends, alcohol and his love for fishing would have better served his family at the home he did a great job avoiding—the place where a butt-load of kids and an exhausted and resentful mom struggled.

Thank goodness for St. Mary's, our local parish. They took it upon themselves to provide for our enormous family. We were St. Mary's single charity. They said we were underprivileged, which meant we were too poor to pay for some essentials, and which was why we didn't have to pay very much to attend their school. And which was also why we got first dibs at some pretty cool perks. Like the summer of 1969, when for two whole weeks I was selected to live with a family of rich white folks—the Utkins! That year St. Mary's had decided to participate in the newly introduced 'Adopt-A-Family' program where a wealthy family from the nearby suburbs brought an underprivileged child into their home. It meant that someone like me could experience a different way of life, one that could conjure up warm, fuzzy memories later on. The folks who designed this program had figured that this kind of influence could turn things around for the child starting at an early age—maybe even sprinkling a bit of that fairy dust onto the rest of the family. I was the lucky one chosen in our school for this fine experiment of economics.

It had all started out really grand…

TWO

It was 2:30pm with only fifteen minutes left until the end of the school year. June 20, 1969. I was antsy and couldn't sit still anymore. I risked making eye contact with my fellow students. Were they with me? I couldn't meet anyone's gaze, but I could tell they felt the same. The build-up to these last fifteen minutes had been momentous. It was great, pure greatness—riding, riding, riding higher with anticipation. It was the last day, the end of the school year. It was the end. THE END.

Then it happened. It was unexpected; a surprise really.

Isabel, please come up to my desk.

Huh? Was I in a Charlie Brown cartoon? I mean, was it just me, or was Sister Eileen speaking that indecipherable language *"Whah, whuh, wheh, whauh…?"* I looked to the front of the room where she sat behind her desk. She was writing with her head still down. I couldn't be sure if in fact she had spoken. Or was it the open air readying itself for my final departure? I looked around again at the other kids for a clue, something, anything. I bet they knew this was coming. It was there in their demeanor. Their fidgeting was meant to conceal another outcome to the end of this day. They knew something—one last cruel joke. I felt it. I looked around some more before I heard my name called out a second time.

"Isabel?"

Now everyone's eyes were on me, including Sister Eileen's. I couldn't believe it was I being called to the front, especially since on this last day Wilfredo, our insufferable class clown, clearly had been the problem. He'd been catapulting paper bombs onto nearby desks, and then during recess he taunted us girls and spiked up the skirt of our uniforms. How could she have missed that? Really, that woman needed to pay better attention. *Look at him, smirking at me. How could she possibly have overlooked our class nuisance? I ought to whack him. I ought to just whack that smirk right off him! Why me, oh, why me? This could ruin everything. This couldn't be happening to me.*

Dear Lord Jesus, please make this one a quick one, please. I'll promise not to swear once all summer. I promise! I promise! I started praying in my head as I got up from my chair.

I walked toward Sister Eileen. My seat was near the front of the class, but not so much so that I was easily called upon to answer questions whenever Sister Eileen felt it necessary. I had my last name to thank for that, even though it was responsible for placing me still too close to the blackboard. It was also responsible for some of the talk that went on behind my back. I started dreading the inevitable delay this interruption would cause. I had spent all day preparing, setting the tone in my mind for the final burst through the threshold that had possessed my thoughts for exactly one hundred ninety-three days. *Why me, oh, why me? I did nothing wrong, I swear, it wasn't me!*

I finally reached Sister Eileen's desk and I stood quietly, waiting for her to look up from her writing. I felt my chest constrict as the clock moved closer to that last moment. I needed to get this thing moving; what was this woman thinking? Had she no clue? I figured this would end badly if I didn't take some action so I coughed. Sister Eileen slowly looked up from her work and seemed to just realize that she had called me. She fussed with her papers a bit, then folded her hands over them and beamed her sweet smile at me.

She said, *"Isabel, you have been chosen to participate in an 'Adopt a Family' program this summer. You will spend two weeks with a family in Trumbull."*

Now I was sure she was the teacher in a Charlie Brown cartoon. What did she say? I leaned down low and offered her my ear. She repeated herself, then smiled. I suppressed my reaction. To be honest, I wasn't sure what this news meant. There wasn't time for questions, for figuring things out. I needed to get back to my seat. This wasn't the right moment for this news. It could really mess things up. Why couldn't she see that more important things were in place—had been all day? I needed to get back to my seat. It was where I wanted to be. It was where I needed to be.

"Okay," I whispered then turned and raced back to my seat before Sister Eileen could elaborate. I sat down quickly in anticipation for my leap into tomorrow, and the next day, and the next.

I knew the final moments of school had arrived because my classmates were now shifting around, openly and blatantly. I joined in. This glorious moment belonged to us. Not even Sister Eileen could harness our excitement. She didn't bother trying. We all rose at exactly 2:45 in unison, laughing, laughing, and laughing. We moved in record speed toward that final door—that opening that all day had taunted us with endless possibilities. We ran and skipped and hopped and bounced and hooted and finally made our last hurrah out into our fanciful world of jubilee. I ran and ran. I didn't offer my classmates any "see-you-laters" or "good-byes." I didn't bother stopping or looking back. I ran all the way home with no one by my side because it was still a time when I wouldn't have to think about coming home alone—before everything had changed. I was sure I beat everyone. I could run faster than most boys my age, and if anyone had stopped to watch the whole gang of us racing, they would have had a hard time picking out the only girl easily making her way to the finish line first. I sprinted through our building's door, #43, and up the last stretch to the second floor. I stopped for the first time outside our apartment door, breathless. I was bent forward with my head down. I straightened up and looked around me, and then walked through our apartment door, #203.

I raced through the living room and into the kitchen; all one room really. It was empty. I sprinted to my parent's bedroom. My mother was asleep. I ran back out into the living room. I was definitely first. That was when I realized it. The moment of truth swiftly propelled itself and smacked me hard and all the excitement of the day crumbled to bits and made its way to the soles of my feet: I had raced home to nothing. Nothing was waiting for me here. I looked around one more time. I was surrounded by nothing, absolute nothingness. This was worse than all the hoopla leading up to the Easter Bunny and the preparations and the anticipation—and in the end there was nothing, no Easter Bunny, no surprise appearance, no nothing.

Early that Easter morning, my older sisters had dressed me up to look exactly like Sarita. Our youngest girl who was only one year younger than me was downright darling. That morning I made dressing me a real chore as soon as I saw two sets of the same outfit being ironed and laid out. I thought if I gave my older sisters a hard time, they would be on their way to recognizing their mistake. I hoped they would wake up and see that I wasn't Sarita. I was the ugly one. I was still gangly at age nine, resembling a boy more than a girl; not even my blondish curls helped that situation. I figured my fussing would help them realize that the narrow long face with features too large, and with a smile so chock-full of misarranged teeth (the same one that often caused them and others to do a double-take), would look ridiculous wearing the same outfit as the family's irresistible baby girl. But my older sisters worked around my fussiness and got the damn outfit on me after all.

Right from the start on that Easter Sunday, absolutely everyone doted on Sarita and looked right through me. I was used to this, but for some reason on that Sunday, I was bothered by the blatant disregard. It hung on me like an overbearing curse and not the gift it often got to be.

The first incident happened after we dressed in our twin outfits. Sarita and I walked into the living room where everyone was waiting ready to leave for Sunday mass. My oldest brother, Sandalio, walked over to us and scooped up Sarita and carried her all the way to church. She and I had been holding hands. Then after mass, the women came up to us both as we held hands, and it was Sarita they bent down really low to squeeze and pinch. Each time she got pawed at, I would squeeze her hand so hard she'd scream and yell something at me. You'd think those plump colorful ladies would then notice me, but no, they merely doted some more on my irresistible sister. That was how things usually worked with Sarita and me, and that sort of thing continued throughout that day. But this lopsided attention wasn't the worst of it.

I had waited and waited for the damn Easter Bunny, and instead only the usual family friends showed up. When I finally asked my sister Teresa, my second-oldest sister, when the Easter Bunny was arriving, she laughed and told me an Easter Bunny wasn't coming.

"Really Isabel, where do you get such silly notions?" she had said.

That was another thing that often happened to me. I would get accused of making things up. I wanted to whack her. I wanted to remind her that she, more than anyone else, had promised me an Easter Bunny. It turned out Easter was about Jesus; it had nothing to do with me, and had absolutely nothing to do with the giant Easter Bunny who everyone had raved about for weeks—the one who supposedly delivered oodles of chocolate. All was not lost, though, because everyone who stopped by did bring us candies of all flavors, shapes and sizes. They brought enough to fill our largest cooking pot, the one that stood well above my knees.

One other good thing about that day; my dad stuck around and my parents got along and were openly in a really good mood, which was rare. I wasn't used to so much joviality from those two, so I kept looking over to make sure they were all right. They both maintained such high spirits all day, especially my mother. She had smoked and smoked and coughed and laughed and pretty much had herself a super time.

But today—when school was officially over, and after I'd raced home more than ready to blaze into my summer vacation—my mother was asleep and I was alone, waiting, expecting. *Expecting what?* I finally asked myself. Greatness, that's what. But greatness wasn't coming. I realized greatness wasn't going to be a part of my life that summer. Instead, I could expect nothing. The truth was I was home for the whole summer with nothing to look forward to. What was so great about that? Why hadn't I made any plans before I took off on everyone? This was definitely worse than the Easter Bunny. I recalled again Teresa's repeated pleas before the Easter Bunny's impending arrival: *"You better get to bed or the Easter Bunny won't come tomorrow."* And, *"Stop fussing and let me get you dressed because the Easter Bunny will be here soon."* I still dreamed about the anticipation that had danced around in my head for days and days before that disastrous Easter.

Then came the rush. The apartment door opened and closed, opened and closed, and all the while I didn't move from where I stood in the middle of our living room as the worst part hit me. I was home for the summer with nothing to do and with all of them, and this wasn't the half of them. It soon got too loud for me. I walked slowly to the girls' bedroom, but then that room got too crowded.

It wasn't until the next day that I remembered. I was folding our entire family's weekly wash along with four of my sisters in our tiny bedroom, which only had one full- and one twin-sized bed, no dressers or anything else. I remembered what Sister Eileen had told me right before I bolted from school, leaving my entire class in the dust to rush to…nothing. Sister Eileen had said I was going to Trumbull, which was one of the nearby suburbs. Only rich white people lived there.

I stopped folding—risking a fight because abandoning a task before it was completed normally started one—and went to my mother who stood over the kitchen sink preparing lunch. I asked her if it was true that I was going away to live with a family in the suburbs. She said yes. I asked when. She said I would be picked up July 10th. And so that was it. In less than three weeks, I would be living with strangers. Doing what? I wondered. And why did I have to go? I walked back to the girls' bedroom and waited just outside the doorway, watching my sisters fold the massive pile of clothes that was seemingly growing by the minute. As I watched them work their way through the endless pile, I knew instinctively I would be folding the strangers' clothes as well. There wasn't going to be greatness in my future for sure.

The days before July 10th crawled at an incredibly slow pace. That morning I woke up hours earlier than usual after falling asleep hours later than usual, and I felt exhausted. I stayed in bed feeling too tired to move. It was Sarita's fault. Last night she popped my bubble, which made me doubt things, which made me stay awake too long, and which made me awake too early.

Two weeks earlier, it had become clear to me after I talked further with my mother about my upcoming trip to the rich suburb, that I was special. No one else was asked to go live in a rich family's house—not my sisters or brothers, not any of the kids from my school. I knew. I asked around. I asked everyone I saw everywhere I went. Only I had been selected, which meant I was special. This new status had me a little worried because I had enjoyed my little knack of disappearing and I wasn't really sure how this special thing was going to turn out. But I plunged forward with my new specialness anyway. I tired out my siblings incessantly asking, *Why me?* They were out of answers, and patience. Then Sarita had told me last night, as we spooned on our twin-sized bed, shifting left to right, right to left, that I was chosen because I was the laziest girl and I needed to learn my lesson. She said she was sorry she had to give me such awful news. And then she turned over and went straight to sleep.

What lesson? My mom told me it was going to be fun, like a vacation. I know my mom said it because I tried to get out of going when I was sure I would have to fold their laundry. Lord knew what else those people had in mind for me. My mother had told me I was being foolish. She clucked, clucked, clucked.

"Oh girl, where do you get such ridiculous thoughts?" Then she assured me it was meant to be fun, like a vacation.

And then last night Sarita convinced me that this whole thing was a trick after all. *Wait! This meant Sarita must have been in on the plan. But she's younger than me! That's not fair!* It was always this way. Oh, so wrong! Most all of it was usually so wrong.

Well, one thing Sarita wasn't in on and never would be was my recent discovery. This was one bubble she would never get to pop. It had come to me a couple of weeks ago: I could swear again. My promise to God on that disastrous last day of school to not swear all summer, when Sister Eileen called on me to inform me of my specialness, didn't count anymore. I hadn't been blamed for Wilfredo's obnoxiousness on that last day, which was why I'd made that impossible promise in the first place. It took me about a week to recall my promise, and when it hit me like a bat on a ball that I was in the clear, I whooped and hollered all over again like on that last day of school. I hadn't stopped swearing ever since. *Shit, shit, shit, damn, damn, damn... fuck.*

I sometimes paused and checked around me before I said the "F" word because it felt a little like a mortal sin, and I never said it more than once in case I forgot to go to confession and I carried too many "F" words in my soul. Sometimes I even swore in Spanish, but usually when I got angry or whenever I felt desperate. I only ever swore inside my head so I couldn't get caught. It was my secret, not Sarita's, not anybody's, only mine. My summer was supposed to turn out okay now that I could swear again, but with Sarita's news last night I wasn't so sure anymore. I still felt too exhausted to get out of bed. *Shit, shit, shit, shit, damn, damn, damn, damn....*

Three hours after awakening, I was still in the girls' bedroom putting the last of my things in my travel bag when Sarita walked in to our bedroom to tell me the rich white lady had arrived.

"Okay servant girl, your rich, white lady is here. You'd better come out now before you get in trouble for making her wait." Before she left the room entirely, she leaned half of her body in toward me and said, *"And don't think I can't hear what you're saying up in that crazy head of yours."* Then she pulled the rest of her body away from the doorway. I stood shocked with my mouth open, which was how I usually held it. That was the day I learned that Sarita could read my mind. I started praying that no one else was in on my secret: not only was I walking toward two weeks of slavery, but I couldn't imagine surviving the summer if I had to stop the one thing that kept me from

living in complete misery.

As soon as I walked into our living room, I was instantly struck by how beautiful the woman standing among my family looked. I had been skeptical that whole morning after what Sarita had sprung on me last night, but my apprehensions melted away as I stared at the woman who would soon take me away. I quickly figured she could surely show me a good time. Everything about her was perfect. Her hair was cut short and styled high, and she wore lipstick—something my mother never did, not even to church. All the other mothers wore lipstick to church every week, but not my mother. She was plain, too plain, nothing like the other mothers at our church, and certainly nothing like this lady. My mother looked monochromatic standing beside the beauty in color. Oh yeah, this woman had it together. She wore a pale blue polyester suit with a nifty flower pattern, and smiled the whole time she spoke. I thought maybe she belonged on television. She looked so much like the mothers on television. Only this mother came in color, and with bright red lipstick. She exchanged words with my oldest sister Celestina, while my parents stood nearby smiling and nodding their heads because they spoke very little English—even after living in the United States for fifteen years.

I finally walked over to stand beside the colorful TV lady. I immediately looked over to where Sarita stood beside my mother, and I could see jealousy was having its effect on Sarita. *Oh glory day, my sister had made up that story last night, I was going on vacation with rich white people.* I moved a couple of steps closer to my savior and stuck my tongue out and smiled teasingly at Sarita behind the woman's back. But then my legs almost went out on me when I realized my mother had caught me, and she gave me that look that said, "I'll get you"—which she always managed to get around to. No one in my family had ever escaped a beating. That was a fact. Only she would have to wait two weeks. I avoided making eye contact with Sarita or my mother, and I averted my eyes to the floor and waited.

I waited, and waited and kept waiting. I was waiting so long my legs were getting tired. This waiting was becoming worse than sitting around anticipating the Easter bunny, although that was a hoax. One look at the woman in color, and I knew this was the real deal. I was in for a treat. I coughed. That got her attention. She looked at me and introduced herself.

"Hello, my name is Mrs. Utkin. You must be Isabel?" She smiled.

Then I smiled my massive smile and displayed my assortment of misarranged teeth. My savior kept smiling along with me, and I watched as with such sweet softness, she picked up my bag and held out her hand for me to take. She whisked me away from our apartment. I hurried down those cement stairs, never once looking back. This was the departure I had been waiting for. This was greatness in pure form. And just like that, I forgot all about my imminent beating.

We drove away in a big white station wagon and didn't reach the Utkin house in Trumbull for what seemed like hours, but was really only twenty minutes. When we finally arrived in the driveway, I got out and stood by the car door. I didn't dare move, or rather, I couldn't. I was stunned. Her house was massive. It was painted white, and the windows were trimmed with glossy black shutters. I looked around and saw that all the houses were enormous. I was sure that houses this size only existed in television, like in *The Brady Bunch* and *Leave it to Beaver*. They weren't real. I hadn't expected all this. I didn't know what I expected. This explained Mrs. Utkin. She wasn't real. I was dreaming. Oh God, I was oversleeping!

I closed my eyes and inhaled a deep breath to be sure I could feel things. I stood there breathing deeply, taking in the smell of the trees and flowers surrounding us. The air smelled sweet like watermelon; it was warm and gentle and comforting, not like the hot stifling air I was used to. The sound of birds and leaves rustling was a stark contrast to the screaming mothers and car engines back home. Oh glory day, I had arrived. I was in heaven. This was greatness, absolute greatness. I wanted to never, ever wake up—not ever, ever, ever!

Mrs. Utkin came around and slammed the car door shut, jolting me out of my reverie. Her four children stood before me. She introduced them starting from the oldest: Cathy, Christie, Karen and Jimmy. Far out! There were only four children, which meant only six people lived in that humungous house! So *this* was a white family. The kids stepped forward and handed me gifts—a doll and a book, The <u>Adventures of Pippi Longstocking</u>. It was my favorite story. *How did they know?* I thought. Then all at once, they began asking me questions. So, what was it like where I lived? Did I ride? Who did I have a crush on, Donny Osmond or David Cassidy? *Ooh, Cathy loves Donny Osmond!* Were any of my brothers drafted?

The attention was overwhelming and their questions became impossible to answer. They seemed to run into each other and soon I only heard garble, which was why I could only stand, still leaning slightly back with my mouth open saying nothing. Finally, Mrs. Utkin walked to me, took my hand, and gently guided me into the house. I followed her up the most luscious-looking soft green stairs that led us up to the room where I would be sleeping.

Again, I couldn't believe my eyes. It was a cheery yellow, like the candy corns I loved so much, and the many windows were covered in pretty ruffled curtains with a tiny-checkered pattern. The floor was covered in more thick soft carpet that sunk with each step. There were two single beds with big white fancy headboards and footboards. The mattresses were neatly fixed with rich-looking covers that matched the curtains. I asked if I was meant to sleep alone in a bed.

Mrs. Utkin laughed. *"Of course. The bed next to the window is for you, and the other belongs to my youngest, Karen."*

I slowly made my way to the bed. For the first time in my life, I sat on my own bed. I wanted only to sit there forever, wishing I would never have to go back home—not ever, ever. Greatness had never looked or felt so good in my head. The real thing was even better than my most extraordinary thoughts that occupied so many idle minutes, often unexpectedly and openly inducing my unwieldy smile.

The Utkins were the best. I played endlessly with all four kids and their friends. We often played in the town lake, where I learned to swim for the first time when one day along with all the other kids, I jumped in the lake and raced to an invisible finish line mimicking a stroke I learned by watching the Utkin kids. I swam out pretty far, which caused me to panic because I knew I was going to drown—until I stood up and realized the water only reached my shoulders. I also learned to ride a bike. We ran around in the nearby woods and pretended we were stranded like on Gilligan's Island. Only we called our adventure Aragon's Forest, named after their street.

We ate lots of ice cream and chocolate, and best of all was McDonalds. Eating out was common for the Utkins but was alien to me. The only times I ever ate out was at lunch in school. My lunch was always a single half pint-sized carton of milk, and a tuna sandwich on two slices of white dewy Wonder bread made by one of my sisters that morning, and my sandwich was always so skimpy because one can of tuna was stretched for eight sandwiches. At McDonalds, I got a burger, fries, coke and a hot apple pie and more of anything if I wanted. Oh Lord, the beauty in ordering more. It was tantalizing—oh, so very, very tantalizing.

When the Utkins dined at home, everyone sat down together and ate at the same time. They would talk about innocuous things like the latest fads and, thanks to Cathy, about my new idol, Donny Osmond. I never before really gave a second thought to Donny Osmond, except to upset my sister Lupe one time by kissing her beloved life-sized poster of him in front of her. That caused us to fight and to get that poster torn up by my mother.

Building excitement for upcoming events at the dinner table was a common Utkin family occurrence. Of course, they were a family of only six that could easily fit around a table. In fact, their family of six lived in a three-level house that had two playrooms. All four children had their own bedroom and Mr. Utkin's office was the largest room of all. I'd walk through the house every morning as soon as I woke up. I got lost every day that first week, and was pleasantly surprised each time I came to the stairs. The pale green-carpeted stairs were my favorite. I found excuses several times a day to go back to my room, which I could only do by walking up those velvety stairs—those sweet, minty, delicious stairs.

But all too soon, it was my last day. Mrs. Utkin helped me pack and the kids gathered around me. I needed another bag for all the new things I was taking home. Earlier, Mr. Utkin had stopped by briefly to wish me luck and to tell me what a pleasure it was to meet me. He had been away on business for most of the time. When he had finally arrived two days ago, he made me question for the first time my personal vow to become a nun, what with his talks of exotic travels. For a slight second I believed my trip home could be delayed permanently by his words but he kept walking toward his office.

I stood waiting after my bags were packed and ready. I looked around to see if anyone else needed to speak. Something, anything, anyone, *PLEASE!* I desperately begged. No one said a word. They all stood around smiling, and saying nothing.

Finally, Mrs. Utkin walked out of the room with my bags. I turned and followed her down my favorite stairs and out the front door as everyone else, minus Mr. Utkin, followed us. Mrs. Utkin slipped into the driver's seat and started the engine. I stood by the passenger door waiting, hoping for a final miracle. *Please, God, let me stay. This time I absolutely promise to stop swearing—for the rest of the year! I'll even give up the "F" word.*

A minute passed before I folded my body into the car. Mrs. Utkin backed the station wagon out of the driveway and onto the street. I turned in my seat and watched as Karen, Chris, Jimmy and Cathy waved good-bye and yelled out assurances that I would be back next year. Their diminishing bodies convinced me that greatness was slipping away from me. I realized that in the end, true greatness was meant to live merely in my head. What a disappointment: what an unbelievable letdown.

This realization was too painful. It was unbearable. I kept looking back at the waving arms, knowing I was never coming back. I started crying. I recalled for the first time in two weeks my mother's facial resolve, my impending punishment. I was owed. I dreaded what waited at the end of our drive.

The trip home was quick. As I got out of the station wagon I could already smell the exhaust and oil from the cars. I started coughing uncontrollably. I coughed and coughed. Mrs. Utkin rushed over to me from the other side of the car and patted my back. She bent down to meet my face and asked me if I was okay. She looked panicked. What could I tell her? What were the chances she would take me back simply because I'd suddenly acquired an allergy to this place? I looked around and realized for the first time the lack of trees and greenery. I scanned the immediate area and noticed the many buildings with people hanging out of windows trying to catch a breeze from the stiff hot air. I found it hard to breathe. Mrs. Utkin asked me again if I was okay. I simply nodded. She took my hand again and escorted me past the many doorways of our building and up the stairs to my family's apartment. These stairs were made of cement and felt hard on my feet—nothing like the soft ones I had just left behind.

Mrs. Utkin knocked on our door and my entire family greeted us. The adults exchanged words and handshakes while the young ones screamed and pushed their way through the crowd. Mrs. Utkin eventually turned to me, kissed my forehead and gave me that perfect smile once more. I didn't move from my spot just outside our apartment's threshold as I watched the dynamite lady in color walk down the stairs and out of my life. I stayed standing in the empty hallway before I became convinced that greatness wasn't coming back for me. I turned and pushed my way past my massive family who were clogging up the doorway of our pathetic apartment, and who eagerly asked me questions, and who were too damn loud.

Oh God, stop the noise! I begged in my head. I ignored their questions as I made my way to the girls' bedroom no longer caring who knew my secret that was screeching in my brain... *Fuck, fuck, fuck, fuck, fuck, fuck, fuck, fuck, fuck...*

I walked straight into the girls' bedroom and closed the door. It was such a short uneventful walk with no stairs, I thought. I looked around the bare room that I shared with four sisters. It was half the size of the pretty yellow room with ruffles. I stared at the dingy white cloth covering the single small window. My eyes moved over to the beds. Worn-out bed sheets covered them. *Why were there no bed covers?* I asked myself. Then I noticed the hideous walls for the first time. The walls in my—our—tiny bedroom were painted an industrial nondescript shade of glossy washed-out blue that always smelled of chemicals. The full impact of my real life struck me through the walls that bespoke acute and total destitution. I no longer could carry my bags so I let them drop. I slowly slipped down to the linoleum-covered concrete floor.

THREE

Throughout my childhood, I did enjoy moments when laughter easily escaped from the untainted reservoir of joy inherent in children. I sometimes was able to experience life through the watery rush of naivete's sweet purity. But even all those moments of delight were tinged with an unrelenting buzz that, years later, I recognized to be anxiety. I'd often try reclaiming the glee from those moments, but the more determinedly I'd grasp the weaker the memory would grow. It was similar to that first instant after waking up from a most satisfying dream that naturally evaporates with each passing moment, leaving behind a wispy wake that always left me feeling desperate and disenchanted all at once.

For all of my life, anxiety and depression were my constant companions, and always there was so much fear and too much anger. I hadn't a clue that this wasn't normal. I knew no other way of being. It wasn't until decades later that I discovered how I was truly meant to feel and think and be.

In my earliest memory (I think I was around three years old), I stood between throngs of people on our apartment's hard concrete floor. *But who are these people? And where is my mama? Where is mama?* Feeling mistakenly transported to an unfamiliar netherworld where the dark forest of shapes caused the tears in me to sprout straight up and out, I cried and cried and cried. I searched through the bubbly film of tears and didn't recognize anyone. I wasn't even sure I was in my home. Someone finally picked me up after the crying transformed into a deafening screech. As this faceless person pointed, my eyes followed her arm through a haze and there at the end of her pointing finger was my mother. She stood some distance from me, laughing and laughing, which felt like betrayal of the grandest sort. I watched as soft grey plumes of smoke rose up all around her and perfectly encase her lively bliss. Spotting my mama in such rapture caused me to cry more forcefully. I wrenched my body this way and that way in a desperate attempt for escape. But that only made the faceless somebody grip me tighter. I never did get taken to her. My mama never heard or saw me that day.

I learned to fear long before my earliest memory. It was fear that permeated the zygote making her way to gestation—which was probably why, almost as soon as I was born, my eyes would shift from left to right and then back in quick, short sweeps then shut themselves tight for hours and hours. Soon enough, fear became the shield I rarely put down. At an unlikely young age, I could sense real danger lurking everywhere and I understood that to not be afraid would surely have dulled me and placed me in precarious situations. Remaining unnoticed inside my home or at school or church didn't ward off danger any more than being outside with strangers. There existed no safe haven, no place where I could relax my shoulders and allow the rapid short breaths I mostly took to flow through my lungs and then into my bloodstream. I deprived my whole body of any real life with an incessant fear that pressed and pressed. I huddled inside myself and ensured I stayed inconsequential.

Except hiding inside my inner sanctuary that was the size of a dust mote didn't shield me that one time—the time I was abandoned too early in life. That unspoken time I lost my innocence to the monster...

Once upon a time, there was a very young and frail little girl whose heart was so completely shattered, she dragged from the sheer weight of so much debris. She was quiet and couldn't share what was on her mind because she couldn't speak. It wasn't that she was incapable of speaking or that she didn't want to speak or that she outright refused to speak. She tried. But every time enough momentum had built up inside her, the force seemed to peter out as quickly as the ignition of that first spark of force that had got her thinking how for sure this time, she could finally speak. Always after working herself up to speak, she would cough up a diaphanous swirl of smoke.

It was her broken heart that really took up all of her time so who could blame her for having nothing left to speak of?

But truly, how could I have spoken? What had happened was too terrifying to speak of, and to allow words to tumble from my lips would only have gotten me in bigger trouble. I was sure of it. I imagined that from the first word I uttered would come the second word, and then the next—and then Lord only knew how many words after that it would have taken before the whole of it was out in the open. Not that I possessed very many words in my repertoire at that young age in the first place. Anyway, did it really happen, or did I imagine it? I was always accused of saying some pretty ridiculous things so maybe my mind was swallowing all the words before they escaped and it was busy up there making up ridiculousness. It could be.

How did the monster get me alone, anyway? Where was everyone? I couldn't find anyone, but how could that be? How could I have been left alone? Were there no people? Was it just me in this world? It certainly felt that way. Except, I definitely was not alone. I didn't move, purposely stiffening my body. I saw shapes and I saw a color but I couldn't really call it anything because it didn't have a name inside my head. What was that? I heard something but I couldn't really know what I was hearing. It was probably all the words my mind had swallowed, getting jumbled up in there. It was garble. Oh, yeah! Garble. There were no real words being spoken anywhere. Was this why I couldn't figure out the sound? And anyway, was I really seeing a color? Was that color outside of me or was I imagining it too? Oh, how could I figure any of it out? I was only a little girl, a baby really. What could I have possibly done or said?

I was minding my own business. I never had many words and I never shared secrets. Could that have been why I was ideal for the monster?

What do you mean I should take off my panties for this part? Oh no! my mind screamed.

I knew I wasn't actually saying those words but it felt very much like the breath was leaving me—and something was coming out.

How could I? Why would I?

Again, I never spoke these words so I guess my mind had somehow managed to swallow my words. This wasn't the first time. I'm pretty sure of it, but I was a baby still. My innocence was all I really had that I could call my own, and now it was being taken from me. How could I even have known this? I was still too young. How could so much wisdom have lived in me?

"All right, now it's your turn, sweet little Isabel," the monster cooed.

Oh no, no, no, no!
Oh come on, this is nothing. It's okay, and it feels good right?
Oh, no, no, no, no, no, no, no!!
Is it my turn again then? Okay, I'll go again, but then you'll have to go next. It's only fair. A tinge of fury escaped from the monster after that last part was said. I stiffened even more.

I'm pretty sure it wasn't the first time, or was it? I couldn't imagine it ever really happened at all. It was all such a blur so how could I really have been sure? It was such a dark terrible blur, like the fitful sleep that kept me pinned down some nights. When I struggled to wake up, it managed to bring me down again and again, and then I finally concentrated my whole mind to wake up and finally I would. Oh, what a relief. What a glorious relief to have finally woken up.

Being molested by the monster was the most damning trauma that contributed to my inescapable downfall, the one that finally came after nearly fifty years of encasing myself in fear and destruction. I had never spoken about the molestation to anyone, not ever. The monster made it clear what would happen if I did. Every time I saw the monster approaching, I'd go running to sit or stand too close to whoever was nearest me. Often, I'd get swatted at like some pestering insect, and like the unrelenting buzzing and pursuit of an insect, I'd swarm my savior pestering and pestering.

After the first time, I stopped speaking. Eventually, people forgot that at one time I could and did speak. Except there was the one time a family friend was visiting and he bent way low to meet my tiny frail body and asked me something. He turned his head so I could respond into his ear and in a raspy voice that I feared would unravel the boisterous bellow that fought to escape I said, *"Karajo! Puta!"*

Well, those two words released a joy in me that stayed dancing inside for days and days. Every time I would visit that precise moment when the swear words slipped from somewhere inside me, I would just smile to myself and then I would run to a closet so no one would see that I was smiling. This was what I meant by fearing to speak. I didn't trust that the first word wouldn't cause a thorough unraveling of what I kept tucked away deep inside me. Who knew what would happen then?

That family friend sprung straight up and ran out of our apartment. Then an extraordinary thing happened. Mama looked straight at me.

"Isabel, what did you say to Mr. So and So?" my mother asked.

I looked up and stared straight back at her. I didn't dare speak, and I didn't dare smile because everything I was pushing deep inside me was struggling to come up. I knew that one word, just one word would let loose the whole fiasco, and for sure I couldn't smile because just the one smile would release from me the darkest ugliest mess.

"Well girl, what did you say to him? He raced out of here embarrassed, you know." Her fists were on her hips.

Oh dear, after those last words my mother spoke my smile started making its way to my lips. There was no stopping its momentum. I needed to run. So I did—directly to the "girls" room where I slammed the door shut then jumped on my bed and lay facedown burrowing my head into the pillow I shared with Sarita. Safe in the smothering darkness, I smiled and smiled and smiled.

It was only months after losing my innocence when my sister Lourdes got her faced burned right off of her. It happened because the deadly incinerator in our building blew up when an aerosol can of hairspray exploded. She had been tossing our garbage bag into the opening when the thing just went off in her face. My sister Lupe, who's only eighteen months younger than Lourdes, had been right by her side when it happened. They sort of became one after that incident. Miraculously, Lupe escaped damage of any kind; her face remained most beautiful. My parents sued the City of Bridgeport after their already sickly daughter ended up with a monster face. That's how, three years after the explosion, we were awarded enough compensation to get the heck out of the projects and into our own new two-apartment, three-story house. But the way my parents saw it, we should have gotten a mansion after what happened to Lourdes, and nearly happened to Lupe. We definitely shouldn't have stayed struggling in our new little house. That explosion was worse than the riot that would occur less than two years later. The noise the explosion created caused us all to die just a little bit more than we would from the gun repeatedly fired at that fatal riot. But it was the explosion that paved our exit from the projects.

It was the middle of the day on a Saturday. I was almost seven years old. Sarita and I were taking a bath together because that's how these things worked in my family. My mom bore no twins or triplets but we were grouped in pairs or threes. We had to stick together and do things together and sleep together and even dress alike. It was as if her only true wish had been to give birth to bundles of kids at a time, probably to avoid the twelve individual ones she did have.

Well, Sarita and I were playing in the shallow tub, making the best of having to take a bath in the first place, when all of a sudden there was a loud *BOOM!* The bathroom shook and rattled and Sarita and I were both lifted from the seat of the tub. The water in the tub splashed up and down, and just as quickly as we were tossed up, we came down hard on our butts. I stared at Sarita. She looked utterly shocked to me and I'm sure I looked completely shocked to her. We spoke only inside our heads because we didn't have the kind of words that normally came out of our mouths. Not that I was capable of speaking yet anyway. If ever there was a way to get me using real words again it should have been that explosion. But we could only use our brains to ask, *What was that? What happened?* We hadn't moved, and we really had stopped breathing… until the screaming came.

I heard my mother first. She was wailing like when one of my uncles had died, only this time it was definitely louder and it reached the very core of my soul. Then it seemed like the world was in our living room, screeching. Sarita and I got out of the tub so quickly, we forgot to dry off. Somehow we slipped panties on and when we crossed the bathroom's threshold, I noticed we were both wearing tee shirts. I couldn't really recall how all that had occurred, because I was still completely wet with only panties and a tee shirt on.

Sarita and I rushed into the living room but we stopped at the doorway. Instinctively we took hold of each other in a tight embrace. We knew better than to move any further into that room because right in front of us, all these people had meshed into one tight bunch exactly in the center of the room. We watched as that crowd writhed and clung to each other, looking like an entire football team huddled to plan their next move. Everyone howled and howled. Then Sarita and I moved our inextricable team of two up and down and over one way, then back over the other way. But no matter how we shifted, we couldn't see above, below or through that dense mass. I had no idea what everyone was crying about but I figured it had to be really bad. Minutes became quick momentary instants.

After only a few more quick instants, Sarita and I gave up on figuring out the bizarre scene before us. We must have felt left out just then because we both clung on to each other even tighter and we started crying, too. I cried so hard I couldn't breathe, all over again. My chest hurt so bad and all I could think of was that one of us had died and everyone had lost their words like me and Sarita had, and the wailing and screeching was all we could manage to get out of us. And on and on this went.

After a while, the mass of people parted a little. And there, right in the middle of that crowd I saw what had caused utter pandemonium. I felt a valve shut off in me. Not only had my words stopped, but so did my tears. I stood gaping, unable to move, unable to think, unable to breathe. I saw my sister Lourdes standing, stupefied from head to toe.

She stood eerily still and erect, resembling a cardboard drawing. My mother embraced her in a hysterical fevered grip, as if this contact could breathe back some life into my sister's still body. I could see my sister Lupe clinging to Lourdes' waist as if she was glued on to it. I couldn't believe what I saw. And if Lourdes couldn't move anymore—which, by the look of her, one could only conclude that too much life had been drained from her—did this mean Lourdes was dead? I really couldn't be sure if it was Lourdes in the first place, but I knew deep down it was her standing there, being draped by the massive crowd.

The scene looked like one of the stained glass windows in my church, this one, depicting all the angels and saints surrounding Jesus, looking as if they all were ascending to the heavens in one fluid motion. And they're all looking directly at Jesus with woeful expressions, as if their ascension was not such a happy occasion. Only this crowd before me was firmly footed to the hard concrete floor of our apartment and their cries were a deafening cacophony, unlike the empty silence the stained glass scene emitted. This crowd didn't look woeful; they looked to be in sheer agony. And it wasn't Jesus everyone was agonizing over. It was my sister Lourdes who was missing her regular face. She had a monster face and she had no hair and her coat and face and hands were all the wrong colors. Her exposed skin was black and grey and red and her skin everywhere looked to be pulsating.

Then I smelled it. Inside our apartment, there was the stink of something I had never smelled before. Our apartment reeked of it. The dreadful smell permeated every speck of space. Slowly I looked around. I could see smoke, and outside our windows I saw smoke billowing higher and higher. When I looked over at Lourdes again, I could see that she was encased in a puff of smoke. How could I have missed all this before?

Finally, a woman walked into our apartment. I didn't recognize this person. She moved right into the thick of the crowd and just like that, she completely parted the mass of people and got to my sister Lourdes. She held my mother and spoke into her ear, and finally my mother let go of Lourdes. The angel wrapped her arm around my sister with Lupe still attached to her hip, and the angel walked my sisters to our apartment's bigger bathroom. When I saw Lourdes's feet move with almost no help, I knew she was alive. She wasn't dead. My sister didn't die!

I suddenly got my breath back. I breathed in huge gulps of smoke-laden air and began crying hysterically again. I kept breathing in those gulps and I started choking on air and mucus and smoke. I don't remember exactly what happened, but I think one of my older sisters eventually walked Sarita and me into the girls' bedroom to get us dressed. While I was getting dressed, I tried figuring out what had just happened because there was no sound—only a hum, really. Whoever helped Sarita and me get dressed was silent. I could see a red, swollen face, wet with tears. It was okay, though. Lourdes was alive. I was sure of it. No one had died. Even if my sister ended up with a monster face for the rest of her life, she could at least be alive. Besides, I had a monster face and I somehow made it through each day.

Lourdes was confined to a hospital bed for three months after her face, neck and hands were charred in the explosion. It caused second- to third-degree burns. She never stopped smelling of burnt flesh, even after she transformed from a monster face back to her usual beautiful face.

One hot summer day when I was nine, two years after the explosion and only one quick month after my stay with the Utkins, all of us kids were outside playing in the courtyard between buildings "11" and "12." Us Puerto Ricans, about a good five families, equaling around fifty kids, were playing various games. I think Sarita and I were playing with a few neighbor girls. The older kids were playing baseball and several other games when the few black kids walked over.

"*We wanna play,*" one black kid said to no one in particular, but to the group playing baseball. He wasn't very tall but he leaned forward like he wasn't taking a "no" from anybody.

"*Hell no!*" one of the Puerto Rican baseball players said.

"*You betta let us play or we gonna kick y'all asses!*" another bigger kid warned. This one looked like he was ready to take care of business.

"*Yeah, well, you all gonna have to kick our asses then because we ain' gonna let choo play.*" This last bit came from Tato, who was the quickest runner of all us Puerto Ricans and the only kid who could beat me in a race. But he was two years older than me so that explained his advanced talent. He stood about one head shorter than the angry-looking tall black kid, but I knew that didn't mean anything. I had seen Tato fight; this tall kid probably was going to find out for himself how he should have gone back to where he came from.

But before that little altercation could get dealt with, there was a surprise outburst of kids screaming and punching and pulling hair and scratching. The fight had escalated too fast for me and Sarita, so we escaped to the closest doorway which was the single door furthest from the safety of our apartment door. We ran up the hard cement stairs to the second floor hallway landing where there was a window that looked out onto the courtyard. Now hundreds of kids were fighting. Puerto Rican kids were running into the growing ball of fury from every which way, and black kids were running in from who knew where; they threw themselves into that ball as well. And wasn't that my sister Maribel kicking the shit out of that girl, and that one, and that one…? And, oh no! The big people started walking over and they looked mad. Then more big Puerto Rican people and big black people walked over, and many were running and throwing themselves in. They all looked so mad.

Sarita and I clung on to each other crying hysterically by this time. The immense fear that normally preceded me zapping my humanness into pure nothingness had grown to proportions I never before experienced. Not even the monster from years before caused me to fear so greatly. I tried disappearing with all my might, but Sarita clung onto me, making it impossible to even move. As my baby sister and I remained glued to each other, crying and crying, we searched the growing mass of human hell. Our teary eyes couldn't pick out our brothers and sisters—except for our sister Maribel, whose Popeye arms flailed and flailed above the storm below. Sarita and I stayed clinging on to each other as we continued witnessing the most spectacular billow of fighting and screaming and blood.

Then suddenly, across from our vantage point, we spotted my tiny frail brother Pablo, our family's second youngest, sitting on a bench. Mayhem bulldozed everything around him as he held his head with one tiny hand; his other hand covered his left ear. He cried and cried while sitting alone and cradling his ear. I searched the entire area and couldn't find my baby brother Manuel nor my little chubby brother Juan. How could I have left my little brothers unguarded in the midst of this hell? To relieve her load, my mother discreetly fostered us kids to form packs and within each pack, a leader naturally emerged. I was the leader of the five youngest, which was an anomaly since I was the least significant member of our pack. With only Sarita by my side, I had abandoned three of my pack.

I suddenly recalled that my first instinct when the fight broke out had been to save myself. I hadn't even grabbed a hold of Sarita before I reached the doorway leading to where we now stood. She had latched on to me. The weight of my youngest siblings being hurt finally propelled me to get moving. I grabbed Sarita's hand and pulled her behind me as I raced back down the stairs.

Sarita and I ran down those stairs crying for our baby brothers, feeling the desperation that was overtaking us. When we ran out that doorway and into the war-zoned courtyard, I witnessed Pablo being scooped up and carried away. Sarita and I ran even faster but this person carrying my brother ran at a much faster pace than us two. Then we saw Juan and Manuel being carried by other big people further ahead, and we screamed and cried and ran behind them. Everywhere I looked there were big angry people shouting and punching and kicking and there was blood everywhere.

Then came the loudest boom. It reminded me of that day a couple of years before when Sarita and I were tossed about in the bathtub—when Lourdes ended up with the monster face.

There was another boom, and someone yelled, *"GUN!!"* All hell broke loose then. Everybody ran every which way. People were banging into each other and knocking each other down on their way to wherever, as one gunshot after another rang in our ears. Someone finally grabbed Sarita and me by our arms and we were practically carried the rest of the way to our apartment.

The riot that had broke out because a boy had said "no" to another boy's demand to be let into a neighborhood game of baseball ended with one dead, several in critical condition, hundreds more being treated at the local hospitals, and with my tiny precious three-year old brother deaf in the one ear he had been holding. A rock the size of a baseball, probably intended for someone else, had been hurled.

After that riot, it became prison-like living in Father Panik Village. All the heavy steel front doors were loaded with extra bolts and locked up by 8:00pm every single night. It was never again safe to walk out our door alone. We no longer stepped outside the confining 1,200-square foot apartment to relieve my mother of the overbearing wails and dissents that twelve kids created, except to go to school. We had to walk to and from school in packs of four or five, which was easy for us Puerto Rican families. Each morning, droves of Puerto Rican kids walked to school together, staring down the packs of black kids staring us back down across the way as they walked to the same schools.

But one time I forgot and I walked home alone from St. Mary's. When I got to the doorway only one away from my doorway, I got snatched and dragged into the hallway. Two much bigger and older black girls punched and punched me. I was screaming and crying and trying to cover my face. They

Part One: Her Beginning

finally shoved my bruised and bloody body out the door. I got up and ran the rest of the way to my family's apartment.

My older siblings got so mad when they learned what had happened to me, because the exact same thing had happened two days before to Lourdes, who had been our family's other monster after her face got burned off. I thought maybe those girls knew we were our family's monster faces (even though Lourdes was already back to being beautiful!) and they wanted to wipe the earth clean of such filth.

My mother shouted, *"Enough! We have to move. And don't let me find out any of you hit someone for any reason. I want this to stop!"*

We all quickly took a step back, because her one hand clenched her hip while her other hand waved a pointed finger directly at us as she stared us down. Her body did that slight bouncie-bounce move that we all knew, too well, meant business. We'd all been at the other end of her hand when we didn't listen. We already knew that the wrath of mama was worse than any black girl's punches.

FOUR

I grew to believe that being born number eight was the most potent ingredient of my curse. That number held no value whatsoever; what was anyone to do with a mere number eight but walk straight past it on the way to number one, or twelve, or three?

Most of the people in my family kept forgetting that I was even in the family, probably because I was one of the few who had nothing of value to contribute—especially after words no longer spilled from my lips. I certainly wasn't one of the ones who were sickly and needed a lot of attention, and I definitely wasn't one of the ones who caused enough trouble to earn a spanking every single day. I was quiet and I wouldn't speak. I was lazy… well, the more accurate word would be listless. I was a listless, frail, ugly little girl with little energy, always taking naps and always living in my head. I mostly walked with my head down. I only looked up with my eyes and never with my head turned up. I rarely let people see me smile and always, they gave me that same perplexed look whenever I did manage to smile.

So I pretty much kept to myself because I never did have much to say, not at home nor at school nor in the playground. This made me an ideal student at St. Mary's where the Spanish nuns preferred quiet children who knew to sit still in their seats. And for little sweet innocent girls to know to keep their knees pressed together tightly. They didn't need to worry about me. I was no longer innocent—nor was I all that sweet, especially with all the thoughts frequently occupying my brain those days. At least I barely ever moved. I rarely spoke and I only ever did the bare minimum for everything, mostly to avoid a spanking. I learned at an early age that I could get a hard swift smack across the face when I chose to be willfully reluctant. I had turned into such a well-behaved girl! Not a good girl, mind you. I could never ever be that again. I was damaged, and there was nothing to be said about that, because then all hell would break loose. So I was more than willing to not make any noise or trouble.

In contrast was my brother Juan, who we used to call Cheo. He was one of the ones who managed to get spanked every day without fail. He was so good at earning the deepest red spankings that I thought for sure he would grow up to be the red child in the family. He also ate lots more than the rest of us, which was easy for him because he was a boy, and boys were golden in my family. It didn't matter that he was born number ten. He was a boy and therefore revered; he could do as he pleased, including eating way too much even with his big protruding baby belly. He was so chunky that when he walked, his practically conjoined thighs pushed his knees too far apart.

At times I feared that if he weren't careful, his feet would permanently turn upward from the outside with all the weight his turned-out legs put on the insoles of his feet. He turned out to be flatfooted, and even though everyone swore he was born that way, I knew better. The kid simply flattened the heck out of those feet with all that extra weight. I didn't exactly blame him, since it was my mom who kept feeding him. Couldn't she see the size of his big fat belly? Wasn't it obvious that his legs weren't looking right? Maybe I could see it because I was closer to the ground than my mom was, but really! This situation was getting ridiculously out of control.

One day, I took matters into my own hands. Somebody had to. I was his leader, after all. Actually, it was my sister Sarita and I who finally decided together to put him on a diet. Sarita and I started Juan on our "Teeny Weenie Diet."

We would make him a super skimpy peanut butter and jelly sandwich and cut it up into itty-bitty-sized bites. I would hold the plate and Sarita and I would take turns feeding him, one tiny piece at a time. If we caught him swallowing a piece whole, we would hold out on him until he promised to take at least ten bites with the next piece, and then we would cut from an already tiny piece a miniscule portion—a crumb really—and hand it to him. The poor thing whined and made all kinds of noises, begging for a bigger piece.

"Aw, come on! This is too little? I'm hungry! This is a stupid diet! Mamaaaa…..!"

"Trust us, Cheo, later on you'll thank us," we would say, willing him to get skinny right before our eyes.

I had figured that the slower he moved, the more weight he would lose and the better chance he'd have of fixing those clumps he called feet. Sarita and I kept this up until my mother stepped in, probably two days after we put him on our "Teeny Weenie Diet," and stopped the whole thing. He was pretty happy about this and, well, deep down I didn't really care either way. After all, it took a lot of work making those sandwiches and for sure it was getting old having to sit all that time while he chewed and chewed, always having to cheer him on, keeping the hoorah going until the last interminable bite.

As I already mentioned, my older siblings, surreptitiously orchestrated by our mother, had formed some pretty tight cliques among themselves before I became the five youngest kids' leader. It happened because not only was I the oldest of the five remaining kids, but the tallest. And so I stood out as the natural choice, even though I was the least consequential, and even though I wasn't a boy.

The day I assumed the role of pack leader, I started speaking again. For days people would stare, then shake their heads, looking completely baffled whenever I spoke. And every time, they'd step around me, creating enough distance between us to ensure my affliction didn't end up in them. It took everyone days and days to get used to the sound that emanated from my mouth, and when finally my voice could be heard on a daily basis, everyone went back to walking through me.

In the beginning, my role as pack leader baffled me because I couldn't get past the 'why me' factor. I lacked any real traits or talents. Unlike my brother Pedro who could sing and dance and needed back-up talent; he apparently found what he was looking for in the three sisters just younger than him. Oh, of course, he was the oldest in his pack…and a boy. *"Well, don't you see dear? Maribel, Lourdes and Lupe are the only ones willing to follow your lead. They're perfect for your fine strong voice,"* my mother coaxed. Nor did I possess the ability to lead like our family's oldest, Sandalio. When he spoke, everyone—including my parents—listened. And since the two sisters just younger than him, Celestina and Teresa, had been a part of his life the longest, they became members of his pack. *"Now, now, son, just prove to them how you're much more inventive and fun than any of those ridiculous girls whose shenanigans they keep cackling at, honestly!"* Plus, yet again, let's not forget the fact that Sandalio was the male!

So not only did I *not* possess any real talent or trait to strut about, I lacked the proper body parts of a real pack leader. I was a girl. I also wasn't my mother's choice. She never spoke a word to me about how the four youngest were eager to follow my quiet hopeless lead. She'd congratulate my pack, never me directly, for a job well done whenever we five weren't causing any trouble—which didn't occur very often, since Juan the spanking magnet was relegated to our pack.

At first, I kept testing my pack's loyalty. But it didn't take me long to get really proficient at leading. If you stood nearby, you would soon detect my knack for giving orders with fierce conviction. I'm pretty sure it was during my tenure as pack leader that I acquired my habit of bulging my eyes when I speak. I definitely communicated more forcefully than our family's other two, older, pack leaders who should have had that ability well figured out, being boys and all. I would tell any one of my younger siblings to bring me a glass of water and, with zero questions asked, they would get up from watching TV or playing or whatever they were engaged in at the time and get me a glass of water.

I decided that my role included teaching my underlings; and since I intended to become a nun someday, I'd swathe my head with a pillowcase before starting the lesson, hoping to epitomize my teachers at St.Mary's. I'd sit them down and teach them how to add and subtract, spell their names, learn the alphabet and who knew what else. My pack's youngest, Manuel, was only two years old then—and boy, did I assert myself when he didn't follow along. I also became responsible for coming up with games for us to play and I broke up any fights among us. I even got to punish them whenever I felt like it.

"That's it! Kneel for 500 minutes!"

"What, no way!"

"Do it!" I'd yell as my eyeballs popped out as far as my sockets could stretch—swinging my habit about just like the nuns did whenever they'd lash out in anger.

My charges would then stop what they were doing and kneel.

Soon after I mastered my role as pack leader, I acknowledged my propensity for mischief—not serious or life-threatening stuff, of course. That came much later in my life. Before I even became my pack's leader, I was keenly aware of my inclination. For example, I could only ever laugh at the mishaps of others, like whenever anyone I knew tripped and fell. I'd double over laughing for too many minutes, never once offering words of comfort or help. Instead, I'd begin walking away, never once looking back, feeling thoroughly satisfied. When witnessing the misfortune of others, I'd finally ease the tightness in my shoulders and belly.

I instinctively knew my slant toward mischief would one day become something more than what lived inside me. I knew I'd someday act out some of my internal urgings, and the four youngest became my guinea pigs for that future.

I'd talk one or all of the four youngest into doing sinful things. There was one time when I was only eight years old. I talked Juan into shouting out of the three youngest boys' single bedroom window to our neighbor, a girl who sat by her open window that was kitty-cornered from ours. *"Oola mala choola, besame la coola, oola mala choola, besame la coola,"* we shouted over and over, until the girl's mom made a big stink about it to our mom. Our mom came running into the room shouting and flailing her arms. She slammed the window shut, then gave our bottoms a proper deep red spanking. Or the time I demanded that Juan hide in a closet with me to smoke the rest of the cigarette my father had just put out. I snatched the half-smoked butt, still smoky and red-hot, from his one ashtray without anyone noticing. Then Juan and I just puffed and puffed harder to get that thing going again.

Or that time on a hot summer day when Juan and I sneaked into the apartment of our oldest sister Celestina and her husband. We stole the yummiest chocolate-and-cream sandwich cookies from where she kept them almost too high to reach. I was already ten years old when we had moved out of the projects and into our new house where we occupied the second floor apartment. Celestina and her husband had moved into the first-floor apartment that same weekend. She always kept the scrumptious cookies in the same cupboard, so it didn't take long on that day to get in and out. It did help our cookie-stealing effort that I knew exactly where to find the cookies; from the first week living in the new house I had been a silent regular in my sister's tidy kitchen, helping myself to those wonderful treats.

One day, Juan and I went our separate ways after my four-year position as pack leader ended. I was twelve years old.

"Cheo, go to the store and get me a Creamsicle."
"No!"

Did he just say no? This couldn't be happening, I thought. My four youngest siblings had never questioned me.

"I told you to go to the store, now go!"
"No, and you can't make me."

He stood up from where he'd been lying on the floor, watching his favorite cartoons. Because he was a prized boy, he got to choose whatever he wanted to watch, and us girls would have to go along with it. He folded his chubby arms, barely able to get them to cooperate, while he simultaneously worked his splayed legs in a near closed-leg stance. He miraculously stretched his fat doughy torso to nearly meet my height, daring me to do something about it.

I didn't have a response. I didn't know what came next after a refusal like that. But I knew that no degree of threat or eye-bulging could get my brother to move. I then turned to my two youngest brothers who both had been lying on the floor alongside Juan. They quickly stood up, folded their arms in defiance and told me I had better not ask them either. They weren't going anywhere for me, anymore. They must have worked this out together at some point.

That was that then. I walked to the corner store, bought my own Creamsicle and I was no longer the leader of our pack.

So, sure, at one time I had a place in the family hierarchy beyond being an insignificant number eight. During that time our family's youngest four could see me for sure. But my tenure as pack leader was disappointingly short, which was why I searched elsewhere to assert my authority. I had gotten hooked on giving orders, you see. And that truly wasn't my fault, because the little bossiness I gained during those quick four years had somehow become otherworldly. I couldn't pull back on my need to boss people around, because the urge kept growing stronger and stronger without any real input from me.

That's when I turned to my friends. I became convinced they were the perfect bunch. The more I thought about it, I realized that not only were my friends the next logical pack for me, but shifting my bossiness from family to friends was truly a natural leap. I felt like I had moved up the arbitrary scale of world domination, and really, this was where my mind kept going. I wouldn't have been surprised to learn that Hitler started out this way, since I instinctively arrived at sensing how these things worked. In my head, I undoubtedly could take on the world once I ruled my friends.

Oh, glory day! Friends, the one thing my mother warned all us kids about. *Friends are no good. Friends are the devil in disguise. Friends will steer you in the wrong direction, for sure! Don't ever bring friends to this house. They're not welcome here!*

Except, *I* turned out to be that friend mothers were trying to keep their sweet kids away from. I was the one that coaxed their young, wide-eyed daughters and sons to skip class and take only that one hit.

"Come on, it's not bad for you, you know. Look at me, don't I look okay? Just watch me do it. See, now it's your turn. What are you, chicken? Will you just try it, maaan?" And always, that last bit, I'd say with a tinge of anger.

I had started smoking pot at age twelve, soon after I lost my spot as pack leader. That was another thing I figured out—world domination needed a leader with real guts, and boy, getting high sure let loose a side of me that could finally be daring. Although instead of daring, the word sometimes thrown at me was uncaring, or selfish, or too bossy. See what I meant about the parallels with Hitler?

I remember precisely the first time I smoked pot. After that first time, I couldn't get enough of the thing. It was really the fault of that girl from my school, Sonny Gail. Or was her name Sonny Gal, or was it Girl? Whatever her name was, she latched onto me one day while we stood waiting for the bus to East Side Middle School, and she must have seen the potential for world domination in me because that girl would not let up.

"You look like you could use sumthin'."

"Leave me alone, Sonny Gail, I don't need nothin'!"

"Yeaaaah, girl, you do!"

"Sonny Gail, leave me will you?"

"Nuh uh, I know you need dis sumthin' das gonna make you laugh, laugh. Den you won' need nothin else, girrrl. You need dis, girl. Jus try it, it ain't gonna hurt choo. Do I look hurt to you?"

I finally dared to look straight at her. I saw that Sonny Gail looked way happier than I felt. She seemed to be floating in a cloud of happiness, while I couldn't feel a pinch of happy in me.

Those days, the depression that weighed heavily on me dragged my body down as I went about business. I had been carrying this weight for too many years, since even before I no longer had innocence in me. Being a member of a family that lost sight of sheer treachery had created pure unadulterated bedlam deep inside me, which only fueled my depression, ensuring its interminable existence. As I stared at Sonny Gail,

I could see how different our worlds were. I imagined that no one could ever be cursed as I had been, living with the most dysfunctional bunch on the planet.

I stood at the school bus stop, brooding over my sorry life and listening to Sonny Gail melodiously coax me into smoking the crooked dirty stick she held at the end of her extended arm. It looked nothing like the cigarettes that my father smoked and I sometimes stole, and I realized that my life was short of the kind of "happy" Sonny Gail clearly had.

"Well, all right then." I finally said.

I took one step back, mostly to get Sonny Gail out of my face because she had edged her way in a little too closely. I figured I needed space for this new kind of cigarette that was dirty as all heck. I plucked the joint from her fingers, brought it to my mouth and dragged in air like I'd watched her do. I immediately began coughing and coughing and pretty much choked like I'd never before choked. Sonny Gail laughed her ass off. She couldn't stop laughing. Then I started laughing. It was infectious, that laughing.

I looked over at her and I hadn't noticed this before, but Sonny Gail was missing some teeth, and she was twelve years old, like me. For some inexplicable reason, her eerily vacant mouth was funnier than anything to me. How her missing teeth could be that funny got me laughing some more, and the laughing in me kept growing and growing. After about five minutes of uncontrollable laughing, I stood up straight from being doubled over and Sonny Gail pushed my hand back up to my lips again. Without us speaking, I took another big drag and got all choked up all over again. Through the tears that wouldn't let up and clouded up my eyes, I could see Sonny Gail's pointy over-sized nose, and I hadn't realized that facial feature on her before either. I instantly stopped choking and switched to laughing and laughing. We both laughed hysterically then.

"Ha-ha! See girl, I tol you. You ain't never gonna be the same, girl. Din't I tell you? Ain't dis shit fun? Come aun, girl, take anothu hit. I got lots more of dis shit."

We were standing off in a quiet spot around the corner from the bus stop where my sisters, Lupe and Sarita, and all the other kids were waiting. And really, I couldn't tell you how we ended up there after Sonny Gail came up to bother me. I stopped laughing right then.

I blinked my eyes a couple of times and looked around me, feeling a familiar disorientation take hold. This sort of thing seemed to keep happening to me. I somehow kept losing the most trivial moments from every day. It was as if tiny drops of memory simply spilled out from my mind, each droplet dissipating before any one of them ever got absorbed back into earth's bottomless reservoir.

And always, I would arrive at the end of the day lying in bed, spooning with my sister Sarita. We still shared the same twin bed with the same twin mattress we had started out in, way back when our younger brothers came along and took over the two cribs my parents kept in their tiny bedroom. I would desperately try to recall the miniscule bits that made up my day, and always, I would fail.

Oh, I remembered things like the huge commotions caused by my siblings, mostly by my sisters—like my sister Maribel defying our mom yet again, coming home hours after she was supposed to, smelling like cigarette smoke with her hair all tousled, causing my mom to screech and smack, smack, smack. Or Maribel being accused by "Queenie" Teresa that yet another piece of clothing was stolen from her room—the only room in the entire new house that was occupied by a single person, because she apparently paid for this status on a monthly basis. "Miss Queenie" one day felt it was necessary to install a lock to keep Maribel's sticky fingers from helping themselves to the piles and piles of clothes that filled that single-occupied room's closet and drawers. These clothes, in time, would be distributed among the remaining five girls when Teresa no longer had any use for them. That meant whatever pieces I ended up with had a hole or stain or were misshapen.

I could easily recall something like the time Maribel ended up having an asthma attack because my sisters Lourdes and Lupe pulled a prank on her. They had waited until Maribel had gone to bed, which was early that night. She was all by herself in the whole dark upstairs in our bedroom where five girls slept. She lay on the full-sized bed she shared with Lourdes and Lupe, those two scrunched deep inside the bathroom at the bottom of the stairs, taking their revenge on Maribel that was long overdue, since she had been pulling prank after prank for years on them.

As Maribel lay alone on that bed, unable to fall asleep, our bedroom's creepy haunted closet blew out its usual wisps of unexplainable cold air, even in the summer. This blowing air competed with the creaking from the old planks of wood that made up our house. Everywhere, there was nothing but darkness and the creepy noises emanating from the house. Earlier in the day, Lourdes and Lupe had tied a string to the door that separated the attic floor from the main floor; this door creaked the loudest in the whole damn house. Slowly, my hidden sisters, pulled that string, and that upstairs door creaked louder and louder as it appeared to open all on its own. In that dark lonely bedroom, Maribel, lay awake, fear-stricken and unable to move, and unfortunately unable to breathe.

When she finally started breathing, it came out in short rough rasps of air that was void of any oxygen as the asthma in her bubbled forth. Suddenly, Maribel appeared at the top of the stairs, afflicted with one of the worst asthma attacks she ever had. My sister Maribel, our suddenly fallen hero, was rushed to the hospital and my sisters got in really big trouble.

So sure, I had no trouble whatsoever recalling *those* things. But it was the little happenings that somehow never penetrated my brain enough to join all my other memories in my mind's vast memory bank. Things like: Did I really cross the threshold of our house before walking to our school's bus stop? Did I beam myself to the spot I stood on, well out of view from my two sisters and the crowd of kids playing or standing or taunting as they waited for our school bus?

I could never recall stuff like that, no matter how hard I tried. No matter how careful I was to walk the day through in my head, I ended up looking at a jumbled mess of things that happened to just about everyone else but me.

It was always the same. Each morning during my middle school years, we all left for school after a harrowing time getting out the front door. And every day, I somehow ended up walking alone to the bus stop for East Side Middle School, even though

I had started out walking alongside Lupe and Sarita. And every morning, I would watch for the boys who would come out of nowhere and push their way in to take positions alongside my pretty sisters, completely ignoring me. There were times when Lupe had three or four boys vying to put their arm around her shoulders. No boy ever tried to put an arm around me, not once. I was the ugly one, and although I walked behind the entourage every morning, willing myself to vanish into complete nothingness, those damn boys still managed to see me. They'd call me "grease head" or "druggie."

"You look like a druggie girl with those ugly black eyes. Who punchoo, girl? Ha Ha, Haaaaa!"

"Are you sure that's your sister?" one boy asked Lupe one time. He had his arm wrapped tight around her shoulder so none of the other boys could slip in and take his place. She looked over his arm and back at me where I walked some distance behind the jeering, and said, *"Nah, that's my dog!"*

"Haaaa Haaaaa Haaaaa! Hey doggie-girl, don't get too close I don' wanna get no rabies! Haaa Haaa!"

Being left behind was fine with me, because I'd get to smoke some pot as soon as I arrived at the bus stop. That was truly a Godsend. I had never laughed much or talked much or did anything much. But with my new best friend, Sonny Gail, I got to laugh and laugh my way to world domination.

FIVE

8:15a.m.

I was at my locker in eighth grade at East Side Middle School.

I had been minding my own business when I was suddenly shoved. My face smacked hard into my open locker and I couldn't imagine how that could have happened. I turned around, feeling a little disoriented, and there in front of me stood five black girls.

One girl from my homeroom class turned away from us and ran. I figured she wasn't the least bit interested in being a part of my gang, especially since she was white and she had nothing to do with us.

I was ten years old when I first realized that my parents being born in Puerto Rico mattered a great deal to "white" people—and that later this would become an overbearing stigma, and a crutch. We had been living in our new house three months when the first incident happened. I was playing outside in our driveway with my pack's four younger siblings.

"Bobby! I told you to get away from them damn Puerto Rican spics! Now get in here!" shouted our next-door neighbor to her grandson from inside her slightly opened window. She then slammed shut that thing, making sure we couldn't fling any poison in. After his grandmother's outburst, little Bobby, who was younger than our youngest, turned to us and spit at us. As he ran toward his apartment door, he shouted, *"Go back to*

where you came from you damn Puerto Rican spics!"

It didn't take five years after moving into our new neighborhood for it to clear itself out of white people. They feverishly packed their boxes and filled truck after truck, muttering to themselves, *"Ever since that damn over-sized Puerto Rican family moved in, our neighborhood got too dirty. And they're never leaving since they bought the damn place!"*

Even though we kept our yard clean, I never could figure out how they knew our house was filled with too many filthy secrets—secrets that made staying inside it so unbearably stifling, us kids would end up outside any chance we could. And unlike the blacks we had rioted with, didn't we have skin the same color as theirs? Had they bothered to stand close enough to my mom, they would have seen how her eyes were the same blue as theirs.

"What?" I asked the angry gang of five, still feeling stunned and disoriented as my face grew hot and bruised from being smashed into the hard metal of the locker.

The fuming group stood staring at me with fiery eyes and flaring nostrils. I never understood why gangs of chicken-shits always picked fights with only one person. I then recognized three of them. I'd never caused any of them any trouble. I stood there confused, blinking and really trying hard to figure out what was happening. *Could they be here because of that riot so long ago?* I wondered. But that explanation immediately didn't make sense. I'd known half of these girls only after that riot. I couldn't figure out why these black girls were standing so close to me with angry eyes, huffing and huffing.

"Yeah, that's her. You ought ta just smack the shit outta her," said the obvious leader, Denise, who I had known for a couple of years. I couldn't imagine why out of nowhere she decided she hated me. I didn't talk to her; we were never close. I knew of her, but I didn't really know her.

"She think she betta than us. Yeah, she think she special. We ought ta just beat the shit out of her ugly face."

All these words came from Denise. I had never bothered her. I never bothered anyone.

"I don't get it, Denise, what did I ever do to get you angry at me?" I asked, trying to make sense of this.

Then she started gyrating practically, and she started swinging that jaw of hers and bobbing her head.

"You fuckin' think you betta than everybody, girl. You walk like you special, well you ain't special, bitch. You're shit, and we're gonna teach you..."

I stopped listening and seeing and feeling and I felt myself shrink further and further... None of what Denise had said made any sense to me. I was definitely still the "ugliest" and in no way special. By the time I started middle school, I rarely bothered bathing the night before school because I already knew soap and water couldn't wash away the suffocating weight that often threatened to zap every speck of breath from me. I also rarely washed my face, and for sure I didn't bother ironing my clothes, and Lord knew the world was lucky I ever even bothered brushing my teeth! I was always waking up to the weight that always managed to make slipping out from under the blanket I shared with Sarita grueling. Even worse was getting out our front door for school every morning.

After the two oldest, Sandalio and Celestina, got married and began living in their own apartments, we were ten kids living at home. You'd think it would have been quieter with two gone, but the noise was always more than I could stand with so much shouting, fighting, and fury. Our mornings weren't any easier despite two less kids taking up space, because we still had Teresa. Every damn morning, never missing one—not one—she took up all the time there was, holed up in the only bathroom with heat and running water. My brothers and sisters would take turns banging on the door and then they would complain how this wasn't fair to my mom, who went about making breakfast as if the whole affair two feet away had nothing to do with her. My mom didn't dare say a word because, well, Teresa had become a working entity in our family. She helped pay the bills, so Miss Queenie got whatever bathroom time she wanted—and just about anything else she decided should be hers.

Every day, she would finally open that door and slowly, oh so maddeningly slowly, step out of the bathroom after forty-five minutes of scrubbing that face of hers. She'd flick her lashes at us and toss one shoulder up and she'd say, *"Tough, if you don't like it!"* Then she'd saunter off toward her room, swaying her hips way more than she normally rocked those skimpy mounds.

I never understood why my sisters didn't beat the crap out of her. Lord knew my sister Maribel could easily have done it! Our fearless hero, Maribel, was most definitely skinnier than Olive Oyl but had muscle arms exactly like Popeye's. She could beat the crap out of anybody who gave us any trouble whatsoever. Seriously, all of Warren Harding High School, which she currently attended along with Lourdes and Lupe, knew better than to mess with my sister Maribel. I also had grown to believe that Sarita and I weren't the only ones who had witnessed Maribel's extraordinary talent that day of the deadly riot. We all knew she could end this thing once and for all, and why she never did I never understood.

As for me, I was happy not having to do a damn thing to myself in the mornings. I also never had a problem taking care of business in the only other mostly non-functional bathroom—the same one where Lourdes and Lupe hid to avenge their long, overdue payback. That's where I got to freeze my butt off sitting on the blessed toilet that flushed with absolutely no trouble. This "other" bathroom as we often referred to it, always smelled of ammonia and mold because it was mostly used to store all our cleaning products—and with a family our size, we never did keep a dry mop. The "other" bathroom worked okay for me, but you couldn't pay my brothers and sisters to step a foot in there except to snatch up the mop. And we couldn't complain anymore to some arbitrary someone about our bathroom not working, because we no longer lived in the projects. We now lived in our own house that carried more problems than anything else, which my mother never failed to point out to us kids.

If I'd let myself listen to my mother's words more closely, I'd probably have noticed how she always said these words directly to Lupe—not Lourdes, the one who got her faced burned off, but our family's prettiest who had stood remarkably close by Lourdes' side when the incinerator exploded. Anyone who dared to pay close attention to what my mother hinted at would have understood that Lupe's escaping of any damage cost us a great deal. As if the folks who quickly slipped that consolation check into an envelope and rushed to get it into my parents' hands with smiles and handshakes had a clue that our prettiest face was worth more. That paltry check my parents received from suing the City of Bridgeport could only buy us a house with nothing but problems, and…

I snapped out of my mental train ride as soon as Denise's angry words came to a halt. I noticed the gang was no longer looking at me. I turned to see what the girls stared at. Mr. O'Malley, my homeroom teacher, had stepped out of my classroom and was speaking some pretty stern words himself, which sent the five black girls on their way. And even though they hurriedly walked away, staring back with angry eyes, I knew that this was only the beginning. I closed my locker door, then walked toward my homeroom as Mr. O'Malley waited for me by the open door. I was shaking so hard I kept dropping my books.

For weeks, I walked everywhere while looking over my shoulder and sprinting from class to class. Every day I made sure I got on the bus home with Sarita. She always traveled with her boyfriend draped around her shoulder, and with his bad-ass sister who flanked my sister's other side and who nobody messed with. She loved calling me "Grease Head" and "Smelly Isabel." So how come she could easily see there wasn't one damn special thing about my ugly self?

The gang of angry girls did find me alone again a couple more times, but those confrontations got thwarted as well. I seemed to keep getting saved. Denise's clear hatred of me followed me through my first year of high school, but somehow that gang grew with more black and Puerto Rican girls. In high school, it was my sister Lupe and me the enlarged gang harassed and I couldn't understand why Puerto Ricans were siding with blacks. *When did this start happening? Couldn't they see that Lupe and I needed them on our side, where they freaking belonged?* I kept asking myself.

Then one spring day, standing in the middle of our kitchen, Maribel decided to put an end to all this *"...damn stupid shit!"*

"What do you mean girls at school are giving you trouble? What kind of trouble?" Maribel asked Lupe immediately after Lupe brought up the topic. I noticed how both of Maribel's hands were quick to form fists. It was as if these appendages only possessed two positions: open and fists. Now those big Popeye fists rested on her skinny hips, and she was leaning forward and she was getting mad.

Lupe was a skilled fighter herself, but she must have doubted her prowess because her eyes were conveying something else entirely. She looked scared. Also, she still had that red scar clear across her forehead from getting jabbed with the drinking glass that had been purposely shattered just two months before. She'd walked away from that fight winning, so if Lupe was seeking Maribel's help, our situation had obviously gotten really serious.

As I stood listening to my two sisters in our family's kitchen, I could see this thing ballooning to proportions—exactly like that riot when my little brother lost half his hearing. Who knew what more damage would come to our family's prettiest face? That red scar, that on certain days wouldn't stop bleeding, too many months later, wasn't going away. This thing really needed to be stopped.

"I already kicked Yolanda's ass, but now she's wanting to fight me again tomorrow at 3:00 after school, only that fucking

chicken-shit told me she's coming with three other girls. She won't come alone, so I need more," Lupe explained.

I looked around, more worried with Lupe's use of the "F" word in our house than what she was actually saying, and more than Maribel getting all worked up. I relaxed when I made sure my mother wasn't around. I only scanned for my mother. Why would I expect my father to be there? He was mostly away until well after we all went to sleep. But his blessed absence gave me a great opportunity to steal butts from his ashtray that he never did get around to emptying. The half-smoked butts would stay exactly in the same spot for days and days—the perfectly scorched-tipped sticks piling up higher and higher. I would suck in my breath every time I watched my mother slow her pace as she walked past the pile of disgusting things. She would sneer at the pile because years ago she had quit that nasty habit; now she wouldn't dream of staining her fingers by touching those dirty little things. But by then, my mother had already ensured she got plenty of smoke in each of us while we stayed in her belly all those months before we came out kicking and screaming. My dad never being home supplied my nicotine craving just fine.

I kept listening to my sisters' words grow more excited, and I nodded in assent, but Maribel and Lupe never once acknowledged me. They didn't once ask me any questions. I never did utter a word to Maribel about Denise and her gang, nor how it was because of Denise's hatred of me that this whole thing got started in the first place. I didn't say anything to anyone, because I had figured something out.

I noticed how Denise would come at me with her gang time and time again and yet, always, nothing really happened.

After some time, whenever she'd confront me, I'd hear her out because it became obvious to me that this girl was angry about something that had nothing to do with me. I still had no illusions about being special like she kept accusing me of. There was enough proof on my side with being "ugliest," and from still being taunted and jeered at by the boys who continued vying for a position on our prettiest's shoulder every morning. That was a good twenty minutes of taunting and jeering. Those boys didn't seem to care or notice that my prettiest sister had that mark scarring her pretty face. Lupe started asserting herself, though, swatting arms off her shoulder and flaring her nostrils. But those boys' salacious fire would only get more stoked by Lupe's repeated rejections.

Once I understood that Denise wasn't going to beat me, my wise brain neatly laid out the situation. I was helping out that poor Denise because clearly she needed to vent to someone. The girl's tirades were a much-needed release, and she obviously needed someone who would listen. I guess she must have picked out that one potential in me because I never bothered saying one word to her and her gang. I even got to folding my arms and nodding along with their gyration dance. Denise would threaten me, she would gyrate and her nostrils would flare and her head would bob and her girls would swirl and dance around her, egging her on, *"Kick her ass, Denise. Kick it! Go on, she think she special. She ain't nothin'!"* Then, almost in perfect rhythm to their dance routine, their fire would get doused by a teacher who happened to walk by. Or somehow the burning flames would go out all on their own, leaving only a smoldering smelly heat behind. And, boy, I was already good at withstanding that kind of heat.

So as Lupe kept explaining to Maribel the events leading up to the next day's fight, I kept to myself, mostly feeling bad for poor troubled Denise.

"What! And you waited all this time to tell me? Why the hell did you wait to tell me? I'm putting an end to this damn, stupid shit!" Maribel said. Lupe continued explaining herself, but Maribel was done listening to her as she flexed her Popeye arms and flared her nostrils. I jumped with glee then. I got super excited that our family's hero was going to take care of the anger and fear that every day made going to school a drag!

The next day at the scheduled time of this four-against-one girls' fight, a pretty good-sized crowd waited down the street from our high school. I could see Yolanda and her girls, and right beside them stood Denise and her shrunken gang of three. I observed the two gangs as they waited and fidgeted some distance away from where I stood hidden. I did know better than to get too close to that crowd. I knew too well that for a reason I could never come up with, my ugly self was not invisible as soon as I left my house.

As I watched those angry girls, I concluded that Puerto Ricans had no place standing beside blacks against another Puerto Rican. It was bad enough that two Puerto Ricans were fighting each other, but now the damn Puerto Ricans were switching sides! And thank goodness, I didn't have to concern myself with any white girl joining our gangs, because it just wasn't done—it was wrong! I stood there shaking my head at the whole thing.

Then I saw my sisters Maribel and Lupe walking up the other

end of the street. They were quickly approaching the crowd, and the excitement grew. I could hear and feel the buzz that the sight of my sisters caused. But wait, who was that walking alongside my two sisters? Was that Maribel's best friend, black Ronda? It was! Best friend or not, I couldn't understand why she was walking alongside my sister Maribel, who had Lupe walking on her other side. I shook my head at the sight of races mixing everywhere I looked, but I stopped moving at all when another thought thundered in my brain.

There were only three in my sisters' gang!

I couldn't see how this would end okay. I feared for my sisters. I was no longer excited. I felt so scared that staying upright became nearly impossible. My sisters didn't know about Denise and her girls. I should have told them. Now they were walking into a fight with two gangs of girls instead of just Yolanda's.

Maribel, flanked by two, whizzed past where I hid, unable to shout my warning. My sister with the Popeye arms went straight into the opening of the crowd, apparently already knowing who this Yolanda girl was. She didn't ask any questions; she just went in swinging, and in less than a minute she beat that poor girl. That fight was the most graceful arrangement of titillating moves I had ever witnessed. My sister's swift dispensing of a most efficient beating was nothing like the riot I had witnessed years prior. Maribel stood tall with her now infamous fists set on her super skinny hips as she stared down at the bleeding girl on the ground.

"I'll tell you what, bitch. I'm going to wait for you on this same spot every day, and I'm going to give you this same beating every

day you dare come back to this school. Got that, bitch? I said, got that, B.I.T.C.H.?" Maribel's nostrils were flaring like never before and her face wasn't even red. She was so calm, which never did happen when she was home. Maribel was a firestorm at home, every single day.

Bleeding Yolanda quickly nodded her head that was being cradled by her two very bloody hands, and she was on the ground in the fetal position protecting her torso that got repeatedly kicked and punched. Having watched Maribel take care of business, I concluded that she fought more impressively than a boy. She never scratched or pulled hair. She flexed her Popeye arms, wound up her punch, and then she delivered such a powerful POW, again and again and again, never breaking once until her opponent was down. You could hear the impact a block away, which was where I had remained hidden the whole time.

It was then I realized it. Not only had no one else moved in on that fight, but the crowd had moved several feet away from Maribel. Only Lupe and Ronda stood closest to her, clearly not afraid of my sister's fury in the least. It was as if sheer proximity to my hero's tight circle would place anyone unwelcomed next in line for the beating of their lives. They all must have sensed this, because that crowd of at least fifty kids took one step further back when my sister Maribel looked up and straight at the two gangs of girls. She didn't look around at anyone else so she must have known something about Denise and her gang as well. Maribel pointed directly at the group that was made up of two gangs of blacks and Puerto Ricans siding together.

Immediately, the gathered crowd, after doubtlessly witnessing the most impressive fight of their lives, moved as far away as they could from that group Maribel had singled out with her laser-red eyes and pointed finger. I could see how the whole crowd cleverly positioned itself behind where Maribel, Lupe and Ronda formed a semi-circle above bleeding Yolanda, and it looked as if the whole crowd was ready to pounce on those two gangs.

"Let me make this clear to all you bitches," said Maribel. *"Myself and Ronda here are coming to school every day from now on, and we're going to wait for all your asses, and if we see or hear you giving my sisters any trouble, you're going to get the shit kicked out of you, too. I promise I will send you to fucking Bridgeport Hospital. So leave this school for good if you can't keep your shit to yourselves. Did I make myself clear?"*

Maribel warned the two gangs as they listened, slightly nodding their heads. No one said anything. It was dead quiet as my hero, Lupe and Ronda turned and walked back in the direction from where they came. This time, I quickly stepped out of my hiding spot and joined them, and so did my two other sisters who were obviously hiding themselves. Us five sisters plus Ronda walked together as one gang, making it clear to Denise that she had better not ever come near me again.

The two gangs disbanded. Yolanda must have transferred to another school, because Maribel and Ronda waited the next day and the day after and for every day after that for about two weeks.

One day, during my sophomore year of high school—which was one year after the gangs disbanded and three years after I started smoking pot—my brother Pedro angrily raced down the stairs and into our kitchen where I sat dazed and very much unacknowledged by everyone who had walked in and out. My mother stopped cooking and walked to stand behind a kitchen chair the second she heard anger spew from Pedro's mouth, probably as a way to deflect his words that on some days could burn down any one of us to a scattering of ashes.

My brother hollered as he paced the kitchen, accusing my sister Maribel of stealing again. My mother stood holding onto the back of a chair, swiveling her head this way and that way. She kept asking my brother over and over what it was Maribel had stolen from him. Pedro continued pacing around her, yelling into the kitchen, and then turning to her and yelling directly at her. But no matter how often my mother asked, Pedro wouldn't name what was stolen. After my mother's fifth attempt at getting to the 'what was stolen,' my brother amplified his voice to redirect my mother's focus toward the real infraction, which was that Maribel *stole*…again!

"Who cares what she stole mama? I mean, really. I mean really!! Why can't you see that's not important? She stole from someone living in this house again? Didn't we just get through dealing with her stealing from Teresa last week? Didn't we? Can you see how that's what matters here? Can you? This has got to stop! That girl has got to be stopped! And if you won't do it, I will!" Pedro screeched this last bit so loudly, our mother gripped

tighter onto that chair back. I could see that she was losing her balance. He then stormed out of the kitchen, leaving my mother and I scorched and breathless.

I had braced myself where I silently sat the moment Pedro started his tirade, fearing the truth would somehow be revealed. He would immediately have recognized the signs. I sat paralyzed with fear that he'd break from his rabid diatribe and let his eyes settle on me. I was afraid because it was *me* who was stealing from him. By that time, I was stealing every day from his many marijuana plants that he cleverly hid around our house and yard.

My plan to only help myself to a little from each pot-plant didn't work out so well. I was helping myself to more and more of those perfect leafy stems, sometimes creating a gap where there had just been a dense overgrowth. I had started out stealing enough for one thin joint a day, but then my wise brain figured out pretty quickly that I could roll up two or three more and sell them. I couldn't imagine my brother ever noticing, since I had been careful to roll super skinny sticks. By the end of the week, I would have enough to buy my own drinks when my girlfriends and I went to the local salsa clubs on Saturday nights, where I would sell a few more.

Had I really paid attention, I would have noticed how the twenty-five dollars I generated from only one night of enterprise was leaving big gaping peepholes back home. I also hadn't realized that I was already a successful entrepreneur by the time I was fifteen years old. This shouldn't have surprised me as much as it did, since my keen wisdom had been devising ways to enterprise since before we moved out of Father Panik Village.

I'd get to work on my first business as soon as I arrived at school. I'd offer the ultra-skinny sticks skimpily filled with the healthy supple leaves that had been plucked from the perfect green stems I had snapped from whatever plants I could get to that morning. I'd hurriedly be grinding then rolling in our new house's "other" bathroom with a perfectly functioning door and toilet that nobody else ever bothered with. I became a master at talking some sweet innocent someone into smoking pot for the first time.

"Come on, man! What are you afraid of? This is some good shit, you don't know what you're missing, girl. Look at me, don't I look okay to you? I'm telling you, you only need the one hit and you'll be laughing for the rest of your life. Shiiiit! It's good stuff!"

And bam! Just like that, I'd have another customer.

SIX

I quit building my drug enterprise the day the Jesus got into me. This happened at the beginning of my senior year of high school. I was seventeen years old. I hadn't known what I was getting myself into when my mom approached me, but the look of determination in her eyes should have been warning enough that I had been singled-out by her, yet again. I eventually understood why the woman, who on a daily basis made it clear to me that I didn't matter much, managed to get me to agree to do some of the most grueling things. All along she'd been trying to zero out her mistake: me. Each time my mom acknowledged my human existence, I'd be so shocked that she could see me that all I ever could do was nod, never really hearing what it was she proposed. That was how this one time I ended up at a high-rolling born-again Jesus retreat, two states away from home during one perfect fall weekend.

My mother invested quite a few minutes trying to convince me that whatever she went on and on about could be fun and would I please, please accompany her. The woman who spoke that day was determined for sure, but she also seemed desperate—which I had never seen in her before. I stared at the desperation growing in her eyes and only caught the word *"please."* As she talked and talked, I thought: *Is she talking to me? Hmm, can she even see me?* I couldn't remember ever responding to her plea because I was laughing so freaking hard—which stopped her begging. I watched her eyes shift and I knew she was really mad, which got me to stop laughing.

But I guess she got the last laugh! Because there I sat, squeezed in between all these loud, over-sized Puerto Ricans as they shouted Jesus' name again and again. All I could think of was how lucky I felt that I'd been smart enough to bring three joints along with me—and not the skinny ones I normally made, because after the first five minutes of being smothered by cheap perfume and holy rollers, it hit me that I'd gotten singled out again by mom.

After the Utkins, I knew I wasn't chosen because I was special. I'd been chosen because I was a mistake. And the aftermath from taking me so high up, then dropping me to the lowest depths of disappointment, was meant to remind me daily of the curse I brought onto my family. And after being forced to attend Barbizon Modeling School when I was nearing fifteen, I figured out I got picked for that particular one because I had become the ugly mistake my mother made—and I had the audacity to grow uglier by the minute. It seemed I was constantly due and my mother knew exactly how to mete out her punishment.

Almost as soon as we entered the dark drafty auditorium, I had abruptly excused myself, walked a couple of blocks, then feverishly smoked one super fat joint down to the teensiest roach. While spectacular for the first couple of hours, it was definitely not doing the job right about then. So I got up, pushed my way through an avenue of plump flesh and walked out and away about a block or two. I desperately lit up the second joint and sucked in a deep drag. I held that drag in until it burned and burned. That was always such a pleasure, that burning. I got through about half of it before the stupid leaf falling from the tree and landing on the ground right in front of me completely cracked me up. I stubbed out the remaining half of the joint and put it back in my bag, because this was a whole weekend event away from home. I needed to conserve my stash if I were to make it through this damn stupid retreat.

I pretty much laughed my way through one and a half days of the interminable Jesus talk, making fun of each speaker, kind of like I used to do to the guest speakers who were invited to speak to us hopeless kids at my high school. My teacher would sit me down the morning of, to warn me that any wisecracks from me and I would be in detention for the rest of the month. Sure enough, I would then ask a question that had nothing to do with the topic being presented, and that stupid old beady-eyed speaker would just stare and blink at everyone, confounded by my idiotic question. Before the response ever came, I would get whisked away to the principal's office, who once suspended me for calling him "Bernie" instead of Mr. Shapiro. And as my teacher warned me, I stayed in detention for the rest of the month. But since there were only two weeks left to the end of the month, it wasn't so bad.

As I sat while everyone else stood swaying and swaying, it happened. Right in the middle of jeering at the big fat sweaty guy up on stage, I got the Jesus in me! I had been laughing and laughing at a wisecrack I'd just made—all under my breath of course—because my mother stood close enough that I could hear her off-key cries over everyone else's. And unlike my high school teachers, she could easily take that hand of hers and swiftly swing it clear across where I sat, and then how funny would that be?

Then my laughing started feeling more like crying. Then the crying became otherworldly and before I knew it, my whole insides started spilling. The whole of my near-eighteen years seemed to rise to the surface right there, with the weight of what I had been keeping buried for too many young years. There stood my darkest secrets, completely illuminated in the open air for all to see, if they had ever bothered looking at me. And, oh, thank the dear Lord Jesus everyone else was busy carrying their own weight. Then I sprung up from my chair and stood up tall alongside everyone. I started shouting *"Jesus"* right along with them, and my left arm shot straight up, and I closed my eyes, swaying from left to right along with the excited mass chanting, *"Oh Jesus. Oh Jesus. Oh Jesus."* I looked over and caught my mother looking and smiling at me and I realized right then and there that she finally could see me.

Two days after my mother and I came home from the retreat, I sat upstairs on my bed. I contemplated how I no longer wished to smoke pot or drink alcohol or steal with my gang of girls who had been calling ourselves "Sticky Fingers" for about three years. I finally decided I would talk to the gang and get them to stop stealing. I would tell them how, for sure, they would end up going to Hell if they continued on their perilous path. I planned to stand above them as they sat on this bed. I planned on speaking to them in the same tone of the speakers who, one by one, had walked up to the podium right in the center of the makeshift stage, gyrating all over it while blaring the words of one scripture after another, proving to me through the obvious meaning of their words how if I didn't change my sinful ways I would suffer for all the rest of time in the burning fires of Hell. I was scared for my friends. I had been saved, but they were in real danger of burning in Hell.

The next day I invited two of my "Sticky Fingers" cohorts over and sat them down on my bed. I stood looking down at my two friends with the most serious expression I could muster, shaking my head precisely as I had rehearsed it in my mind the day before. I began reading from my crisp new bible which I already had opened to the Scripture of Corinthians 6:9-10, the very one that had sprung me up and on my feet and swaying that weekend. I read to them: *"Know ye not that the unrighteous shall not inherit the kingdom of God? Be not deceived: neither fornicators, nor idolaters, nor adulterers, nor effeminate, nor abusers of themselves with mankind, nor thieves, nor covetous, nor drunkards, nor revilers, nor extortioners, shall inherit the kingdom of God."*

After I finished reading, I went about preaching, preaching, preaching with bulging eyes to my two scared-looking friends how not only did they have to stop stealing, but they had to get rid of all the clothes and jewelry they had stolen. I shared how I had discarded all of my stolen goods the day before, right after I had resolved to save them. I paced from one end of my room to the other, and their heads followed my excited movements in perfect unison. When I finally was finished preaching, I found my two friends stretched out and lying face down on my twin-sized bed, crying for their sins. I was sure I was getting the Jesus in them, just as surely as I had gotten them hooked onto pot just three years prior. They sobbed and sobbed and left my upstairs bedroom vowing to throw away their stolen stash of goods, of which they wore a few pieces. They swore to never again steal.

"Next we'll talk about the drugs," I had said to them as they walked out of my parents' house. *"Yes, yes let's do that, we want to be saved!"* they had called back as they walked out the front gate with their eyes still red and swollen from all their crying.

I probably should have gotten to them the next day, and probably again and again after that. Because the following week, they replaced me in the "Sticky Fingers" gang that I had been a part of since its inception. They were also busy replenishing their damn stash of stolen stuff they had given away while in some crazy trance, and *what the fuck was that all about?* they had thought.

It wasn't until months had passed and I was graduated from high school, and I was working at my first real job, that the Jesus craze that had overtaken me wore off. Graduating high school was still such a surprise to me after having been sat down one day after school by my Science and History teachers. They'd stood close together in the front of my near empty homeroom class. I had stared up at them as they told me flat-out that it was looking like I would be staying back and not graduating with my class. After all, they hadn't received one piece of homework from me all year and, *"We've been warning you all year, Isabel. This shouldn't come as a surprise to you,"* and what did I think this was, because *"This was serious business, young lady,"* they stressed. *"Get your homework caught up and we will pass you."* But I got away with this sort of thing with all my other classes, and I had scored really high on all those tests. Not for Science and History, though. And so I worked night after night those last three months of school, checking off each assignment as I completed them from the never-ending lists.

Months after the Jesus craze no longer kept me spellbound, I still didn't dare smoke pot. And still I repeatedly refused to accompany "Sticky Fingers" as they worked their perfected craft through each shop at the nearby malls. I had even almost stopped drinking. It wasn't until I went to my first "white people" party, when I found myself straight back on my eternal path to Hell. Glory Hallelujah!

A co-worker from the bank where I had started working one month after I graduated high school invited me to her house for a party she was throwing that Friday night.

"So come ready to party!" she had eagerly said.

I smiled and said, *"Okay, I will."* But inside I knew I was done partying. I was only eighteen years old and I had given up partying after quite a few years of it.

I arrived that Friday night at my co-worker's house and I waited and waited for the party to start. More people would arrive and I would stay standing and really doing nothing else but talking to more people. And all these people just stood around and talked and talked their asses off. About two hours into the party, I noticed I was still holding the same cup of beer that had been jammed into my hand when I first arrived. I didn't see any rum or vodka anywhere. But that was fine by me, because I wasn't drinking very much any more ever since the Jesus had gotten into me, and even after it had fallen away. And what the hell was this music? How was anyone supposed to dance to this shit? I finally walked up to the hostess, my co-worker, and asked her, *"So when is the party starting?"*

She looked at me as if I were the dumbest object in the

whole entire world, which she tended to do everyday at work. *"What the fuck are you talking about, you're at the fucking party, you fucking idiot!"*

I stood dumbfounded and thought, *Oh hell, so this is a "white" party!* I immediately put down my warm cup of beer and walked through the apartment and out the back door to the backyard where a keg was being pumped for its cold pale yellow bitter liquid. I grabbed a cup from the stack sitting next to the keg and I stuck out my cup as if I were in a soup kitchen line, waiting for my turn to get my empty belly filled. As I waited in line, I saw that a joint was being passed around and in that second, I knew I would be stepping right back on to Hell's path. I reached out and grabbed the damn thing even though it wasn't my turn. I quickly rammed it into my mouth and sucked in the biggest drag ever, and I let it burn, burn, burn.

The next day I woke up feeling painfully hung over. I reeked of beer and cigarettes and pot. I lay in bed feeling completely spent. Never had I felt so out of sorts as I did that morning. I tried recalling the night before as I lay there unable to move, but only itty painful bits would come up for me. Then I remembered all the white stuff the hostess' husband had divided into skinny lines. One by one, people would sit down in front of the very low table where the white lines had been formed in near-perfect marching order. They would grab one of the tiny straws strewn about the table, bend down really low, and they would then hold that straw perfectly still at the opening of a nostril, and then finally they made a perfect line disappear. I knew what it was they did, and what it was they made the disappearing act with, but I had never gotten up the nerve to try that one. But on that night, already well on my way to Hell, I decided to make the devil proud.

Well, no wonder I feel like crap today! I thought. I had too much fun making white lines disappear. I'd gotten incredibly high from the first line, which instantly zonked me with inexplicable valor that got me believing how incredibly invincible I truly was. I had never before felt that strong. So I went back for seconds and then thirds, hoping to grow more and more and more powerful!

I checked the alarm clock on the dresser and saw it was almost 1:00pm; not morning at all. Thank God I'd had the wherewithal to open my window last night because I reeked. When I finally could get myself out of bed, I went downstairs and saw that Sarita had gone and my mother had left for work. My younger brothers were watching TV and my dad was outside tinkering some. I sat at the kitchen table, not moving.

And all I could think about was finding a way to get more cocaine. I was sure I could repeat the high that overtook me with that first snort. I never could get the other snorts to repeat the high of the first... God, but that first one was pristine. It took me to the highest high I'd ever experienced!

I picked up our house phone and called around to see if I could "hook up" with anyone who knew anything about purchasing some cocaine. How much did the thing cost anyway? I had no clue and I didn't bother with figuring out how I would pay for the damn thing. I was getting real clever with my words, though, as I spoke to each new person, making my offer too good to refuse. But no one I called had what I was looking for.

I grew obsessed at that point. I wanted the white lines! My

need to get this drug brought me so far down Hell's path again that it reminded me of when my mother would manage to lose fifty pounds. Immediately after she'd declare that she was staying skinny, the weight would slowly make its way back. Not any one of us kids would dare make a comment like, *"Gee, those pants don't seem to fit you anymore, mama."* Or *"Hey, doesn't your diet require half the portion you've got in front of you now?"* Before we knew it, she'd end up with the fifty pounds she had just lost, plus another twenty. We all knew not to point out her downfalls because instead of ending up in Hell, we'd end up crippled from one of her deadly spankings. Even getting the Jesus in her hadn't seemed to take away her anger any.

So there I was again, well on my way to the burning fires of Hell—only now, I was definitely securing Hell's most deadly room.

In the midst of my desperate attempts to procure the perfect white drug, one of my friends called and asked about the party I had gone to the night before, while she and all my Puerto Rican girlfriends had gone dancing at our local salsa club.

"Holy shit! You won't believe it. It was a bunch of dumb white people just standing around talking and drinking fucking lame beer and listening to disgusting hard rock music. I swear, man, nobody danced, not one time. And can you believe they didn't even have rum or vodka?" I told her.

"Get out! No fucking way!"

"Yup! It was the worst party ever. I ain't ever going to another "white" party again, maaan. That was too painful."

Then I was instantly struck with an idea: Since these lame white people seemed to be the only ones with the white drug, I needed to be talking to them—not any of these dumb-headed Puerto Ricans who didn't seem to know the first thing about the miracle white drug that made me capable of doing anything I damn well felt like doing. I immediately ended the phone call with my friend and dialed my co-worker's number, hoping to catch another white party, even if they were painfully nothing like the fun parties I was used to.

Only six months before attending my first "white" party, we had celebrated our tight-knit group of friends' first eighteenth birthday. Our friend's father hired an entire salsa orchestra to play for the event, which was held in the apartment they lived in above the variety store they owned. There must have been at least a hundred people crammed into that small apartment, dancing and dancing while drinking sweet concoctions of rum and coconut juice, and rum and coke, and vodka and orange juice, and big swigs of plain vodka or rum, (It was at this party when I broke my abstinence from alcohol! I'd prayed and prayed, and cried and cried the next day repenting for my sin.) and on and on we danced and drank until practically the next morning.

Toward the end of the party, that one guy, Herberto, kept grinding and grinding into me during the slow dances. *Where was my boyfriend?* he wanted to know. By the end of the night, we had all drunk too much to make it home, and we had all danced our asses off, and we all slept wherever we'd dropped!

So, just like that, Jesus left me for good at a "white" party. I was relieved because I had been having all the wrong thoughts for a Jesus-fearing follower to make it into Heaven. If the nuns from my years attending St. Mary's were right, my thoughts alone had already granted me passage to Hell. While I had the Jesus in me, I had tried hard every day to rid myself of the sinful thoughts. Sometimes I'd pray so hard, I started crying all over again like I did at that retreat. It was a relief to no longer pretend that I wasn't having sinful thoughts. Only now, along with these thoughts, my brain was crammed with the years of my mother's ruthless rule, the years of the guilt-inducing teachings of St. Mary's Spanish nuns and priests, my most recent acquisition from the three days of holy-rolling Jesus freaks' messages, and God with the long white beard in a most pissed-off state. I was so well on my way to Hell that I thought I would die exactly where I stood if I didn't fucking get some cocaine in me soon, and my heart had raced hours before I even got the stuff in me.

Part Two

Her Relationships

SEVEN

There are no instructions in life to help guide one toward waking up. It just either happens or it doesn't come at all—that is, until death comes knocking. It was after finally arriving at death's door that I could see my whole life clearly. And even though it was after my marriage to Harry that death came looking for me, I can now see that death had been following me decades before Harry, and that he and all the rest of them had only been death's pawns.

In the following pages I'll walk you through only some of the romantic relationships I endured—the very ones that led me to Harry, then death, then divorce, then waking up, then finally to my divine, glorious, happy life. Oh, and I used the term endure in its most literal meaning. I only ever learned to go about life with a most acute degree of endurance that kept my mind dulled, and wisdom stifled. After Harry, I realized that all my relationships were stepping-stones not to any place up or good, but straight down to Hell—where eventually I would discover the door to a glorious life.

Through my relationships, I learned how nothing had changed the day I left my parent's home to marry, the first time. I learned that I simply recycled the parts of me that kept me in perpetual suffering with each relationship, regardless of years gone by that should have armed me with a basic know-how of living.

I'll start with my first relationship.

EIGHT

One month before my fifteenth birthday, my mother talked and talked about this place that could be good for me. Her co-worker at the factory she worked at had sent her daughter there, and it had done wonders for her little baby girl. After attending this enchanting place she couldn't keep the marriage proposals from coming. How lucky was this co-worker's beautiful darling girl, and the same could happen to me if I were willing to give it a go. So I did. I let my mother sign me up at Barbizon Modeling School.

Every weekend for six months I would take the train from Bridgeport to Stamford. However, after four months of that nonsense, mainly because it wasn't helping wipe away my ugliness one bit, I skipped Barbizon Modeling School altogether. I would catch the train to Stamford and smoke pot and hang around town all day. Then at the regular time I'd take the train back to Bridgeport, walk from the station to our house, race up the back stairs to our apartment and tell my mother all about my trippy day at modeling school as she prepared supper. *Oh, and yes, yes, it's really, really helping me,* I'd reassure her. But I could see she wasn't convinced. She would examine my face and it was clear that I was just as ugly as the weekend before.

Then the letter came. I hadn't been expecting it so it was jolting to be yanked down hard on the kitchen chair as soon as I walked in after my extremely enjoyable time that Saturday. I had just finished devising the perfect excuse as to why I was so late this particular Saturday in the first week of February: *The train was so late, I froze waiting out there,* which explained why my eyes were bloodshot and why my sallow skin was so blotchy.

"Really? Well, that's interesting because this letter says that you stopped going to school a month ago. Where have you been going all these weeks, girl? And please don't even think about lying to me!" My mother shouted, as she leaned way down and stared me down with the most menacing look. I sensed my life would be ending soon, and so I closed my eyes.

But in the next instant, I was shocked to hear myself yell the words that angrily spewed from my mouth even before I reopened my eyes.

"I hate going to those stupid classes!" I had never yelled at my mother. I had never dared to. I waited for her to beat me as I cowered, but she didn't even raise her powerful hand to me.

"Humph! They are good for you, and you are going back, and you are going to finish." My mother straightened her body and turned her back to me. As she walked away, she said, *"And I will be taking you to class from now on."*

So, that was that. My mother accompanied me to Barbizon School of Modeling every Saturday thereafter, and waited until I spent the extra hours making up for the Saturdays I missed so I could graduate from ugly to beautiful. And wouldn't you know? Both she and my father attended the graduation—the only graduation those two ever bothered sitting through.

Exactly three months after graduating from Barbizon Modeling School, I began grooming myself properly, which was why I no longer looked hideous when I finally snagged my first boyfriend at age fifteen and a half. This age was considered to be in the red danger zone; everyone knew you needed to be engaged by age sixteen in order to follow a proper courtship through a wedding day scheduled some time around the age of eighteen. I got myself a flattering haircut that had been highly recommended by my brother Pedro, who was enrolled at the local beauty school. Every morning I bathed, blow-dried my new hairstyle, and then applied quite a bit of make-up precisely as I'd been taught at Barbizon. Some mornings, I reluctantly acknowledged that perhaps my mother's persistence did help me some—like looking good enough to no longer be taunted by the boys that still every morning fought to wrap their arms around Lupe's shoulder on our way to school. I started receiving compliments about my appearance, which I had no clue on how to graciously accept. Everyone kept congratulating me, and I'd ask for what, and they'd assess my appearance with their roving eyes and say, *"You look new!"* or *"Wowweewowwow, girl!"* and afterwards I'd shout, *"Liar!"* or *"Shut up!"* instead of saying a polite and ladylike, *"Thank you."*

Without my mother ruthlessly ensuring I completed that course, I probably wouldn't have snagged a boyfriend either. My prince walked up to me one day after school, miles away from his own school and began talking sexy to me. His name was Rafael. Rafael wasn't just any boyfriend; he was the guy too many girls coveted. And, oh Lord, it was me he clung to for three years. How special I felt in my first boyfriend's arms—even if he was a no-good chcat!

We'd spend every weekday together after school. During that first summer together, I'd sneak away from home and spend hours with my dream guy until school started, and then again

I'd meet him outside my school every day. Then it was during our second summer together (three months before the whole Jesus thing), on one of the hottest days, when I learned about my prince's cheating ways.

And really, it was quite a shame, since it happened just when we were getting in sync with our drug-dealing enterprise.

On that unfortunate day, I skipped up the back stairs of our house to my family's second-floor apartment after a long day at the job I held that summer. My mother yanked me to stand directly in front of her immediately after I entered the kitchen. I could see she was livid. I didn't need her to utter one word, because her red face and flaring nostrils and bouncie-bounce was all I needed to know that I was about to die. My knees went out on me and I almost fell to the floor; I would have, had my mother not been gripping my arm so tightly. I was sure she'd discovered my drug enterprise. I was sure my brief life was over. As she spoke, I raced through all the scenarios in my head that could have enlightened my mother to my burgeoning business.

"Listen girl, you don't know this but that boyfriend of yours has been sneaking every day into the corner house where that woman lives and he doesn't come out of there for hours, and if you think they're sitting around drinking coffee and talking then you're more stupid than I thought you were for picking someone like him in the first place. Now, either you break it off with him or I will tell him myself that I know what's going on."

My mother moved in closer and closer as she broke this news to me. I couldn't figure out how her news explained her discovery about my drug enterprise and…What? Boyfriend? What?! I should have felt relieved when I understood my secret business was still safely hidden from my mother. I should have started breathing normally again, but the bits that did manage to penetrate my brain warned me that something just as damning as being caught out about the drugs had occurred.

"Did you hear me, girl!?!" my mother screeched, and she repeated her news with so much force I almost went down but for the chair back that dug into me.

She still gripped me by the elbow and I swear she was getting ready to crack my head open so she could get some common sense in there. I tried pushing myself up off the chair she pressed me onto. I had trouble making out exactly what she said. No way would my beautiful boyfriend cheat on me, I finally allowed myself to reason. By this time in my life, I had swiftly kicked my wise chamber down to the lowest depths of reason, where absurdity smothered it like a dark noxious tumor. Which was a shame, because had I kept my wisdom up on the surface of reason, I could have arrived at a completely different conclusion. As in, I never, ever again should have accepted all the swooning over me that was soon to come from my Puerto Rican cheat.

I immediately figured my mother got her eyes all clouded up, because that corner woman she referred to was only a girl. I automatically assumed my mother was talking about the girl that lived there with her aunt. Absolutely, no way could my mother be referring to the aunt who was at least 30! And no way could my doting boyfriend be sleeping with the girl because she only ever slept around with older men, including a seventh-grade teacher when she was only in sixth grade. That rumor made it around the whole school the same day that stupid teacher came in to her classroom and told her what he planned on doing to her. What could she want with my boyfriend when he was months younger than me, and I was two years younger than her? My mother must have gotten it wrong.

"Are you sure it was him you saw? Are you positive?" I asked her.

"Oh really? You think I can't see, girl? You think I'm now some stupid old blind lady?" she yelled.

She really was beyond mad now. She tightened her hold on my arm, and she dragged me from the middle of the kitchen to her bedroom window. It jutted out far enough so that I got a perfect unobstructed view of that corner house's back door, and she held me there. My insides were getting all churned up. I wasn't sure I was ready to give up this beautiful boy that all the girls kept trying to steal from me. Sure enough, he came out the unobstructed back door and in plain view, I watched him give that corner girl a real sexy kiss with his arms wrapped tightly around her, nothing like the way he kissed me. And didn't he just get through kissing me?

"There!" my mother said as she roughly released my arm and stormed out of her bedroom, huffing and puffing. I was practically choking on the vapor smoke my mother left behind. It was so hot, my eyes burned and I couldn't stop my tears from flowing.

The next day I broke it off with my beautiful Rafael, even though I really didn't want to; who would ever want me again, being "ugliest" and all? Even though the people in my life continued telling me how good I looked, my brain would expel their words and my brain would buff until it sparkled the one word that had explained me since the beginning: UGLIEST.

Well, at least by this time I knew not to yell at anyone for giving me a compliment and to say *"thank you,"* or what more often slipped from my lips, *"Uh-huh, whatever."*

I couldn't stand it. I ran home after I broke it off with my first, and most likely last, boyfriend. As soon as I got up to our second-floor apartment, I ran up the stairs leading to our third floor's creepy attic. That's where the girls' bedroom at that time was only Sarita's and mine—and how I loved that I had my very own bed. I locked myself in our bedroom's closet that still blew out cold air. I cried and cried and worked myself into a hysterical tizzy. Then from deep inside me came the cry I could no longer contain. I knew this would happen one day if I weren't careful. I knew the whole ugly mess that I spent year after year burying would some day make its way out of me.

Then I heard my mother. She was wailing somewhere in the house. I thought my ugly secret had reached her and the words that I worked so hard to contain over the years had managed to sprinkle all over her. I heard her cry get closer. I opened the closet door and ran out of my bedroom and through the attic and out the top door that closed off the upstairs from the downstairs. I watched as my mother, now in the middle of the stairway leading to the attic floor, wailed. I watched as she struggled to climb the next step, and she clung onto the banister using both arms to hoist herself up onto the next step as if her sad life depended wholly on that one step. I noticed how weak she looked, compared to the fury she'd flung at me the day before when she informed me of my boyfriend's cheating.

She looked up then and saw me standing there. She stopped her wailing.

"What's happened? Are you hurt? What's happened?

I heard her words, but I knew deep down that I didn't matter much to her. Even worse than being "ugliest" was me still being invisible to her. Sarita was whom she saw, which I had long ago grown used to. Sarita still cooked for the few of us left at home, and I was busy enterprising with my head literally in a cloud of smoke.

"I'm fine. I broke it off with Rafael like you said. I was just crying, that's all."

"What!!" She screeched. *"You made me think someone was up here killing you and it was only that you broke up with that damned idiot scoundrel?"*

Then the impossible happened. My grossly overweight mother suddenly got her energy back and in one swift move, she miraculously made it to the top landing where I stood. She came at me with her fury and struck me hard across my face. I fell back and smacked my head against the door that divided the upstairs from the downstairs before I went down completely.

"Idiota!" She yelled to me as I fell to the floor. She turned and walked back down the stairs, huffing and puffing like mad, not once looking back, and this time she left the whole upstairs clouded by her fiery trail. I couldn't see through the smoky haze, and once again I couldn't stop the tears from blinding me entirely.

By the end of the very next day, after sweet promising words of devotion were desperately spoken to me, I got back together with Rafael. I figured I might as well hold onto him, even though I didn't believe a word he said. My wise chamber tried warning me all that day, especially after too many words were whispered in my ears each time I shared the news of our breakup. It seemed that everyone I saw in those twenty-four hours, as I hid my swollen pulsating red cheek from them, already knew Rafael and I were broken up. They also knew how the girl who lived in the corner house was hardly the only whore Rafael had been cheating on me with. He was having himself a good time, while I couldn't decide whether handing over my virginity to him was a matter meant only for marriage.

After I heard the full scope of my irresistible boy's cheating ways, I figured he couldn't help himself. For nearly eighteen months more, I tolerated him having his way probably as soon as he dropped me off at home. My mother not only stopped talking to me then, but she went back to not seeing me—until I redeemed myself in marriage.

NINE

My first marriage to my Iranian savior, Reza Shapur, came sixteen years before Harry. It marked the first time I lived with a man. Except for the two weeks I spent with the Utkins when I was nine years old, I had never lived away from my parents' home. Leaving my second childhood home to marry felt like the first real grownup thing I would be doing. Not even securing my first real job at the bank at age eighteen felt all that grown up.

But really, Reza was merely my ticket to getting the heck out of my parents' domain. I was only nineteen years old when we started dating, and I hadn't thought of him as husband material whenever I watched him coming in and out of the house that he, his youngest brother Masoud, and their college buddies rented across the street from my parents' house.

It was about a year after he began living in that house that I spoke to him for the first time, but it wasn't anywhere near where either one of us lived. My girlfriends and I were at a bar named Barnaby's near The University of Bridgeport (UB). Reza, his brother and their other roommates were engineering students at UB, and they all frequented this bar. In walked Reza. For months we had been giving each other "googly" eyes—me from my front porch and him from his car to his front door. There at this bar, he noticed me right away. He then smiled at me and my heart melted.

In that brilliant moment, I felt unbelievably lucky for being the one singled out from my group of friends, since I was always the last one to be asked to dance whenever my girlfriends and I went to the salsa clubs. Little did I realize, though, that at the time I was Reza's savior. Only after it was too late did I learn that once my Iranian 'prince charming' graduated from college, he would be immediately shipped back to Iran, from where he desperately hoped to avoid going to war.

He walked directly over to where my friends and I sat.

"I know you," he said, pointing at me.

"Yeah, and I know you. You live across the street from me, well my parents' house."

"Yeah. Do you want to dance?"

"Sure." I jumped from the stool I sat on and ran to him.

Later that night outside of Barnaby's bar, Reza and I made out, then talked and made out some more, and then rested long enough to talk some more. I only ever had kissed three guys before that night. It was clear that Reza had lots more practice than those boys I'd been with, including my Puerto Rican cheat.

The first time I made out was in fifth grade. This girl in my class, Mary Alice I think her name was, organized "kissing time" every day in the back of Garfield School. I had been transferred there halfway through the fifth grade because St. Mary's was too far for Sarita, Juan and me to walk to after we moved into our new house. My new school had a remarkable secluded patch of yard that was hidden from every single building surrounding it. We would climb the fence and jump down onto the yard that was perfectly surrounded by the tall fence. There were about ten of us who would go back there for kissing time, which lasted about a good fifteen minutes. I only got invited because Edgardo wanted to join and he repeatedly threatened to tell on the group if he couldn't come along. So then I got invited and was relegated to the one guy everyone stood really far apart from. That made him a perfect partner for me, because in fifth grade I was definitely still the ugliest one in my family, and in my new classroom, and for sure I was even uglier than Edgardo. So how lucky was I to have even gotten invited in the first place!

After that magical kissing night with Reza, I knew he could be my ticket out from under my parents' rule; really, my mom's tyrannical control. It didn't help that all my sisters had gone off and got married and I was the only girl still living under my mother's glares and disapproval. Even Sarita, who was one whole year younger than me, was married and soon to be a mother. There I was, nineteen years old with no boyfriend to speak of—clearly an old maid, a status every woman who came to visit us never failed to confirm.

The morning after kissing Reza, I started planning my escape from my parents' home. I decided immediately upon awakening that I'd never again be bullied by my mother. Her bullying lately had reached a whole new level, like that night when I arrived home from the most fun weekend of my life.

I'd entered the front door reminiscing about the splendid weekend holiday in Wildwood, New Jersey with my two best friends. Midway up the stairs to our apartment, I heard my mother call out to me. I slowed my pace, already expecting the worst. When I finally opened the door to our apartment, the rooms were dark, so I wasn't really sure that anyone had called me. But then she said, *"In here."* She called from somewhere in the living room to the right of the apartment's entry door. It was completely dark in there. It was about 9:30 on a Sunday night.

"Where have you been all weekend?" she asked me before I stepped into the darkened living room. I hesitated, then slowly stepped inside and hovered near the entryway.

"I told you I was going away for the weekend," I finally responded, sounding more like a fifteen-year-old teenager sneaking in after curfew rather than a nineteen-year-old adult.

"So just what is it you think you are doing, girl?" I knew she was getting closer to her point with that question. I could hear in her voice that she had gotten herself all worked up into an angry state. The fifteen-year-old in me didn't even hesitate and answered her again.

"Um, coming home?"

"Don't get fresh with me, girl. I don't care how old you are I'll slap you to bits. I'm curious to learn how you expect to find a man who will respect you when you're up and down every weekend partying and Lord knows what else you're doing out there?"

My mother was desperate to eradicate her home of the curse that I was. She knew, moments before I was born, that I'd someday douse our family with damnation. She'd declared my curse so loudly on the birthing table at the hospital that a nurse ran to get another dose of the fine needle to quell my mother's delirium. But nothing the doctor or nurses did stopped the damming words from escaping her lips—the unbearable pleas to make this one go away. She'd learned she was pregnant with me only two weeks after she'd heard about my father's other woman, the one who wore skimpy, tight clothes—and who had a growing belly. Even after my mother confronted this woman who denied the whole thing and, in fact, did not have a swollen belly, she'd rearrange our heaviest furniture, desperately hoping to rid herself of me. I was the dirty mistake that kept reminding my mother that filth lay beside her night after night after night.

She also observed throughout my nineteenth year that I had shed myself of Jesus and was back to shaming my family's name further with whatever filth kept me from getting scooped up by a man, and out of her house. She even sometimes hinted at perhaps *my* mistake in giving up the Puerto Rican cheat too soon.

"I'm only nineteen, mom. I want to have some fun. My friends and I didn't do anything wrong, we only went away on a weekend vacation. What's wrong with that?" I explained, still hovering by the doorway.

"What's wrong with that is you won't be nineteen for long, and before you know it you'll be too old for any man to want you. Not to mention you keep taking off in the middle of the night to do Lord knows what. You think I can't hear you sneak out? Do you think a man is going to want you damaged? And how much longer are you planning on waiting to have children because if you think you can easily have kids when you're older you are most definitely mistaken. By my late twenties each pregnancy got more and more difficult, girl. You're not making this easy on yourself, you know. You will be sorry you didn't take life more seriously."

It was immediately after those words that I vowed to get the heck out from under my mother's ruthless dominion. All I could think of as I walked away from my mother, who stayed sitting in our darkened living room, was how less than one year before I'd let the only prospect for marriage go because he was a cheat. And considering my looks, I knew he was the best I could have ever had—and I let him go anyway. I also knew my mother could see that. Not even her sneaky tactic of forcing me to attend Barbizon Modeling School had helped cover my ugliness. That was a fact I always knew she held against me.

Having given up my only marriage prospect to my first boyfriend, Rafael, I attached myself to Reza. Over the next few months, I was especially careful to say and behave in ways I believed appealed to him. This time, I was determined to not relinquish my sole means of escape.

And here's the thing: I was obsessed with being a good girl, even though the absence of innocence by then was a vapid imprint that kept my soul completely broken. But this having to hold out all over again after the fiasco of my last relationship—being pre-engaged to the Puerto Rican cheat, wearing that tiny speck of a diamond that marked me as taken while he went off and did as he damned well pleased—was not going to work so good for me this time. So I knew I needed to get this boyfriend to ask me to marry him. And all my efforts were worth it, because eight months after we kissed that first night, he did.

We were visiting Reza's best friend and his wife in Washington D.C. for the weekend. That first night we lay on the living room floor in sleeping bags because there wasn't an extra bedroom. Almost as soon as Reza's friends closed the door to their bedroom, he whispered the magic words in my ear, *"Will you marry me?"* I think I let him ask the whole question. At least I hoped I did, because otherwise that would have made a perfect night a bit awkward. I immediately said, *"YES!"* and felt so happy.

I was saved! No longer would I be referred to as my family's "old maid."

I was twenty-one when we married, only six months later. The day we married I still felt lucky, even if the weather didn't bother to cooperate.

It was raining, pouring really. Only the day before, the weather had been spectacular. But what did I expect for April in Connecticut? I was lucky it wasn't snowing and I didn't need to wear snow boots. And even if I had to wear snow boots, it would have been fine, because it was finally, finally happening. In a very short time I would no longer carry the awful stigma that had been pressing down on me ever since Sarita left my parent's house a married woman.

About one hour before it was time to leave for the church, I was still waiting in the dining room, completely dressed in my wedding gown and with a damp towel still wrapped around my wet hair. I stared out our dining room window as I waited for my brother Pedro's car to pull into the driveway. *Why had I assigned him something so important?* I thought. Hadn't I already expected him to let me down? My brother Pedro, my most trusted and devoted ally over the years, was also the most unreliable member in our family. Yet we all constantly entrusted him with the most critical duties. Where was he?

Finally, I watched him quickly turn his car into the driveway and stop. He stepped out of the car. At least he seemed to be in a hurry as he ran and pulled his case out from the back seat, slammed the car door shut and ran to the front door. I heard him race up the stairs leading up to my family's apartment.

"Where have you been, Pedro? Do you have any idea what

time it is?"

"I'm so-so sorry sweetheart, I overslept. But I'm here, ta-da!"

"You overslept? On my wedding day? I'm supposed to get married in forty-five minutes. What's wrong with you?"

"Listen girl, don't give me no shit. I made it, didn't I? Now siddown so I can get your hair done."

This was just like my brother to completely screw up and then turn the disgruntlement on whoever stood in front of him.

I rolled my eyes as I twirled and plopped down on the chair he pulled out for me. He immediately got busy working his magic, which almost everybody in the City of Bridgeport knew about. He could make anyone look beautiful, simply by working their mop of hair into a masterpiece. But now I begged him not to bother with working too much magic, because there just wasn't enough time, and it was raining and what if it got wet? After about thirty-five minutes, I stood up from the chair even though Pedro wasn't done yet. I was clearly risking a big fight with him because nobody interrupted his work, NOBODY!

"Just get my damn head piece on, Pedro. Don't worry about making my hair look beautiful," I said in my don't-fuck-with-me tone with my fists on my hips, looking like the angriest bride in white. And, oh God, how I needed a drink right then, and why had I given up drugs!

"Are you kidding? It's your freakin' wedding day, of course I'm going to make it beautiful. Now sit the fuck back down because it's your wedding day and everyone has to wait for the bride!"

"Forget my hair! I'm late!" I shouted as I ran into the kitchen and looked at the clock on the wall. *"My God, I'm supposed to be getting married in five minutes. Dammit! Give me my Goddamn*

head piece!" I was screeching and I felt the tears rising.

I leaned over the chair I had sat on for thirty-five minutes and snatched from my brother's hand my wedding headpiece with the delicate silk flowers I had glued on only two days earlier. I then pushed my headpiece's attached comb through the top of my hair, not checking to see if it sat right, nor did I bother making sure it stayed on, and I… oh, Lord God, I suddenly realized what had been bothering me most as I had sat and sat.

"I don't even know how I'm even supposed to get to the church!" I screeched.

It was only me and Pedro in the house. I couldn't recall who I had charged with that one detail, and it must have been that I hadn't even thought of it, and wasn't that how this whole wedding was working out!

"Pedro! Take me to the church! Will you stop what you're doing? Who cares how clean the fucking floor is? Get me to the damn church!"

And before Pedro finished talking, I was already out our family's apartment door and racing down the front stairs.

Pedro raced us to the church. Finally we arrived and I jumped out of Pedro's old jalopy before he even stopped the stupid thing. I ran up the stairs of St. Mary's and I knew I was in trouble with Father Collins. He hadn't wanted to marry us in the first place because he had his doubts, and he'd shared them with me again and again and again. When he realized I stopped listening, he then made us take Pre-Cana classes. Instead of taking Fr. Collin's hints that all was not as it seemed, I asked him if we could skip all those useless classes because we didn't need them; no matter what he said or did to try and stop me, I was marrying Reza. So he let us skip the remaining two classes.

I yanked the heavy solid wood church door open and found my bridesmaids in the vestibule looking all worried. The groomsmen smiled at me in that way that said, ...*second thoughts, eh?* I gave them my "fuck off!" look, and down the aisle we raced, and there at the alter stood my husband-to-be looking terribly handsome.

Our wedding constituted one of the most magical days of my life. But almost as soon as we married, Reza began demanding all kinds of stuff from me, like his dinner. Only, I didn't even know how to boil water because I never bothered to learn to cook. I had long ago decided that if the boys can be lazy, then so could I.

It was my sister Sarita who took it upon herself to feed the family when my mom finally had to start working nine years before because my dad had gotten laid off yet again. At that point, there weren't any real income earners aside from my dad and Queenie Teresa. And well, when you looked at things closely, my dad barely made enough to pay all the monthly bills even after almost thirty years of working at the factory— especially after he was done drinking and doing whatever else it was he did that kept him away from home almost all the time. Teresa was a secretary working in a bank, and after figuring things out, it was decided that she barely had enough to offer. That was my mother's cue to start working.

My hard-earned marriage, starting from the first week was far less than perfect. Actually, right from the start my marriage was awful! I quickly learned in that first week that when I walked alongside my new husband, I should not be caught looking around with my ugly face in case I somehow attracted a glance from another man. If that happened…well, in that first week it did happen. Only I wasn't looking at any man. Mostly, I was enjoying our walk feeling elated that I finally got a man to marry me, and how lucky I was, especially since I was a whopping twenty-one-years old, almost too old for any man to bother with. At our wedding my mother kept giving my new husband the biggest hugs; I swear she thanked him a couple of times. I must have been impossible for her to see even on my wedding day, clinging onto the man she wouldn't stop hugging. She'd only smile in my direction, then her smile would fade as she blinked and blinked.

I didn't complain one bit about that or about having to wait so long to get snatched up. So I was feeling especially lucky walking alongside my new husband, when all of a sudden Reza started shouting at this guy. He let go of my hand and rushed over to this man and got in his face then shoved him hard. The poor man didn't know what was going on, so he took off running. Reza watched the guy as he ran away, then he turned and walked right up to me, and he brought his face right into mine and said, *"If I ever catch you looking at another man again, I'll kill you."*

"But I wasn't looking at anyone. I was just looking around!" I said incredulously.

"You keep your eyes down from now on! Khari!" He shouted this word at me, which I later learned meant stupid in Farsi.

So I did. For three years I kept my eyes down. I quickly learned I was meant to be a subservient wife. I no longer felt lucky after that first incident. And I no longer wanted to have sex with the psycho I had to introduce as my husband. I didn't think I could stay married to him but I knew I couldn't run back home; my mother would make living in her house more miserable than living with a psycho.

About six months after we were married, though, I couldn't stand living with my husband any longer and I called my mother and explained to her how I had made a mistake. I told her I didn't love Reza, and that I really, really, really hated being married, and worst of all was being expected to have sex.

Then she said to me, *"Do you think the rest of us like it? Did you think this was supposed to be fun? This wasn't meant to be another one of your careless weekend vacations with friends, Isabel. You need to grow up, girl. You need to focus on making a proper family and start having your children. That is your responsibility now."* She hung up right away, because she wasn't the least bit interested in any more nonsense from me. She also made it clear I was never to taint her home again.

For two and a half more years, I endured the sex and Reza's tyranny. Something else I never told anyone, especially not anyone in my family: I was back to snorting cocaine after having given it up years before—not that anyone of my close friends or my family knew about the first time. I'd gotten a bit out of control that first time I tried it, and well, talk about seeking world domination! A year later I was sure the universe was mine, and forget measly old planet earth! My heart would race so uncontrollably sometimes, I grew scared the thing would burst. So I quit it. But then I started up again because being married to Reza was a nightmare.

I hadn't known Reza snorted cocaine when I first married him, and I never told him about my drug years. But about eight months after our wedding day, I walked straight into the back guestroom of our apartment. And there he sat on the edge of the guest bed, leaning over the night table cutting the white powder. He looked more shocked than I felt. I hadn't known he was home. I stood there completely confused by his presence, and it took a minute for my brain to process what I saw.

I knew in that instant of realization that I would be back to making the miraculous white lines disappear. I walked over to him and told him he'd better cut a line or two for me if he didn't want me to call my friend, who was a police officer. He simply laughed and made room for me on the bed and we had ourselves a grand time. I realized the next morning that cocaine would be my outlet to marriage, and I gave myself to it wholeheartedly.

But after almost three years of hell on earth with the bastard, I decided my once again overly hyped-up heart couldn't withstand any more misery. I decided that even tolerating my mother's glares and harsh words was better than staying married to the Iranian bastard. In the turn of an instant, I decided to leave my first husband.

It happened on a quiet Saturday morning. I woke up early that morning as Reza snored beside me. I could also hear everyone else in the house snoring. It wasn't only the two of us any more. We now lived with Reza's two brothers, his mother and nephew, all in that same apartment we started out living in as newlyweds.

About six months before, Reza had sat me down and explained that his family in Iran needed to get his nephew out of the country before he was drafted for war, which would be in another year or two. By then, this was a very familiar topic for me; only three days after our wedding day we'd received a letter demanding we report to the Department of Immigration. For six whole months, along with the attorney we were forced to hire, we sat through interview after interview, week after week, before the United States of America determined that my marriage to the Iranian who was due to go to war upon graduation was, in fact, valid.

Still, it took one year after we married for me to realize my husband's true motivation in marrying me. One night after flying high on cocaine, my husband explained that of my girlfriends at the bar that first night we'd kissed, I appeared to be the only desperate one. He detected my eagerness the moment he saw me. He told me it was never about love.

Reza asked if I would be willing to host his nephew and Reza's mother, and if it would also be okay if they lived with us. I didn't hesitate for a second; I quickly figured that more people would create the buffer our marriage needed. I also figured his mother would step in and discipline her despicable son. Oh how wrong I was! On the day of their arrival at the airport, I noticed a third person in their group. I turned to Reza.

"Who is that man walking alongside your nephew and mother?" I asked.

"That's my older brother, Habib," he simply said.

"I don't understand, you never told me about him. Are we all supposed to live in our small apartment?"

"They're used to sleeping on the floor, so don't worry about it."

Before I got to ask my next question, which was how did

his older brother get into our country if I didn't host him, Reza's family had reached us. His mother rushed to me first. She grabbed me in a tight embrace as she released a high-pitched cry, saying words in Farsi that made no sense to me. She finally turned to Reza and held on to him, all the while crying out words in Farsi. Then she turned to Reza's younger brother, Masoud, who had moved to the U.S. with Reza, and who only the week before moved into our apartment because his wife had left him and she had been the bread winner. I greeted Reza's nephew and older brother, who both spoke no English. After a long time hugging and crying, everyone finally turned toward our car in the airport's daily parking garage.

As I walked behind Reza's family, I could only think about how six people living in our tiny apartment would mirror the life of my early years living with too many people. I wondered if I would become just as invisible to these new people as I already was for my husband. Then my mind drifted to the nightmare that recurred too often—the one where I was right back living in the same projects where the deadly riot occurred, and where fear had grown to such exorbitant proportions it kept me trapped inside the shrinking apartment, where walls dripped with chemical-smelling blue paint and thick doors of steel remained permanently locked with hundreds of bolts everywhere I turned.

That Saturday morning, the day I finally had enough, I oh so gingerly slipped out of our bed so I wouldn't wake up Reza, still dreaming and snoring in harmony with his other family members in the nearby living room. I softly walked out our bedroom door and I slowly and quietly closed it behind me. I walked straight into the kitchen situated outside our bedroom, and sat at the kitchen table for a long time. I sat not moving, only thinking about the absolute mess I had gotten myself into by marrying Reza. I finally stood up and walked to the coffee maker and began preparing coffee. I waited by the machine for the full pot to brew. I once again found myself asking the one question that seemed to be the only thing I could manage all these years: *How did I get here?* Then I followed this question with: *At least I'm not pregnant. Thank God I'm not pregnant!*

Just like that, the realization that I was not truly tethered to the bastard hit me. I saw how easy it would be to leave, since there were no children to hold me back. I realized I could get a divorce. How relieved I felt at that understanding! I no longer cared what my mother or anyone else thought about me being divorced.

In the next instant, before even pouring myself a cup of coffee, I decided that I wouldn't take another day living with Reza and his clan. Life with the whole bunch hadn't insulated me from my husband's tyrannical ways, after all. My hope that his mother would straighten out her son was quickly quashed. She was used to being trampled on by the men in her country because women there were considered to be lower-class citizens. So instead of standing up for me, she merely turned her head.

I had been a prisoner every single day of that marriage. I wasn't allowed to do, be, say, or think—even though I did, said and thought in spite of the threats. Reza never actually laid a hand on me, and lately I'd been telling him if he dared touch me I would kill him. I was starting to think I could kill him, especially after snorting some lines. I really wanted him to die. But it seemed that as recklessly as he lived his life, God somehow kept protecting the bastard. I even took out lots of life insurance on him, figuring it was only a matter of time. Now, time had finally run out.

I turned away from the brewed coffee and raced into our bedroom and woke up Reza. Before he was fully awake, I told him I was leaving.

"Don't bother waking up for this, Reza. I'm leaving and I'm not coming back."

I quickly walked to our closet and started taking out some clothes. Then in two short steps I was at our dresser and opened drawer after drawer, plucking pieces of clothing, not really thinking about which ones. I filled two duffel bags and walked out the room with them. I put the bags down on the kitchen floor near the doorway and began scanning the kitchen for anything I needed to take with me. As I continued scanning, I heard a flurry of noise in the bedroom; drawers were being slammed shut after being yanked open. Finally, Reza swung the bedroom door open and stormed out. He swiftly moved to stand two inches from where I stood.

"Where is my gun?" he asked, in a low menacing whisper.

My heart sank.

"I don't know," I said.

I didn't dare look at him as I continued scanning the kitchen.

"Listen, Isabel, don't fucking lie to me. I kept it in the underwear drawer and it's not there. I'm only going to give you this one chance. Give me my fucking gun. NOW!" He shouted this last word and I jumped and finally looked at him. His face had turned the reddest I had ever seen it.

By this point, everyone was awake, in the kitchen and speaking in Farsi. Reza and I stood challenging the other with our angry eyes as we ignored them.

"Fine," I said, and I could feel my body start shaking. I walked out the back kitchen door, down the back steps that led me out to the garage. I stepped through the side garage door and walked straight to the rusted old toolbox that was discarded there long before we arrived. I opened it and took the gun from where I had hid it beneath the top layer. I emptied the gun, watching the bullets drop to the bottom of the toolbox. I knew there were no other bullets in the apartment. I walked out of the garage and back up the stairs to our second-floor apartment. By this point, my clothes were soaked in sweat; I nearly dropped the gun because my hands were slick with sweat.

"Here," I said, handing him the empty wet gun. The bravado I'd felt only moments ago vanished and I stood barely upright, shaking. In a moment too late, I realized I'd just retrieved a gun and handed it to an angry man with a deep red face—the same man who for three years had so easily discarded me time after time after time.

I thought for sure he would point the gun at me and pull the trigger. I stood there thinking how stupid I was to have agreed to give him the damn gun. But immediately after I handed him the gun, he turned from me and leaned over the kitchen table and grabbed his set of house and car keys. I watched the nightmare whom I'd once naively considered a celestial blessing, walk out our kitchen and storm out of our apartment of three years.

His mother stood in the middle of the kitchen crying and crying, and his nephew kept begging me to tell him what was going on. I told him I was leaving Reza. Then he turned to his grandmother and told her what I had told him. She started wailing and speaking directly to me in Farsi. I didn't understand a word she said except my name, which she cried out over and over again.

"Isabel-joon, Isabel-joon, Isabel-joon…!"

"But you don't have to go because of us," Reza's nephew said.

"We are so close to moving into our own apartment," Reza's younger brother, Masoud, said. His older brother still didn't speak English so he stood off to the side, just staring into space and not daring to look at me.

"Oh, no, trust me, my leaving has nothing to do with any of you. I have to do this. I have to go, and I have to go now." I heard myself shout that last part as panic spread across my chest, then up to my brain, silently seeping like the monthly flow of blood.

What I had really meant to say to the frantic group swarming around me was that I had to go because soon, very soon, Reza would realize there were no bullets in his gun. He would know I purposely gave him an empty gun, which meant he would soon be back with most likely the rage that knew no bounds. I'd already witnessed several more explosions when my delusional husband believed that some stranger was looking at his "ugliest" wife.

"Are you fucking that guy? Because he looked at you like he knew every inch of you really well," Reza had said more than once.

"You're crazy. You know that right, Reza? You're fucking crazy!" But even while daring to say these words to my crazed husband, I did whatever he demanded so I could get the cocaine from on him to inside me. Then I would wait until the fear in

me could transform to courage. Then I would let the fairy dust grow me wings, and I would fly fearlessly and boundlessly into never-never land.

Reza's imminent outburst was the impetus that finally got my feet moving from the middle of our kitchen toward our front door. I quickly snatched up the two duffel bags, grabbed my handbag from on top of the couch, and ran out the apartment door. I picked up the pace as I raced down the front stairs and when I arrived at the main door, I struggled to open it, even after three years of opening and closing the damn thing. I felt the panic in me grow stronger and I started breathing faster; my hands started shaking uncontrollably.

Finally, the door opened. I sprinted to my car before I realized my car keys were still in my handbag. I dropped the bags and frantically searched for them. As I practically emptied my handbag, my mind expertly convinced me that every car driving by belonged to Reza, especially the one that came barreling down the street toward our house. My head had grown so hot it burned. When I finally found my keys, I scratched my car door a bit while unlocking it. I picked up whatever contents from my handbag that had fallen out within close reach, along with the two duffel bags. I threw everything into the open car door and jumped in after them.

All the while Reza's family followed closely behind me. His mother kept wailing and his nephew and brothers kept trying to talk me out of leaving, and talk about 'leaving a trail of dust.' They remained standing behind my car as I slammed my car door shut and drove away, tires screeching. I watched how the excited group appeared eerily shadowed in my rear-view mirror as smoke rose up and around them, blurring their edges and seemingly shrinking them out of my view.

TEN

I only ever lived with three men in my life, which I realize may be one or two more than the average woman's experience. Let me tell you about the second man I lived with—who, by the way, closely resembled the cowboy in the cigarette ads I grew up with: the Marlboro Man.

My Marlboro Man wasn't a bad guy. He hadn't realized what he had done when he stepped onto my perilous path. And really, I had quietly but swiftly lured him to me. He was six years younger than me, and at twenty-six years of age he looked too adorable to pass up. This wasn't the first time this sort of thing had happened. There was the subordinate at the bank I had once worked at. I only ever addressed him as Mr. Subordinate. I never once used his real name. One time I trapped my scrumptious-looking Mr. Subordinate in our building's only elevator. I stopped that thing on the top floor and I pretty much had my way with my sweet, younger Mr. Subordinate.

My two-year relationship with the Marlboro Man didn't turn out to be the kind of relationship where two people piled up experiences that fostered getting to know each other better, so then they could grow to respect and love each other. Ours was nothing like that. He and I had a "slam-bam thank-you!" kind of experience all the way around. For two years we kept up this torrential pace and after I ended things with the same kind of vigor, I decided to give up on ever dating—feeling too exhausted and no longer trusting that I could keep my hands from destroying.

The Marlboro Man and I met through mutual friends over three years before I met Harry that dreadful first night. My introduction to the Marlboro Man culminated into the most explosive sex I ever had, which followed a crazy night of drinking after a wild day of sailing from Westbrook, Connecticut to Sag Harbor, New York.

There were five of us sailing: two guys and three gals, with the Marlboro Man being the only experienced sailor on that forty-foot Beneteau we all chartered. After a long and tiresome day at sea, we took turns showering inside the boat's tiny-sized head. Us three girls immediately dolled ourselves up in short shorts and skimpy tops and big hair, and we filled our bellies with lots of alcohol, which made us say tantalizing, naughty things and move our hips this way and that way. All this looseness from us girls lured all the guys from all the other boats. I knew how playing hard-to-get piqued a guy's attention and I played that up big time, too.

The men from the sailboat right next to ours who were headed for Fire Island walked over to where we were prancing two docks away from our boat, drinking someone else's perfect Daiquiris. Those Fire Island men moved right in as if we weren't already being talked to. They tried hard to convince us three alluring girls into ditching our guys, the ones with the perfect Daiquiris, and leaving with them. We teased some more and laughed and sashayed right back to our boat where our real guys waited. There were only us five on our boat, but you'd swear with all the raucous noise we made over the next hour that we were twenty drunkards.

We took off on foot to a local bar and we stayed there until it closed. At some point, us girls were sitting at the bar with our fine, skimpy, lacy panties fitted on our heads. We took off our bras and tied them onto our two guys' heads. The whole place gathered around, trying to get a piece of us.

"Hey, bra head, bra head, can I buy you a beer?" one guy offered.

"Do I look like another beer is going to do me some harm? Sweet face, don't ask me silly questions like that and just put the damn thing in front of me!" I said, never even looking at the guy.

"Haa Haaaa, you are something, girl," he said.

"Yeah, yeah, and wouldn't you like to know. And can't you see I'm wearing panties and not a bra?"

"Haa Haaa, yeah, I can see. I can see alright, and I like what I see." Right then I looked at him and I could have sworn there was more than one of him talking to me. And when did I stop being the "ugliest?"

As I mentioned earlier, the Marlboro Man and I had an explosive hooking up of sorts that night back at the boat. For two years we didn't slow down on blowing each other up just like that first night—only there was a shift; we used our spiteful words instead. Then I'd slap him or punch him in the stomach. We moved in together into a darling townhouse on a five-mile-long marsh in Clinton, Connecticut, where we caught eels in our backyard and stripped off their tough scaly skin and fried their tender meat. Some nights, he didn't come home. I'd often turn on him in the middle of being out with friends while we were having a good time and laughing.

There was no telling how much worse things would have ended up had I not one day decided to walk out the door and driven my butt back to Milford. We were headed for real trouble, since I found myself wanting to beat the living crap out of the guy every time he even walked into the room. I still refer to that two-year relationship as my dark years.

My Marlboro Man was the one man who had unleashed unadulterated recklessness—the kind that I later realized had been trying to escape for decades and decades. And after this relationship, I vowed for a second time in my life to stay single and free of all men.

ELEVEN

So by the time Harry entered my life, there was an inordinate amount of clues that should have kept me oceans away from him. Plenty of signs had started coming from day one. But not one of those clues ever managed to knock me over enough to get me to pause and listen or see. In fact, plenty of relationships before Harry had already openly offered the precise lessons that could have turned things around in my life. Had I heeded any of them, I could have avoided the immense suffering altogether. But decades earlier, suffering had seeped into my unique strand of chromosomes, influencing the devastating outcome of my every action.

The first time I met Harry, suffering's forewarning climbed up and out of whatever cells it had been holed up in. It knocked forcefully on my heart; I merely swatted at it.

It was the end of October 1996. It had been a mild fall and the quaint beach house I'd been renting in Milford, Connecticut filled itself each day with warm sweet sea air. It was my favorite time of year. My sixteen-year-old niece Emily, Sarita's daughter and my goddaughter, was staying with me for that last October weekend. My beach home was the perfect place for hosting her, what with the oodles of sunshine and water and sand right outside my doorstep. I envisioned us lying out on an over-sized blanket, wearing loose warm sweaters and sweats, and settling in for hours, listening to waves roll and crash only a short distance from our feet as we read and napped our way through the entire blessed weekend.

That Friday, I picked up Emily early from Sarita's house. My niece and I talked the whole way to my beach house. I described to her the perfect quiet and lazy time I planned for the two of us. We had barely walked through my front door when the phone rang. I ran to the kitchen and picked it up. It was my new friend, Dana, who I first met along with her husband Tom years before. They didn't become my friends right away, not until our mutual friend Julie got married. We grew to be good friends from hanging out at all the bridal showers and celebrations leading up to Julie's wedding.

I was one of Julie's bridesmaids. During the actual wedding, some time in the middle of the reception after the dinner was finished and cleared away, Dana and Tom came walking through a doorway and into one of the two rooms where guests had just finished eating. They found me in the middle of that room, exuding my then well-honed world domination bossiness in front of an audience of women I coerced into smoking cigars. I had long ago given up my daily dose of pot or cocaine or pills or a combination thereof. I had clearly advanced from polluting mere young sweet innocent girls to the more tenacious older moms, who were parents to my friends and were well into their fifties and sixties. And really they were a blunt bunch!

"No, no, no, not like that! Like this." I practically shouted to the thick-headed group of moms, and I demonstrated the art of cigar smoking yet again.

My bridesmaid gown was hiked up above my left knee, and

that foot was planted up on the chair's seat, exposing a good part of my leg and my high-heeled shoe that had been skillfully spray-painted the same color as the long skirt of my bridesmaid gown. With my elbow resting on my bent knee, I sucked on the cigar I held between my thumb and index finger. I tossed my head back and swiftly released perfect grey swirling smoke circles. My friends' moms once again cheered and giggled and clapped their hands and did little mama dances.

"Okay, now you guys try it, exactly like I did. It's not that hard, for God's sake!"

In unison, they gave it another go choking and coughing and getting all teary-eyed from inhaling yet again. At one point during my cigar-smoking lesson, the bride's mom had walked in and watched the scenario of grown women making fools of themselves. She'd yelled to me, *"Isabel what are you doing?"* She didn't wait for a response from me; she turned away, shaking her head in disgust.

Oh gosh, this group really was a hopeless bunch, I thought!

This was the sort of reckless thing that drew Dana and Tom to me. They'd stood just inside the doorway the entire time, watching and laughing at the debacle. Finally, they walked straight up to me and put their arms around my waist, and in unison, walked me away from an impossible situation.

"Oh, hi Dana. It's great to hear from you. How are you and Tom?" I said into the phone. My niece waited by the phone with me.

"We're great. Julie's wedding was loads of fun, huh?"

"Yes, it's four months later and I'm still recuperating."

We laughed a bit, then Dana got right to her point. *"Listen, we have a friend visiting and we got this great idea that maybe we could all go out to dinner tonight."*

"Really? Oh wow, well, I'm not sure. I have my niece with me and she's spending the weekend with me and I just don't know. We were planning on having a quiet weekend on the beach. I just don't know. Let me talk to her and I'll call you back, but I really think we're going to hang out here. I'll talk to her, though."

"So, how old is your niece?" Dana asked as I started pulling the phone away from my ear.

"Uh, she's sixteen years old. But she was really looking forward to just hanging out with me." I was still pulling the phone further away from my ear as Dana continued speaking.

"Okay, but talk to her, I bet she'd love to go out to dinner with a bunch of fun grown-ups," Dana insisted.

"Okay, I'll talk to her, and call you back."

I hung up the phone and turned to talk to Emily. Before I even said anything, she bounced and bounced, giving me the biggest happiest smile I ever did see; she even squealed a wee bit. With her hands clasped together and her shoulders pulled up to her ears, she said, *"Sure I'll go. Sounds like fun."* She'd obviously heard both ends of the conversation. I realized I'd never once considered that the teenage girl might be hoping for a more fun weekend than the relaxing one I'd described to her on the drive home.

"What? But I thought we were going to lay on the beach all weekend and rent movies and eat popcorn. We're going to have the most fun girls' weekend at home talking, reading, napping and watching movies, just the two of us. Doesn't that sound like more fun?"

"Sure it does, but dinner out with your friends tonight sounds fun, too. Ooh, ooh, are we going to Millie's again this year?" Emily was lining up her own fun-filled weekend as I tried to get us back on track.

"Oh gosh, no. Her neighborhood is having their big annual beach party this weekend. We're definitely not in the mood for that craziness."

"Oh, really?"

"Oh yeah, I'm real sure about that one!" I said.

I hadn't heard Emily's disappointment in the car but could suddenly see in my niece's deflating bounce, the real hope she'd had. I felt exhaustion creeping its way up my body. I took a deep breath and continued trying to pull my niece back.

"About dinner, Emily, are you sure you want to do this? It's going to be a bunch of old people hanging out probably just talking and talking. Are you sure you want to spend time doing this? They're inviting some friend who's staying with them and I have no idea who this person is. Are you sure? Because I'm just as happy staying in. We could jump in the car now and pick up a movie rental and pick up some Thai takeout and hang out, just the two of us."

"Oh no, no. I don't mind going out tonight. I'm sure I'll have lots of fun at dinner with you all. Besides, we have all weekend to hang out, right? And you're not old, Titi Isabel, you're only 35. And how old are Dana and Tom, around your age?"

I let my sixteen-year old niece talk me into going out to dinner that evening. *"Well, okay, if you insist,"* I said, already feeling too exhausted for the upcoming evening.

I guess I could have avoided a second divorce altogether,

had I insisted on staying home and not letting myself be swayed by Dana's uncanny ability to get people to do anything she wanted. Oh, Lordie Lord, I really should not have called her back. I should have stayed home. But all Dana ever needed to do was open that mouth of hers, and out the words flowed that invariably put people in a trance and got them moving in whatever direction she wanted. I guess when I think back to that phone call, I really didn't stand a chance. That Dana really ought to bottle and sell that little knack of hers!

"Hi, it's me, Isabel." I could hear the exhaustion in my voice.

"Heeeey!" Dana said, in that lulling tone she uses to snag you.

"Emily says yes, yes, yes! So where do we meet you and what time?" I asked. I heard my tired voice say the words I would regret years later.

"Great! How about you come to our house around 6pm and we can all drive to the restaurant together?"

She gave me the address to their house in Stamford, Connecticut. Oh, how I really didn't want to go! I especially wanted to get to bed early that night since I had been out partying all week, and I had a busy week work-wise. I'd been feeling strung out and really needed to rest.

Emily and I got in my car and drove the forty minutes from Milford to Stamford. We parked in the driveway that could easily have fit a dozen cars. We got out of the car and walked toward the front door and up the steps of Dana and Tom's lovely old Victorian home. They both immediately came to the front door to greet us. We hugged and kissed and said our hellos. I introduced my niece to them and they bubbled over her. Then we all walked through the front door and past the pretty foyer with the sweet wooden bench jutting out from the old regal staircase. We turned left into the front parlor and Dana asked if we wanted a glass of wine. I looked at Emily and she beamed that smile of hers that said, *Ahh, this is what I was hoping for,* and I said, *Sure,* for both of us.

When Dana returned to the front room with our glasses of wine, this other person came bounding in behind her. I immediately noticed how the tips of his fingers were tucked into the front pockets of the washed-out 80's styled jeans he wore. His shoulders were hiked up so high, they practically touched his ears. He was clearly shy as all heck. I saw that demeanor and stared at his glasses that were more suited for a square sixty-year-old. I noticed the hairstyle that surely could not have been meant for him but the grandpa who probably sat next to him at the barbershop. Well, everything about him rubbed me the wrong way. I absolutely didn't want to go out to dinner with this bunch anymore. What work the evening was going to be, and how completely exhausted I felt!

"Sooo, Isabel, this is our dear friend Harry," Dana said, again lulling me into her trap.

"Hi," Harry said, looking and sounding nervous. For some reason, that brought up the gush of anger inside me that I had been working so hard for two years to keep under control.

"Hi," I said rather curtly, and quickly turned away from him. Then from behind me I heard him say *"Hi"* to Emily and she said it back to him. Oh boy, did I start chugging my glass of wine. It was at times like these that I thought having given up any drug wasn't such a great idea. But by that point it had been

over ten years since I had given up drugs and cigarettes. I'd tried quitting drinking, but I'd been drinking almost every day of my life since I was fourteen years old. I couldn't find any way to give that one up. And thank God I hadn't, because at that point there was nothing left to say. I practically downed the whole glass of wine and was clearly ready for a second.

I continued talking to Dana and pretty much kept my back to this Harry guy. He went on talking to my niece, who found everything he said enthralling; they kept talking and talking. Then Tom walked in and immediately started talking to Dana and me. Finally Dana announced that it was time to go. We all got into two cars after withstanding a full five minutes of Dana's insistence that we all squeeze into their SUV. I thanked God yet again for being able to win that battle. Emily and I followed Dana, Tom and that square guy to the restaurant.

In the restaurant we were seated at a table large enough for ten people. I took a seat next to Dana, and my niece Emily sat on my other side. Throughout the entire dinner I talked to Dana and Tom and mostly not to my niece, and I didn't utter one word to Harry.

If months earlier, I had kept my mouth shut, I could have avoided that tragic dinner altogether.

It was at Julie's "Jack and Jill" party, where I socialized with Dana and Tom for the second time. I'd met them the first time through Julie at a bar in New Haven one night, years before. I instantly liked them that first night. They're the kind of people you want to keep in your life forever, with so much sweet spirit, joviality, and doggone goodness pouring from them. When they arrived at the "Jack and Jill," I was thrilled to see them again.

That Tom made me laugh and laugh the whole time at the party. At some point he asked me, *"So why don't you have someone?"*

We'd been talking about geeks and what a geek he was and weren't geeks grand, and so I said, *"Cause I haven't found the right geek yet."*

Well, that comment must have stuck with Tom, because sitting across that restaurant's dinner table was Harry, exuding goober geekiness. And no way would I talk to him. I didn't need any warnings clamoring inside me because I wasn't talking to anybody!

In the parking lot after dinner, Harry walked straight to me and said, *"It was really nice meeting you."*

I still wasn't making eye contact with him. I quickly said, *"Same."* Then I looped Emily's arm in mine. I couldn't wait to get many miles away from this crowd, and I hurriedly moved toward my little red car as if sheer proximity would fill me with poison. Again, it wasn't that I didn't like Dana and Tom. My hope and plan was to become close friends with them. But something inside me had been knocking ever since Dana's phone call, and this knocking had stayed with me even after my niece and I walked into that charming Victorian home.

I felt great relief spring up and spread inside me as my zippy car created more distance from the restaurant and propelled us toward the quiet beach house in Milford, where the pounding would surely stop, and where I could finally get some rest. It seemed that no matter how much sleep I got those days, I still woke up feeling completely spent, as if I'd worked all night and had not just slept eight whole hours. I couldn't wait to walk into my dark and still bedroom with its own bathroom, where I could lean over the full, round sink and finally wash the evening away.

"Soooo, what did you think of him?" my niece asked me as soon as we got onto Interstate 95.

"Think of whom?"

"You do know you were being set up with Harry tonight, right?"

The relief I had been enjoying instantly vanished and I felt my chest constrict. *"No way, I'd know if I were being set up and that was not a set up. The guy barely talked to me. He only said something to me twice, the whole time…'Hi!' and, 'It was really nice meeting you',"* I said in a mocking tone. *"Trust me, that was not a set up. Besides, he's definitely not my type."*

"Okay, but you were being set up, and I can't believe the sixteen-year-old has to point this out to the thirty-five-year-old," my niece said, with the soft glowy smile she got after ingesting a bit of alcohol. I could see she was feeling good. Meanwhile, there was a desperate rage marching up inside me, trampling all over whatever good feelings had me smiling only moments ago.

"I know who would know if I were being set up, Julie would know. I'll call her as soon as we get home." My car picked up speed at that point. The second after I crossed the threshold of my beach house, I was on the house phone dialing Julie's number.

"Do you know anything about me being set up tonight with a guy named Harry?" I spoke with that hard-lined Isabel tone that said "don't fucking mess with me." By this time, Julie knew better than to evade a question from me. I'd come at her and stay on her until she spilled her guts.

"Dana called me this morning and asked what I thought about it. So I take it you met him. What did you think of him?"

"No way, no fucking way! He's not even close to being my type." Which, for some unfathomable reason, seemed to mean everything to me that night. I immediately hung up on Julie and called Dana next. It was still too early in our budding friendship for her to have gotten even a whiff of my "don't-fuck-with-me" tone.

"So was this a set up tonight?" I asked, huffing and huffing, without allowing Dana the chance to even say hello.

"Ahhh, what did you think of him?" Dana said.

I barreled straight through that damn lulling tone of hers.

"Okay, just so you know, never in a million years. He's not my type. I mean, God! I'm not even a little interested." I could hear myself huffing and I was sure that my new friend-to-be Dana could hear it, too.

"Okay, then." With that, we said a few last words and hung up. But unbeknownst to me, during our conversation, Harry was waiting right next to Dana, most likely with his fingertips still tucked into his pathetic outdated jeans pockets.

After Dana hung up the phone Harry asked her, *"Well, what did she say?"*

"She likes you!"

∾

Had I known all I know today, I never would have taken the call that came three months after that terrible night in October. I hadn't thought of Harry once after I hung up the phone with Dana. Yet he called me all the way from across the globe after he moved to Tokyo only two months after we met, even after I had clearly said no and closed shut that particular door.

"Hi, do you know who this is?" the tentative voice on the other end asked.

"Uh, hi. No, who is this?" I answered. I honestly couldn't recognize the man's voice.

"It's Harry, remember me? I met you at Dana and Tom's."

At his mention of his name, all kinds of alarms when off inside me, and I screeched in my mind, *FUUUUCK! Noooooo!* I was no longer concerned if God or anyone else could read my mind. After quite a few seconds, I finally was able to speak. *"Oh, yeah, um, how are you?"* I said, but *No, no, no, no, FUCK!* was what I continued screeching in my head.

"I'm in Tokyo now. I didn't get a chance to tell you that night we met that I was moving, and then I was busy the past two months with the move. I wanted to call you sooner. So is this a good time?"

Pause.

"Uh, yeah, sure." The pounding and knocking that often accompanied me those years reached a crescendo, and *'yeah sure'* was not what was in my brain. *Nooooooooooo!* was definitely what I heard screeching inside there. I couldn't figure out how or why I sat in my tiny office, tucked inside the quietest corner of

my beach house, talking to the man I swore off that exhausting evening in Stamford, Connecticut.

Sigh. *"Good. I wasn't sure if this would be okay. You really made an impression on me when we met and I've been wanting to talk to you ever since."*

"Really? But we didn't talk. How could I have made an impression on you?"

BULLSHIT! BULLSHIT! FUUUUUCCCCKKKK! I continued screeching inside my head.

"Yes, I know. I gave Dana a hard time about that. She monopolized your time the whole night and didn't take a breather. I really didn't get a chance to squeeze a word in edgewise with all her talking."

Asshole, it was me who didn't let you in, I thought.

"So what's Tokyo like?" is what I actually said, while my brain continued warning me to end the damn call.

Two hours later, Harry had me laughing and hoping I would see him again. He worked his magic (that I later learned was actually poison) and basically got my insides turned all the way facing in the other direction, the absolute wrong direction. After two hours, I found myself needing to hang up because at that point, I was, oh, so tired, so completely exhausted, there was no way I could hold the phone for another second.

He literally charmed me to exhaustion.

We talked again and again after that first call from across the globe. I was fascinated by all his travels. He was apparently a brilliant skier and scuba diver and sailor. He loved wines and had lived all over the States and had been preparing his move to Tokyo after temporarily living in Argentina, and he was funny as all heck. He also knew a lot about a lot of things. Most notable was how the magician with deadly poison knew precisely what to say to get me excited.

When Harry returned to Connecticut for a visit early February 1997, it was only two weeks after that first phone call and three and a half months after I wrote him off. I struggled to keep my hands off him. That first night after he arrived, we kissed for six hours straight. I don't know why I didn't tear off his clothes, but for some bizarre out-of-Isabel-body reason I kept things pure between us throughout his entire trip. But I could only keep that charade up for so long.

Another three months passed by the time Harry returned to Connecticut in May to visit me a second time. In March, two months before this second trip, I had cervical cancer surgery. The surgery was an unexpected event that further weighed me down most days with debilitating exhaustion.

I'd received a call from my gynecologist five days before the surgery. She explained my pap test showed irregular cells were present, and she needed to biopsy the area. Two days later the biopsy came back showing levels 3, 4 & 5 cells in my cervix, which meant surgery, and possibly a hysterectomy. Two days after this report I was wheeled into surgery.

All the while, I behaved as if this was a major inconvenience, since I was forced to cancel my long-awaited Mohab, Utah trip that I'd already planned and paid for. Before this surgery, I was already feeling an unfamiliar exhaustion that felt more like being swaddled by overbearing arms. I didn't like feeling physically powerless, and after surgery, I became nearly incapacitated. Every day, I struggled with ordinary life.

I didn't take the whole cancer scare seriously, which today I believe to be the more beneficial approach since the very focus of cancer could have potentially landed me prematurely without certain female organs. But at the time and for most of my life, I tended to treat most anything with flagrant indifference. My capacity for offering and receiving indifference was so deep, it sustained itself straight through my upbringing. By the time I started developing relationships outside of my immediate family, indifference had weaved itself into the fabric of my being and became a nutrient my physical body craved. It was the foundation from which my thoughts and words sprang. My friends, colleagues, lovers, my jobs, my businesses, and even my illnesses were all drawn to me because of indifference's call to arms. My survival depended on indifference. I would have died without it.

I hadn't realized all those years going about my life that, like my mother, and like her mother, and like the mother before her and so on, I'd been infused with a very core substance of survival. For too many generations it swirled in the bellies of the women of my family. If you sat and talked to any one of my six sisters, you would easily detect this same indifference in them as well, with some of us bearing it more heavily than others. If I were required to describe it, I'd say it's the emptiest, most hollowed cavern. Certainly it can never be satisfied and only after great effort can it be destroyed. And for sure, if I had never been breastfed, I could have escaped all the suffering that for most of my life I unwittingly sought with such fervor.

During those three months before Harry's second visit from Tokyo, and especially while I laid in bed convalescing after surgery, unable to move a fiber in my entire body, Harry devoted many hours on the phone and on email. He described in delicious detail what he planned on doing to me the next time he visited. When he finally stepped into the living room of my beach house after three months of tantalizing promises, I had to restrain myself from tearing his clothes off. I'd had to summoned energy from some unknown reserve, because most days I had difficulty standing upright. Yet there I stood, ready to pounce on the man.

My roommate Sandy stood next to me. This was her first time meeting the "Mr.-Too-Good-To-Be-True" whom I'd went on and on about for weeks and weeks.

Sandy smiled her way through all the responses Harry gave to her many questions. I could see she was impressed. I also noticed how once again he was shy toward me. After about ten more minutes, Sandy left the house, probably settling in her mind how this Harry guy indeed fit my breathless descriptions of his staggering marvelousness. But with only the two of us in the house, Harry pulled back even more. I wasn't having any of it. I took him to bed and I seduced him. But we only did some of the things he had gone on and on about, phone call after lengthy phone call. Afterward he was quiet and I didn't understand. I just didn't understand.

"What's wrong?" I asked him.

"Nothing. I don't think I was ready yet," Harry said.

"You're kidding right? You sounded more than ready on the phone the last three months, and your emails definitely sounded like you couldn't wait. What happened?"

"Nothing, I hope this was okay what we just did."

How was it not okay? I wasn't asking the guy to marry me. I'd only wanted some of what he tantalized me with phone call after phone call. Where was my cyber lover from across the steel blue ocean? That man clearly lost in guilt was not him. But little did I know then that this was how things usually went with Harry, ever since his heart got completely poisoned by his parents' divorce at age eleven.

In the years to come, he would say or do one thing one minute and then he'd make a complete about face on me the next, saying or doing the complete opposite. I would stand there dumbfounded, time and time again. And, oh dear lord, in those early days, I was so unseasoned about how much Harry relied on destruction to ensure chaos ruled his world. Still, I called him "Mr.-Too-Good-To-Be-True" to everyone I talked to. On and on I went about this guy Harry, who later I switched to calling "Bastard" and "Two-Mouth."

After Harry flew back to Tokyo, things slowed down quite a bit between us. Harry didn't call or email for two entire weeks and I couldn't figure out why. I kept asking myself, *What did I say or do to make him run so hard and fast from me?* It was my first thought upon waking every damn morning.

During that time, I was fatigued beyond anything every day. At the start of Harry's second visit in May, a spark of energy had risen straight up and then dwindled days before he left. Before he stepped onto that plane back to Tokyo, I could barely lift a finger.

It was mid-May, two and a half months after the cervical cancer surgery, when I finally returned to the entrepreneurial center where I'd been consulting business owners for nearly two years. That morning, first thing, I sat across from a client whose words only sounded like garble. *How was it that he was talking but I couldn't make out a word he said?* I thought. On my first morning back working, after ten weeks and after five minutes of hearing garble, I excused myself from my very first consultation and went home.

I walked through the front door of my beach home and walked directly to my bedroom. I took off my shoes and nothing else. As I slipped under my bedcovers, I couldn't understand why I'd only heard garble earlier that day. Then, as I started falling asleep, I tried recalling exactly what was said the last time I talked to Harry. And then he called, right in the middle of my nap.

"Hi, how are you?" he asked, as if things were no longer the same between us.

"Hi…" Pause. It took about a minute to wake from the haze that blanketed me. *"Um, so I haven't heard from you in two weeks. Is everything alright?"*

"Yeah, I told you I was going to Thailand and I wouldn't be able to call while I was away." He sounded more than okay.

"Really, Thailand? Are you serious? You went to Thailand? Why don't I recall you mentioning Thailand to me?" I responded, and I was fully awake then.

"Yes, I told you I was going with my roommate, remember?"

"No, I don't... Wait, you have a roommate?" The old disorientation with wisps of black smoke rose up from wherever it had been hiding all those years. I shook my head repeatedly, trying to clear the haze that moments earlier had swathed my body and enveloped my brain.

"Yes, my friend here lost her apartment and I told her she

could stay with me until she found another one."

Loud, clamoring warnings started shooting off inside me and panic swiftly took over.

"And, what—in less than two weeks you guys decided to go to Thailand? And, and…your roommate's a woman?" I asked, incredulously. My voice had noticeably risen in volume.

"Yes. I told you we were going. I told you about her."

Along with the knocking going on inside me, there was this tug yanking on my heart with such great force that words started falling from my brain. I was quickly becoming speechless. And in the *un-stillness* of that next moment, I made a decision. For some time, ever since I'd been unable to wake up with any real coherence in my head, since words had transformed themselves into maddening garble, I would feel a fragmented gaseous swirl swoosh its way up from my soul to my brain. Then it would exit through my pores with such force, I would fall straight to sleep.

I knew time was running out. I cleared my throat and took a deep breath, summoning my words before I spoke. *"I've been wanting to tell you the whole time I hadn't heard from you that I love you."*

Silence.

I was about to speak again, to backtrack a bit. In the moments of sheer silence I convinced myself that, like that night of seduction two weeks before, I'd scared off my savior again.

"Why are you telling me this now? Why didn't you say this before?" Harry asked in a whisper. Pause. *"Do you mean it?"*

With his hopeful-sounding words, I stepped right back onto my original track. *"I really do,"* I said feeling anxious, and already sensing the wrath of damned words.

"Why didn't you tell me before?"

"I'm not used to falling in love in three months, Harry. In fact, I've never fallen in love before in my life. And you do realize we've hardly even seen each other, right? I didn't say it before because I was afraid it was too soon for you, especially after your last visit." Which was the only honest thing I had said thus far.

Silence throbbed again inside the vast distance separating us. Then I felt the moment when the words I spoke took hold thousands of miles away, which was an instant before he spoke.

"This is really great news because I love you too," Harry finally said with exuberance.

So just like that, less than four months after that first phone call from Tokyo, and seven months after I'd slammed the door shut on the pathetic square geek, we started planning our future together.

First we talked about me flying out to Tokyo for a visit. By the end of the following weekend, we decided I would move to Tokyo. I gave my notice at the entrepreneurial center where I sometimes worked and where I still only heard garble. I called friends and told them all about my move. Then over the summer, our talks escalated from me moving in with Harry to getting married. I wouldn't really commit to that one, until finally Harry tossed me his first ultimatum.

"I'm not interested in just living together, Isabel. Sorry, that's just not for me."

"But we haven't even started living together. How do we know if this will turn out right?"

"I love you and things will turn out great."

"I don't know about marriage, Harry."

"Then we can't do this because I'm not interested in just living together."

Oh gosh, that conversation really exhausted me. I hadn't the strength to hold the phone any longer. Most days it was exactly like that. After I woke up and finally got out of bed and went about my day, I would begin feeling too exhausted to do another thing. Whenever this happened, I'd take a three-hour nap. Immediately after waking up I'd run a couple of miles to get my blood flowing. But each time I'd end up feeling completely wiped out for the next two to three days, and on and on this went.

The truth was, I instinctively knew there was illness ravaging my body. I kept thinking the cervical cancer was never fully eradicated and now it raged inside me with a vengeance. I reasoned that only cancer could submit my body to such a total capitulation. Not even my internal pleadings that coaxed me through most of my life could get me going. It didn't take my wise brain long to grasp my predicament; still only being able to hear garble in the center that paid the bills, and only being able to stay awake a few hours at a time most days. Lord knew how much longer my knight would be willing to put up with my unbearable baggage. I knew I had no choice but to acquiesce. Time had run out.

"Well, then okay. Let's get married," I said, more than ready to hang up the phone and get myself back in bed.

"What? Wait. Are you sure? Because I don't want to talk you into anything."

"I said yes didn't I?" I responded as I huffed and flared my nostrils, angry as all heck.

For some inexplicable reason, from that day forward, I

became angrier than I'd ever before felt. I barreled through the next few months leaving scalding black trails of scorched earth behind me, and everyone would run as fast and far as they could.

For the remainder of the summer we talked about marriage. Well, actually, it was Harry who did most of the planning while I repeatedly grunted my agreement. Harry decided I should move to Tokyo in the fall, and he immediately bought my plane ticket. He planned to stop in Connecticut in September so we could share the happy news with my family and all our friends. And then he decided we would fly to Indianapolis where his family would next learn about our wonderful news. Harry immediately bought these plane tickets. And wasn't this all, oh, so grand! Except, deep down it didn't feel grand at all. The week before Harry's September visit, I grew exhausted beyond the usual "can't think, or get out of bed, or eat, or do anything" exhaustion. It also was impossible for me to pinpoint when exactly I agreed to any of these plans. The exhaustion, confusion and fury had all meshed into one coagulated pressure ball right in the center of my chest, and when the pressure peaked, I'd explode. Afterward, I'd peter out for hours—that is, until the unbearable pressure built up in my chest again. And on and on this went.

Later, when I finally gathered the pieces about my agreeing to marry Harry, I realized it wasn't that I didn't want to marry Harry. It was marriage itself I had trouble committing to. After my first marriage to Reza, I had sworn I would never again slow down enough for anyone to catch me—not ever, ever, ever!

TWELVE

Fear still followed me everyday, even decades after the molestation, the explosion, the riots and Denise and her gang's pursuits and threats. It was only much later in life during therapy that I understood how fear had claimed ownership of every cell in my body well before any of the events. I hadn't been aware of this across the span of my lifetime.

I went about my days unconsciously doing the things that helped keep fear's buzz from overtaking me, like numbing my senses with alcohol and drugs or forcing myself to escape waking hours through sleep. But none of these ploys could stymie the buzz from growing. As soon as I'd awaken or the high wore off, there fear pranced as if I'd merely interrupted its speech in mid-sentence, and a quick clearing of the throat was all that was necessary to get it back on track. Then there were those times fear's fury exploded so loudly that even my long-time close circle of friends would go off running. Finally, after too many blow-ups, my closest friends had run so far away, I never heard or saw them any more, and I kept saying, *"Fine! See if I care!"* Then I would blow up some more, always emitting deadly sparks of fire.

By the time Harry walked onto my path that warm October day in Stamford, Connecticut, I could sometimes get the ever-expanding fury to not rage too out of control. But even before I boarded the plane to Tokyo, only a few months after the day we decided to marry, my fury was back to exploding unprovoked. And after always having lived in Connecticut, and only in Bridgeport and in Milford, and the one very short while in Clinton, I didn't feel so self-assured anymore the second my feet stepped onto Japan's soil. I had never felt so naked with only anger and fear in me, even after too many glasses of wine. It seemed this pure nakedness stoked my fury further.

As soon as I left my familiar surroundings and landed in Tokyo, I instantly grew self-conscious, unable to speak the proper words that could convey what I thought or felt. It was like that time when losing my innocence had instantly zapped words from my tongue; and when I did finally manage to release a mere two words, it induced one unsuspecting family friend to run and run and run. Had anyone leaned in and put their ear close to my lips during my most self-conscious days in Tokyo, they probably would have been whipped by a slew of angry words, sending them on the run of their life.

But no one got too close to me in Tokyo. Only Harry dared try, even during the many months when I began digging the trench that kept him away. And after having lived through a deadly riot and years of abuse and gangs circling me with teeth bared and claws poised for the kill, and after having lost my innocence so long ago, I was suddenly afraid to walk out our apartment door. Whenever people would ask me questions, I would stutter then cough, hoping that would help loosen things up. But only a few useless words ever stumbled out.

After a while, I became convinced that people were staring at me. I would look around and sure enough, all these Japanese people were staring at this tall, fair-skinned, light-haired Puerto

Rican woman. I had never felt more like a minority than in that country, where we westerners sought each other out as we went about our business. Often in the middle of the street somebody would call out in English to another ex-pat. And there, in a foreign land, a friendship would start that would last for the rest of their days, even if there weren't a speck of common ground to stand that friendship on. This was so unlike what living in predominantly white neighborhoods back home was like.

Being a minority in Tokyo was nothing like that time I walked into a dining room in Monroe, Connecticut so many years before, when the end of a fine dinner arrived as soon as I walked through the archway. The one young woman smiled and said hello from her seat, and her sweet husband only nodded. After too much silence floated in that room, they both began asking questions about the weekend their brother and I had just shared. I knew better than to walk in any further, even though I spoke to everyone's parents. I did smile at them, but those two never did look up at me. It was clear to me and everyone else in the room that their parents weren't happy to see me. Afterwards, it was said that I should never come back to that house. It had all boiled down to me being a low-class citizen, a Puerto Rican, from that low-class city where they themselves had been born, and had lived most of their lives.

So I had long been aware what people thought of me being born Puerto Rican. Living in Tokyo should have been a relief since all the white people there were more than willing to band together, regardless of where our parents were born. We were all westerners in Tokyo, and nobody was avoiding or spitting at a Puerto Rican there.

But it didn't matter where anyone was born. Without my familiar surroundings and friends and routine, I felt more naked and ill-fitted than ever in Tokyo. I wasn't sure what to make of this new me—who still could burn the heck out of anyone who dared get too close. And sure, I was able to talk more freely after the second or third beer or glass of wine or vodka and tonic or martini, and sometimes the combination of all these. After enough alcohol, I would become capable of speaking whatever nonsense I damn well felt like speaking. I had zero trouble exploding when my inhibitions took their leave from my brain. With enough alcohol in me, it was easy to go back to spewing fire.

I mean, how did I know I would grow more afraid as soon as I left Connecticut? I thought it would be another adventure, even though I arrived in Tokyo with the most recently acquired secret in my chamber clamoring warnings of deceit and destruction. I thought it would be more like opening a new business—which, after opening and closing several over a fifteen-year span, I could do without thinking twice. Or I thought it would be just as easy as all those nights I had walked into a bar and I had drank and drank along with everyone else, and I gathered an entourage to follow me home for some more fun. I had no clue that what would happen after I arrived in an unfamiliar land would be an unraveling that left me speechless, and with no charm whatsoever.

In that land one vast ocean away from the only home I ever knew, I grew so dull that I became invisible again. I grew so invisible that Harry would grow obscured merely from his proximity to me. In restaurants, we would sit and wait and wait for someone to take our order. But no one would ever come. And when we finally stood up after waiting and waiting, and we finally got a server's attention, they would stare at us open-mouthed and blinking, looking so surprised that anyone was even occupying that table. This kept happening everywhere. People everywhere kept seeing straight through me.

How was I supposed to know that the second I stepped foot in Tokyo, I would become just as inconsequential as that frail newborn baby girl who got carried out naked from the hospital on a cool October morning.

THIRTEEN

By the time Harry stepped onto my rampant path of destruction, it had been twelve years since my vow to never marry again, to never again be forced to avert my eyes downward with lips smacked shut. When Harry had insisted on marriage, it was my first marriage I was resisting every time he brought up that nasty subject. Then the ultimatum came, and from there the threat of leading a wretched life became clear. I was propelled to do what was necessary. So three months later I had moved to Tokyo.

And less than ten months after Harry's ultimatum, on an overcast cool Saturday in June, I was back in Connecticut, pacing in a room on the second floor of the most quaint bed-and-breakfast in Westbrook. One hundred and fifty guests milled around downstairs. The energy they generated rose high above the ceiling and seeped through the old wooden planks and flowed and swirled in the large room where I couldn't stop my feet from pacing. My niece Emily opened and then closed the door of the magnificent room I had sequestered myself in. She walked over to me and handed me the uncorked bottle of wine I'd asked her to fetch.

"Titi Isabel, if you don't want to be late again for your wedding, you better get dressed now." She paused and waited for my response. *"Do you want me to ask the guests to start making their way to the garden?"* My niece looked worried after asking

that last bit. *"Do you want me to stay here and help you?"*

I could feel all that swirling energy start seeping through me. *"No, I'm fine. Yeah, please get everyone moving to their seats in the garden. Thanks,"* I responded breathlessly.

I turned from my niece and placed the full bottle of chardonnay on the table near the empty glass. I waited for her to close the door behind her before I slipped on my wedding dress. I made my way to the mirror and stared at myself. I repeatedly reassured myself as the lady in white glared back at me. I should have felt giddy. I should have been excitedly talking with a maid of honor as we dressed side by side. I hadn't even bothered with one. I repeatedly ignored how I didn't feel right in the dress, and I refused to recall how many years before I had vowed to never again marry.

After my first divorce, I'd made sure every boyfriend was clear about my intention to never marry again. And to ensure they got the message, I'd get really mean with them. I'd say things like:

"You know you're not that good looking, right?"

"Ha! Don't know why I even bother sticking with someone like you!"

"I could get myself a better-looking guy, if I wanted to."

Quite often I did help myself to any other guy I wanted, even while I was in a relationship. By this time, I'd figured out that being "ugliest" didn't seem to bother very many men anymore.

And my mother was wrong, wrong, wrong! Marriage was not for me and when I waited six months to tell her that I'd left Reza she had said, *"Ah! Girl, I already knew this. Everyone's told me already."* She then squeezed her lips shut and turned her face from me. But, oh boy, that was okay. I was used to her not caring about me or seeing me. I had my freedom and she wasn't taking that away from me, not ever, ever, ever, ever!

But then Harry's ultimatum arrived precisely when the energy in me had become shreds of tenuous breaths, and words had turned to mushy garble. I was without options.

I stood before the mirror lamenting how I was in another damn ugly wedding gown. I knew I would soon be walking down the stairs, out the French doors, and through the B&B's colorfully adorned garden. The one hundred and fifty guests would soon begin fidgeting in chairs that had been meticulously fitted in fine cream-colored linen covers and watch me pass them on my way to getting married, again. I stalled. I tilted the open bottle and filled my empty glass with wine again, and I didn't bother sipping the delicately flavored liquid.

And there was this one secret Harry and I hadn't told any of the guests pacing and pacing in the fine rooms below. Should that overwhelming crowd downstairs find out that Harry and I had already married three months before in Tokyo, they would probably shake their heads and complain that it sure did cost them a lot of money to take those lengthy trips to get there. *What do you mean you're married already? So this wedding is a hoax?*

I gulped more wine, sneering back at the pathetic woman in the mirror before me, replaying once again an even more damning secret. When Harry had visited in September that last time before I moved to Tokyo, I'd learned something about him that I shared with no one. It was the second clear warning about "Mr.-Too-Good-To-Be-True." I knew I should have stopped things with Harry before they ever got moving after his call from Thailand, and certainly I should have gone running in the opposite direction after his visit this past September. If I were honest with myself, I'd acknowledge that in the past year I'd been with Harry, plenty of warnings both inside my secret chamber and out in the bare open, had knocked and knocked. But instead of growing wiser and taking proper action, I simply grew angrier.

I was well aware of why I married Harry. I was well aware of what I was getting myself into, months before boarding that plane to escape my old life.

It was a sunny and warm September day and I was still living in the beach house in Connecticut. Harry had just arrived from Tokyo—his third trip to visit me since his first phone call from Tokyo nine months earlier. His arrival carried so much promise and hope for my future. He was the hero who came to save this distressed damsel from her cursed tower. But even though months earlier I had started referring to him as "Mr. Too-Good-To-Be-True," a nagging tug in my chest kept trying to get my attention, as if it were trying to tell me something important—a secret that could shatter my lovely rose-colored dream. I ignored it.

On that day of his arrival from Tokyo, in the middle of us calling our friends to share the news of our impending nuptials, Harry excused himself to the adjoining room that was my bedroom. He called his roommate in Tokyo to check up on her. And even after I heard his words and the tone, and especially after I understood, I slammed the door shut on the tug. It had been yanking at my chest so forcefully, I thought it would shatter my heart. I smiled after he walked back into the room where I usually conducted business. We moved on to the next person on our list to share our happy, happy news.

I should have ended things then. I really should have. It would have been the decent thing to do for both of us. But I wanted out of my current life. I decided in that fleeting whisper of time to thrust the truth out of that room, even as the truth that "Mr. Too-Good-To-Be-True" was most definitely an imposter zinged through my thalamus and straight into my cerebral cortex.

So I boarded the plane to Tokyo a couple of months after I understood, because I had already planned the perfect life for me. And nothing was going to stop me from getting it, not even the truth. Just then the secret deep down in my psyche no longer tugged at me; instead it chastised me with repeated tsk, tsks.

I had arrived in Tokyo on November 1st 1997, and everything was ideal. Really, Harry and I were doing just fine. I brilliantly went along with the master plan: Live together to measure our compatibility…check. Marry in June…check. Well, except that we didn't quite mark two months of this blissful period when something inside me snapped.

This wasn't the first time I'd snapped out of utter delusion, so I wasn't surprised when that old familiar overpowering determination to get to the bottom of things surfaced and completely overtook me. I should have shoved that mighty resolve way deep down, and kept moseying straight on with our lovely plans that were so carefully calculated and laid out. Living together in Tokyo could have been a once-in-a-lifetime-dream-come-true kind of time for me and my "Mr. Too-Good-To-Be-True." Instead, that otherworldly force bulldozed my secret chamber and all hell did break loose, I tell you.

It was the lipstick under the bed that did it. That worn-down paled shade of coral sheathed in a most pathetic tarnished case was what finally brought me to my senses. My wrong senses, that is, because if I'd had an iota of smarts, I would have quietly snapped it up and tossed it in the trash bin, along with the extra-extra small-sized panties and the dust balls. What was I doing cleaning in there anyway? I knew it used to be *her* room. What was I really looking to do there? I hadn't cleaned my own home in over ten years because I'd been too busy with my businesses, sometimes working thirty-six consecutive hours with very few breaks.

I'd been an entrepreneur most of my adult life. At age twenty-one, I bought an existing business and started this sidelined career while I worked at the bank eight hours every weekday, clearly having stepped up the ladder of enterprise. It had been years since I stopped rolling the super-skinny sticks that I sold for one dollar each, but the fire that endeavor had ignited stayed burning deep inside me, never once going out. So I wasn't surprised when I found myself exchanging a product I'd assembled for dollars once again.

Admittedly, I had years of experience in enterprise from selling marijuana to unsuspecting souls, but I hadn't a clue on what to do with "brick and mortar." Until I was steeped in it, I didn't know how much I'd hate it. But that was how most things tended to work out for me. I usually barreled into a life-consuming, forever-altering choice, never really weighing any part of it, at least to measure or feel whether it was a good fit.

Giving up cleaning was easy for me, because this was the chore I hated most—ever since I was a young girl. In childhood, I was forced every damn Saturday morning, well before I was ready to open my eyes for the day, to take up the mop or broom or scouring pad while the five precious boys in our family got to play, watch TV or hang out. I decided that the thirty-five dollars spent every week for the previous ten years to rid my house of every speck of dirt was by far the smartest money I ever paid out.

It was meant to be a quick cleaning in that tiny room, but it turned out to be the unraveling of a perfectly good thing. When Harry came home from work that unfortunate evening, I flat-out asked him if he and his roommate had an affair. He squirmed and squirmed, the poor thing.

"Why do you ask?" he said.

He looked as if he was having trouble breathing, and his face had turned an alarming shade of pink. I should have helped ease his discomfort. I should have taken a different turn and said something like, *"Oh, I'm just kidding…psyche! Ha Ha!"* But instead I pressed for the truth in a very "me" relentless kind of way—sort of like the ketchup bottle that won't spit out the gooey sauce no matter how hard you smack it, and really, a knife through the opening gets things moving a lot more swiftly.

When he finally said, *"Yes, we had an affair,"* my legs grew weak and I couldn't see straight. I couldn't breathe. It was truly the first time I had gotten the wind knocked out of me. Being punched repeatedly by two large angry black girls hell-bent on exacting an un-named revenge on the one day I'd forgotten to make sure I was accompanied by a Puerto Rican gang had not knocked the wind out of me like this. It was only meant to be a quick cleaning. What did I think I could accomplish in that room with only a bed in it? Really, how dirty was it in the first place? I saw my perfect life crumble before me and there seemed no hope of getting it back.

And then, Harry said, no longer daring to look at me, *"I'm so sorry. She and I hardly spent time together, and I was lonely, and you weren't very responsive. It just happened."*

"You are a little, little, pathetic man!" I shouted.

"You're right," he responded right away. *"I don't think we can fix this. Maybe you should go back."* The bastard still wasn't looking at me.

"I'll decide what I'm going to do next, and right now I need to get the fuck away from you!" I shouted again.

Our neighbor was away on a business trip and had entrusted her spare keys to us, just in case. I grabbed our neighbor's keys, stormed out of our apartment and ran straight to hers. I spent the next few hours on her bed unable to move, crying and crying, and thinking and thinking and crying and thinking. I figured I couldn't go back to Connecticut where family and friends would surely say:

"I told you so."

"I knew it was too soon."

"Oh, Isabel, you did it again."

"What did you see in him anyway?"

I vacillated between moving to a whole new state to staying with the bastard, bouncing from hope to despair, back and forth, back and forth.

Okay, and here should be where I finally take responsibility for already suspecting the very thing that Harry just admitted to. None of this should have been a surprise, and for sure my reaction should not have been what it was after the truth was spilled. To be honest, there's no explanation for my reaction. The best I could explain my reaction to Harry's admission would be like when my brother Pedro died of AIDS. For two years before his death he suffered tremendously, and there was no turning back because he would be dying. There was no escape, no change of events to expect other than the transformation from living to dying. And on the day he died, the shock and hurt was so great that I couldn't breathe properly again for months that then turned to years. The knowing never fully prepared me for the brutal thrust of destiny.

I was still suffering from debilitating fatigue, which had worsened after the cervical cancer surgery. One month after surgery when it became impossible to get out of bed, I went back to my doctor and tested positive for Ebstein Barr Syndrome. But my symptoms seemed more severe than everything I had read about EBS. One of the more severe symptoms was how my brain decided to stop functioning. At an untouchable place in my psyche, I had been expecting this after so many years of ingesting drugs and alcohol. I guess you can say I fell into a real "pickle" about supporting myself.

I eventually concluded after hours of wallowing in my heartbreak on my neighbor's bed that I had no choice but to stay in order to pay the bastard back. Then I'd get the heck out of Tokyo. Meanwhile, the force in my secret chamber was frantically cleaning up and making the necessary preparations, because…I had some secrets.

It didn't take long for me to pick up where I left off with our master plan. But I grew exceedingly more fatigued, some days sleeping eighteen whole hours. And, yes, I was drinking a bit more than usual. But when I think about it, I got through that time pretty okay. It could have been a lot worse. I could have ended up back in Connecticut with no possible way of saving myself from absolute wretchedness. Some would refer to my predicament as being stuck. I guess that was kind of how I grew to see it, too, which was why I grew more distant. My angry outbursts, which already were too frequent for me to handle ever since I arrived in Tokyo, away from my familiar territory, became quite destructive.

In the weeks following Harry's admission, I kept asking him a million questions about his affair. I pretty much cornered him with my increasingly pointed questions. He kept saying he was sorry, again and again, answering my questions with the very details that kept fueling my bouts of anger.

"So, how often did you two have sex?"

Sigh. *"Hardly ever."*

"Oh, come on, you two lived together, how could it have been hardly ever?"

"Well, maybe it was more like sometimes."

"You mean sometimes as in twice or three times a week?"

"Like once or twice. Why do you keep asking me for details? I want to forget the whole thing and move on. You said you could move on."

"Yeah, except you keep lying to me. How am I supposed to trust you? First you say hardly ever, and I have to press to get once or twice a week, which only means you two fucked just about

every goddamn day! How could you make me close my business, sell everything, pack up all my things, leave my family and friends, and move across the world as you were fucking her? What kind of decent man does that to someone?"

"It didn't mean anything. It's you I love. I don't want to marry her, I want to marry you."

"Oh, God!"

"I knew it would be too difficult for you to get past this. Maybe we should break up. You probably should go back."

"Fuck you!"

For months we carried on this way. I invariably found my way back to the damn master plan, only I added one short appendix: pay back the bastard properly, but not before enough time passed to redeem myself… for the sake of all the folks back home.

I shouldn't have been so affected, because it was I who kept on stomping toward destruction. What else did I expect from a man who thought nothing of convincing me to leave my life in Connecticut to start a new one halfway across the globe, while he remained in a relationship with another woman? Long before pacing the upstairs room in the quaint B&B, and most definitely before the secret wedding no one back home knew about, I knew exactly what I was getting myself into as I stepped onto that plane toward the new life.

I should have been willing to run far, far away from the whole truth: Harry liked to play with women. He always had women, lots of women "friends." Before we married and were living together in Tokyo, he would approach a woman, a complete stranger, on the train on his way home from work. On the fast-moving train he would sweet talk his new "friend," exuding his poisonous charm and wit. *Oh my, he's so intelligent and confident,* she would think. *Gosh, this guy really knows so much about everything,* she would whisper to herself. These were the same deadly arrows he had shot to snag me not so long ago during that first phone call that I never, ever should have taken. Later, when he'd finally get home, he'd tell me all about how he made a new "friend" on his way home. I never understood why he couldn't go up to men and strike up conversations with them.

"Oh? I'm just curious, Harry. Why did you go up to a total stranger and start talking to her?" I would ask him.

"She seemed lost."

"Mmhmm. I see. And when do I get to meet your new friend?" I asked each time, feeling like a possessive mom.

"Soon. You'd love her. I thought of you the whole time I was talking to her because she's a lot like you," he said, every single time.

"Did you now? So then she's just like the last 'friend' you made?" I would ask, letting him know I was keeping count of his many supposed friends.

One time, only four months after I moved to Tokyo, and only two months after he admitted to the affair, I knew something wasn't right when on a Saturday morning, I waited and waited in our apartment. Two hours passed and Harry still hadn't returned from helping our neighbor with her computer problems—the same one who entrusted us with her spare keys.

I grabbed our keys along with her keys and walked down to the first floor. I knocked on her door and waited as it took her some time to walk through her itty-bitty apartment to open it. I was poised to slip in the spare key she so easily had handed to us only three months earlier when she finally opened her door. I walked in past her. Harry sat at her computer desk with his back to me.

I turned and looked at my neighbor. Her face was a cherry red and Harry still stayed glued to the computer. I said *Hi*, and asked Harry what was taking him so long. As I waited for his response that never came, I noticed that this neighbor had no bra on, and she was covering her breasts with her hands over her very see-through t-shirt, and she wore no pants or shorts or skirt. She stood in front of me with slightly swollen lips and a fucking guilty smile on her face, and, oh God! how I wanted to smack the shit out of her.

Instead I turned to Harry and said, *"Okay, I think it's time for us to go, Harry."*

"Huh? But I'm not finished here yet. Give me a minute," he said, still not looking at me.

"Yeah, I think you're finished."

I walked to her door, opened it and waited just inside the apartment. Nobody said anything about anything. I stopped looking at my neighbor because I was that close to getting physical with the bitch. Harry and I walked out the door and took the elevator back to our floor. We walked back into our apartment.

"What the fuck was that?" I shouted as soon as the door closed behind us.

"What the fuck was what?" Harry asked, looking at me incredulously.

"You, and her. She's standing there with her breasts practically exposed, and she's practically naked, and she's

embarrassed as heck to see me, and you won't even look at me. You think I'm going to believe you were just fixing her fucking computer after that?"

"What the hell? Nothing happened!" Harry shouted.

"You expect me to believe that you were down there this whole time... no! Take that back, holed up with her in that tiny apartment for two whole fucking hours trying to fix her computer while she pranced around in see-through skimpy clothes practically naked the whole fucking time, and nothing happened? What. The. FUCK!"

"Nothing happened!" Harry insisted. *"I knew you'd never get over it. This is how it's always going to be, isn't it? You're going to accuse me of cheating every time I'm near another woman. You're never going to trust me, again, are you?"*

"I'm trying to, but you make it impossible with what I just saw."

"Isabel, you didn't see anything!" Harry shouted again. He stormed to the back room where we kept a desk and computer and he slammed that door shut. Harry asserting his innocence with a bit of anger always got me quiet again.

Standing in the middle of our living room, having stripped off a bit more of whatever semblance of sanity I had erected after Harry's affair confession, left me feeling like a caged-in animal. I paced my way to one end of the small room and turned and headed in the opposite direction. My mind raced in every direction as I paced and paced. I knew I couldn't go back to Connecticut and that I would have to stay stuck in Tokyo with a cheat. Wasn't that always the way, though? Didn't all my exes cheat on me? Didn't all my exes treat me with utter disregard?

Then I froze, because it suddenly hit me that I had always been destined for this kind of relationship. *What else had I expected?* was all I could ask myself. I kept repeating this one question to myself, accepting my fate effortlessly.

Oh, but didn't I have secrets of my own? The tugging in my chamber where I stored my secrets had been frantic with worry that I would start talking—and then for sure I'd end up in Connecticut with no way to support myself, because I definitely couldn't get out of bed all those dark blurred days in Tokyo. The pounding in my chest was deafening and I felt exhausted. I walked to the couch and sat, which became too much effort. I stretched my body and laid my head down. Then I slowly turned and faced the back of the couch and lay there for hours, too tired to move, just too damned tired.

I certainly had all the proof I needed to know better than to don the ugly dress I wore. I yawned and yawned, and tears formed in my eyes and started falling. Luckily I'd thought to apply waterproof mascara.

I stared at myself in the mirror, chastising the ugly streaked face for making such a mess of life yet again. Why did I even choose this ugly dress with its high collar that clearly didn't belong on me? How pure I looked! Ha!! I'd arrived in Connecticut two weeks before our wedding and spent days and days sewing each of those ridiculous little pearl beads.

Harry arrived from Tokyo at the end of the first week before our wedding. On the evening of the day he arrived, he settled into the tiny marina house my good friend extended to us as a wedding gift. Several of my close friends came by with lots of alcohol and food and cheer—and a plan. About halfway into our fun time, my friend stood. I braced myself, because wasn't this what you did with your closest friend when she was about to get married? Only I had my secrets and they had theirs.

"So I think this is a good time as any, wouldn't you all agree?" said my dearest friend, Julie.

"Yeah! Oh, Yeah!" the rest of them responded, egging Julie on. I went from bracing myself to shrinking down to the finest thread of silk dust. I had never told Harry about the looseness, about my indescribable wild past. I had never once uttered a word about all the nakedness and the many men and women and drugs and alcohol and parties and destruction. Thank God these friends didn't know most of that. There was even more than all that; how lucky was I to have kept all that locked away. Oh, thank God I never let loose the first word that would have unleashed the whole of what lay buried beneath the belly of absolute filth!

I suddenly realized in that moment that I was still trying to keep our relationship pure by not staining it with my past. But how could it ever be pure with so much infidelity, deceit and anger already a part of our very short story? I knew some of my secret chamber would be emptied that night. I felt the pounding before my dear, dear friend uttered her first word.

Standing alone before the full-length mirror with all those damn pearls suffocating me, my mind replayed how Harry's expression grew increasingly stunned while my friends kept on spilling very naughty "Isabel stories"—not once noticing the short pants Harry had started making about half-way into their unfettered tales.

Before the last of my friends left, I could tell he no longer saw me the same way. In fact, he stopped looking at me altogether. The unsuspecting guy had gotten a big chunk of my secret chamber dumped right onto his lap. I could see that it was all he could do to not wipe the whole damn mess off and go running back to Tokyo. Oh God, and that hadn't been near most of it.

I recalled the indignation I'd felt at his reaction after all the destruction he'd dumped on our path, all those months leading up to our wedding day. I was fine with how he turned from me since I'd already closed the door on him.

What a mess, what a complete mess I've made of my life, again, I thought. I remained glued to the one spot in front of the mirror after once again replaying in my mind the entire mess.

Sigh.

As my wedding guests made their way to the cheery garden, checking their watches again and again, trying to gauge through the faces crowding near them whether it was time to start worrying, I again picked up the bottle on the sweet antique table. It so innocently sat beside the regal-looking antique mirror where so many brides before me had probably placed their treasures—imprinting the most precious memories of this day for all their days to come. I emptied the bottle of its deep yellow liquid and I emptied this last glass of wine in one gulp. Then I slammed down the glass on the delicate old table. I turned and finally walked toward the door to do this wedding thing…even though we were already married.

FOURTEEN

Harry arrived at home from work one day, three months before our June wedding, and only a couple of weeks after I'd snatched him from our half-naked neighbor. I'd conveniently started having doubts about whether she in fact had done anything with Harry, because he worked his magic again and got me believing how "nothing happened." I had my own secrets, so who was I to judge him?

He told me he had a surprise for me even before he walked through the front door. Once inside, he urged me to get changed and to hurry. His excitement was contagious and I couldn't help but feel excited. I ran to our bedroom, got dressed and met him in the living room of our apartment. He grabbed my hand and led me out the door, all the while looking into my eyes giving me that "I'm so in love with you" smile he gives to every damn woman he likes. I let myself get swept away by him, again.

Forty-five minutes later, after lots of walking and a train ride, we stepped out of the train station in our Tokyo neighborhood's prefect, Shibuya. We walked toward the prefect's town hall, and when we finally stood across the street from the building, I noticed ten of our friends waiting out front with champagne and flowers.

"Surprise!" they all shouted with such glee when we finally crossed the street and reached them.

I didn't understand, and oh, I suddenly felt unbearably

tired. I turned to Harry. I struggled to smile, but he was smiling a big happy grin, and then I watched it falter.

"You agreed we could get married before our June wedding so you could get on my insurance." Pause. *"You told me to take care of it. Remember?"* He wasn't grinning anymore. He looked nervous. *"I took care of it,"* he said, with not much enthusiasm.

"This is great," I said, although it was clear that it wasn't.

"I don't want to make you do anything you don't want to do, Isabel."

"I said it was great, didn't I!" Instead of those words reassuring Harry, they swooshed out of me with so much blazing heat, they scorched his spirit. The fire in me continued blazing and I could have punched him. I recalled in that moment how years before, I'd fought to quell the same blaze that raged hell in me. Back when the ghastly beast bared her teeth, desperate for the taste of blood from an unsuspecting twenty six-year-old in Clinton, Connecticut.

I quickly turned to our friends who stood waiting with frozen smiles. I smiled back, and oh, I felt completely spent. I didn't have any stamina left. How was I supposed to do this now? I had a big dilemma pressing down hard on me while exhaustion threatened to overtake me in the middle of Tokyo's busiest prefect. I stepped closer toward the waiting group. I offered my hand and accepted the full glass of champagne extended to me. I quickly drank the whole thing before any toast was offered, and everyone laughed. Then I laughed and I could feel the tears coming. I begged for more champagne and it flowed and finally there were toasts…

"To the happiest couple in all of Tokyo!" declared the neighbor

woman. I felt a tinge of something as I stared at her bright smile. I wondered in that brief instant how many more times Harry had stopped by to tinker with her computer. Clink. Clink. Somebody poured me another full glass of champagne and I downed that one too.

"To my wife-to-be. I've waited my whole life for you," Harry said, as he stared into my eyes with the softest smile. With all my doubts and secrets and rage and exhaustion and outright chaos clamoring in my secret chamber, I let Harry walk me toward the town hall entrance to get married. Our entourage followed closely behind.

Later, right in the middle of the carefully planned after-party, I walked into the bathroom and threw up all the food and champagne I'd consumed that afternoon and evening. I rested the palm of my hand on my forehead, which felt hot, really hot. I got sick again and again. I finally came out of the bathroom about twenty minutes later looking like a real monster bride. One look at me, and our host took a quick step back.

"You okay?" he asked.

"No. I've been throwing up in your bathroom. I'm so sorry. I feel like crap, and I'm pretty sure I've got a fever." I turned to Harry, who was standing beside me looking concerned. *"We need to go, and now. I'm so sorry, Gene. Really, this was wonderful. Thank you for everything."*

"Hey, no problem. You look sick," he said.

"Thanks."

Harry and I left our Tokyo wedding celebration without saying good-bye to any other guests. As I withstood the rattling of the train on our way home that evening, willing myself to not get sick again, I looked over at Harry. He seemed genuinely concerned for me, sitting so close with his hand on my knee, searing the heck out of my skin. All I could think was: *How did I get myself into this mess? How was it that I would be marrying this guy twice when I never wanted to marry ever again?* Then I decided that everyone's constant joking that day about having gotten married on Friday the 13th being risky stuff was dead right.

FIFTEEN

After Harry admitted to his affair, my Ebstein Barr Syndrome symptoms morphed into severe depression for the remainder of our time in Tokyo. I mean, really, how was anyone supposed to feel good with so many damn secrets bottled up inside, wreaking irreparable damage? Like that one that got me to stoop so low, I picked out the dirtiest trash from under a bed.

It was this same secret that caught me by surprise as I floundered through blurred days. I should have heeded its obvious significance and stayed under the covers in my quaint beach home in Milford that sunny September day. Instead I kept, illuminated and cleared, that same road I'd blindly stepped on that day a little girl was stripped of innocence. Void of innocence, and infused with indifference, and having sent wisdom to eternal confinement, I was perfectly poised for getting crushed by life itself.

I slept most days up to eighteen hours, and would often be still asleep when Harry came home from work. The entire apartment would greet him in total darkness. He'd walk into our dark bedroom and turn on the light. Then he'd walk over to my still body and pull me out of bed. Then he'd walk to the kitchen and cook dinner while I clawed my way to the darkest corner in our living room. I would sit dazed, not moving, not thinking, and definitely not looking. Eventually I would crawl back to our bed and sleep until the next evening. He complained incessantly that I needed medication to help me get through depression's darkness, but I countered with how there was no medication to treat EBS. He'd look at my stubborn face then sigh and walk away.

One year after living in Tokyo, Harry landed a new job that took us to Sydney, Australia. By the time we arrived in Sydney, I felt better and more optimistic. I figured we needed a change of scenery, especially since my secret chamber had been sending me warning signals that sleeping my life away was taking me further away from my original revenge plan. Payback was, after all, why only three months after Harry admitted to his affair, I moved forward with marrying him in Tokyo's busiest prefect town office.

Harry was due and I had vowed to see my revenge plan through. I was starting to think that perhaps I would have an affair right back. But considering that in those dark days in Tokyo, I couldn't summon up the energy to get out of bed most days, getting dolled up and out the door was unlikely.

Moving to Sydney seemed more promising in every way. But not even Sydney's clearest, purest blue brilliance could help us. Today I can see how it wasn't entirely Harry's fault that our marriage still couldn't move in a positive direction in Sydney, even after the umpteen hours in couples therapy, or after the many fun-filled adventures we'd go on, or even after the times we'd laugh until our laps were drenched in tears from catching up on *Frazier* reruns. Today, I'd love to blame Harry and say that he thwarted every effort I made to turn things around for us. I'd also like to be forthcoming and tell you that the bastard was a conniving evil no-good doer. But then, I'd embody that idiom "the pot calling the kettle black."

You'd probably blame him anyway, especially after you read about some doozies like how he never once, not one time, ever treated my visiting friends and family all that well. He always managed to behave in a way that caused them to feel uncomfortable and unwelcomed enough to set their feet walking back toward the guest bedroom each night instead of "hanging out" with us. Their eyes would move in quick side glances that spoke more clearly than their lips ever dared speak.

When my friend Sandy came to visit us in Sydney, she'd been looking forward to a fun time—the kind we used to have in the old days when we were roommates living on the beach. Back then, we went out drinking and laughing and pretty much enjoyed raucous carefree fun. Often, we returned to our place with some friends we'd rake up along the way, drinking and partying some more until it was practically time to get up and go to work the next morning.

Sandy kept mentioning how she was really looking forward to getting to know "Mr.-Too-Good-To-Be-True" a little better since my move to Tokyo. It didn't take her long after she arrived in Sydney to figure out the truth, though. I can still see the dazed look she couldn't shake off her face as she wished me good luck instead of saying, *"Good-bye, I'll miss you,"* when I dropped her off at the airport.

Sandy arrived about a year after Harry and I were already living in Sydney. By this time, I had been receiving treatment for my symptoms, which went from being called Ebstein Barr Syndrome to Chronic Fatigue Syndrome. During her visit, I was able to stay awake for a good part of the day, and had enough energy to show my dear friend some of the city's wonder and beauty. It was probably her third day and we had just gotten back to the apartment from a fun day out. On this day, I'd been feeling especially alive and clear-minded, which only occasionally occurred. So we decided on a place for dinner. We were coming home to get showered and changed. Harry was going to meet us for dinner. But as soon as we walked into the apartment, Harry came out of our bedroom. He stood there glaring at me, looking very agitated. I knew that what came next was not going to be good. Then the bastard spoke and changed everything for my unsuspecting friend.

"Where the hell have you been? I've been calling you!" he asked accusingly.

"I was out with Sandy," I said, suddenly feeling the familiar exhaustion and fuzziness seep out and wrap itself around me like a confining deadly web.

"I came home from work early because I've got a migraine, and I've been trying to call you. I don't see why you have to be gone all the time."

"Sandy is visiting this week. Of course I'm going to be gone more. What the hell is wrong with you? Can't you see she's right here?"

"Oh, hi Sandy."

By that point, Sandy was tiptoeing to the guest bedroom.

"Why do you always have to behave badly in front of my friends and family?" I asked him. *"I take care of your family whenever they visit. I'm nice to them. Why do you always have to be such a shithead with mine?"*

"I'm not being a shithead. I had been calling you all afternoon

to tell you that I came home sick and you wouldn't return my calls. You were supposed to tell me where we were going to dinner, and you never did."

"What the hell difference does it make where we're going to dinner if you're in bed sick! Sandy and I are going to dinner, so go back to sleep."

I ran to Sandy's room, knocked, opened the door and went in. She was sitting on the bed looking stupefied. I could see she was having trouble speaking.

"We don't have to go out, it's okay. You need to stay with Harry," she finally said.

"No, we're going out. I'm getting dressed. I need to get the hell out of here!" I left the room.

Then there was the time my sister Sarita spent three weeks with us. Harry and I had been married a year and a half. On one particular day, it was Thanksgiving and it was only nine months after moving to Sydney. Sarita and I were cooking and getting ready for the thirty-four mostly non-American friends soon arriving to feast on an American Thanksgiving dinner. Then Harry walked into the kitchen and pretty much chewed my head off for something I did. Or was it something I didn't do? I really can't recall his exact words that precipitated Sarita's outburst.

After Harry left the kitchen, Sarita yelled, *"What the hell is wrong you? Why do you let him talk to you like that?"* I don't know why she bothered saying the words when I knew exactly what she was thinking. She'd been trying to say these exact words for a couple of days now. But I kept slipping out of the room, or I would beg her to help me get dinner started or something, anything to keep her from speaking the truth. But now she stood waiting, and there was no running this time.

I was about to redirect my sister's focus, when I saw it. I hadn't seen it that whole time we'd been working in the kitchen. But there Sarita stood with her arms spread wide, gripping our sharpest butcher knife in one hand as grease dripped from her other hand. She had on one of Harry's old button-down shirts to keep her clothes clean, only she was wearing the shirt backwards. And as she stood there, menacingly gripping our largest knife and looking like the unhappy housewife I was, I got the most brilliant idea: I could make maxi aprons!

This seemed to happen a lot to me that year. I would be in the middle of doing something and unbidden, in popped an idea that would convince me how easily I could make millions. I could see how perfectly that backward shirt could work in kitchens around the world.

The one side of my brain was already thinking of the full range of colors and materials as soon as that bright yellow with a glossy stiff plastic finish had flashed. But the other side once again blared *"Escape!" "Escape Now!"* I focused on only the one side, as I often forced myself to do. I could see happy housewives around the world hosing themselves and their kitchen clean, never getting wet in one of my aprons. Oh, and perhaps a clever catchphrase should be imprinted on the front side like *My Kitchen!* with a bull-faced housewife sporting a sparkling gleaming butcher knife, and…

"Well?!" Sarita screeched.

"Oh, he's just tired." Sigh. Merely saying those words made me feel more tired now than I had the past two days, with all the work Sarita and I had done to prepare for the special

Thanksgiving meal.

Sarita didn't bother with using her mind; she continued yelling.

"Bullshit! The Isabel I know would never take that crap. He's been treating you like shit all week, and you're just letting him. What the hell?"

"I think we need to just focus on getting dinner ready, Sarita. I can't think about this right now."

Sarita rolled her eyes and clucked and tsked. Then she pressed her lips together really tight, shook her head, turned her back to me and went right back to her plucking, still shaking her head. She was obviously disgusted with the truth that surfaced in my brain, because she could still see what was in there ever since we were little girls sharing a tiny bed in a tiny room.

After she turned around, I noticed that I was looking at Sarita's back yet again, only it was her real back. Gosh, that looked really strange, and just like that, I decided that two backs was maybe not such a good idea. I shook my head and I tsked-tsked myself. Then I pressed my lips together, squeezing the heck out of them. And once again a brilliant idea popped straight out of my head, leaving behind the singular cry for escape.

You see, it sounds like it's all Harry's fault. I'm not saying he wasn't a shithead. Oh, for sure, during most of our marriage he was a shithead, and a bastard and conniver all rolled into one big ball of hell. I put up with his "crap," as Sarita very aptly coined it, just about every day of our marriage. But who was I to complain or feign innocence? A victim…me? No, I knew what I was getting myself into the moment I heard that voice divulge deceit and infidelity on that beautiful sunny September day in

Milford, Connecticut. I never once uttered to anyone about all I knew before I embarked on that journey toward the other side of earth. I gave everyone all the room they needed to come to their own conclusions.

And well, there was still my one little problem… I was quite ill and unable to function so well most days. At least my brain flat-out refused to cooperate. What were the chances I could support myself with so much illness keeping me attached to our bed most days? Who knew for how long I would be ill? So, shithead or crap-dishing bastard aside, I had to stay, and in many ways I had it pretty good. Oh sure, by this time I often had to quell the desperately screeching call in my secret chamber, since my secrets were becoming no match for what the bastard kept dishing out. I should have bailed, but to be frank, I did get my way sometimes. I did get to call a few shots, and I did enjoy a little autonomy, which was a far cry from how my life started out when I was inconsequential, ugly, and invisible. For sure it was nothing like my first marriage where I was forced to cast downward eyes and quell desire and hope.

SIXTEEN

One day, right in the middle of couples therapy, five months after Harry and I moved to Sydney, Australia, and about eighteen months after Harry admitted to his affair, I shared something. I shared how through writing everyday, just writing and not thinking about what I wrote, the deep truth revealing how I really felt about the affair surfaced all on its own. There was quite a bit more that surfaced on those pages, but I tore those particular pages into tiny pieces and tossed them in the trash. But not before I hurriedly dropped the scraps in a tub full of water and then scooped up the soggy pieces and slipped the whole inky mess in a bag.

I shared in that therapist's room how, after months and months of assuring Harry that I was fine, *"No, I'm not mad about the affair anymore, and don't I look like I've fucking gotten over it?"* that I was, in fact, super mad about the affair. I became aware of this only after having read back what I wrote on some of those pages. Not only that. I admitted sitting in that therapist's office to having held out on Harry the past eighteen months by keeping all the love between us blocked. Not that there was real love there in the first place, but I hadn't figured that out yet. I felt a weight lift from me in that therapist's office, sitting on the most uncomfortable chair. It was a weight that week after week had caused me to squirm and fidget. I was pleased with myself for having revealed how I really felt, instead of making up some story that wasn't real and had been living in my head.

For many years, I told untrue stories as a way to protect what really dwelled in me, and often I'd get confused stumbling over my own words. Then I would invariably forget what I originally said, and I would say the wrong thing after having just said something completely different. Time and time again, I'd backtrack and work my way forward again. Or I took a long while responding to questions, getting the story straight in my head before my lips committed to real words, and gosh was that always so exhausting.

That dreadful day in the room that had grown to feel safe, I finally spilled some truth straight from my secret chamber, and it felt wonderful. I felt so good inside I immediately started thinking I could have saved those other pages. Perhaps I would even blow open my entire chamber and set the whole of my insides free.

"What? What! All this time you've led me to believe that you were okay about the affair and now suddenly you realize you were not okay? How am I supposed to feel now? You've been lying to me this whole time we've been together and you expect me to feel okay about that?"

As Harry spoke these words, I stared straight forward with my mouth gaping, never even glancing his way. I couldn't believe what I was hearing. Weren't these sessions all about finally sharing openly? Wasn't it good news that this truth, so long bottled up was finally out in the open? Didn't my admission offer oodles of room for reconciliation? Isn't that what the therapist repeatedly assured us needed to happen? And didn't I take that first step?

"So how do you feel about what Harry just said, Isabel?" our therapist asked me next, as if it wasn't one fucking ridiculous piece of crap.

"Like it's completely unsafe to open up about anything. It feels unsafe to be with Harry," I said, speaking lingo that only weeks before the doctor had taught us to use. I wanted more than anything to hurt someone and not sit there, contained in the chair that was now hurting me.

"Oh, so now this is about me being wrong?" Harry said. He was up and already slipping on his suit jacket, and he was clearly done with this session.

From that day forward, Harry wore an anger that would spew from his mouth completely unprovoked almost every time we were together. It didn't matter that on the coolest days when wearing a sweater was necessary, my sister Sarita or my friend Sandy while visiting were wringing their hands and clearing their throats and fanning themselves in the same room where he erupted. Or, we might be out having a lovely quiet dinner, just the two of us with no worries, enjoying some sweet moments together, when Harry would lash out and deeply wound me with damning words!

Time after time, Harry said the cruelest things reminding me of all the heartless words I had so often spewed, making sure people knew they were getting a little too close to me. No matter how many therapy sessions we sat through, Harry held onto that one admission I made.

After the one time when I dared spill a sliver of what writhed in my secret chamber, I knew never to speak truthfully again. I knew to never open myself in any way whatsoever

ever again, and I was quite good at it. For most of my life I had practiced dwelling within the confines of a deep knowledge that the curse of my birth was perilous and my only protection was to cloak myself in silence, assuring an absolute invisibility. And, oh, oh, oh, thank God I held on to the rest of it. How lucky I felt to not have spilled any more bits, even though a couple of big chunks had been dropped on Harry—first that one night in Westbrook, Connecticut, and then in an unsafe therapist's office in Sydney, Australia.

Harry and I would get pretty close to breaking up, but then we'd somehow talk each other out of it because, well, how was I supposed to support myself? I was feeling better, but far from well. Each time, right in the middle of marching toward the overdue breakup, Harry would suddenly remember that he did love me in some way, and I'd acquiesce again, feeling relieved at being saved. Then once again we'd be fine for about two more weeks before I started begging for sex.

By this time we were approaching almost a year since the day of my admission in the therapist's office. Now, without speaking a word, Harry would mete out my punishment, turning his back to me and falling straight to sleep. Why he used withholding sex from me as my punishment, I never fully understood. With illness debilitating me those years, sex was usually the furthest thought or desire for me. But having it dangled, then snatched away time and time again, made me ravenous for it. Every time Harry would deny me sex, I would lie awake listening to his irregular snores. He'd turn over again and again in his sleep, as I remained awake, suppressing my deepest desire to run. And I would realize yet again how we were exactly where we had

Part Two: Her Relationships

started after his, then my, admissions.

Then with much flourish, my surprise fortieth birthday gift was presented to me right in the middle of a romantic dinner by the ocean. Harry chartered a sailboat for two in the Whit Sundays. One week later, we picked up our boat and sailed off.

On the penultimate day of our sailing trip, we were having the most perfect time together, sailing into the most picturesque harbor as porpoises performed their playful dance behind our boat. And right in the midst of laughing and loving the day, he whipped out an anger so fierce, it left me breathless and in tears.

From out of no fucking where that I could tell, he bludgeoned me. As I stood at the helm crying, when only seconds before I was filled with such glee, the truth hit me. I finally realized how I would always blindly allow Harry to guide me to this safe-feeling place that usually brought me so far up, I wouldn't dare open my eyes. Kind of like the tens of pigeons my oldest brother Sandalio blatantly tracked into Warren Harding High School one fine spring day. That dim-witted bunch pecked at the crumbs of bread he laid out for them, desperate for the next crumb—blindly following his trail into the bowels of a period where hundreds of kids were racing to get to their next class on time. That prank ended up being the "last straw" that finally got the insufferable Puerto Rican kid expelled from the school.

Harry once again dropped me from way up high . . . take that!

I finally opened my eyes and decided that I was done… again. The tears instantly stopped flowing and I felt my face grow hot. I finally saw, as I gripped the helm, that he was using my admission to somehow wipe out his admission. Only, my admission came after realizing I was harboring bad feelings, and wasn't it great that I finally allowed myself to get vulnerable and talk about what bothered me, exactly as the marriage therapist suggested? While his fucking admission was that he fooled me into giving up my life and everything back home while carrying on with another woman.

Oh, well, never in these moments did I acknowledge that none of this would have happened had I ran when I should have…the first time, then the second, and so on. Never mind that.

Instead, I replayed how before agreeing to marry him, and before finally stepping on that plane, the bastard led me to believe he loved me and only me. On and on he went about how I was the only love in his life, and never had he felt such deep love for a woman, and how he couldn't wait to get me to Tokyo, and how he was never going to let me go once I got there. All the while he was having a full-blown sexual relationship with the "girl" who allegedly needed a place until she got her own, and who he absolutely never told me about before they took their trip to Thailand to consummate their budding relationship. I was livid!

I yanked the helm this way and then that way, jerking Harry a bit as he sat on the stern's narrow seat. I finally let emerge what I was most angry about, which revealed itself on those pages I wrote, just spilling and spilling. We were planning our future together while the bastard was already living the promise he repeatedly offered me with the girl living in the room right next to his. Then I not only stopped crying, but I stopped talking.

For one full day before we stepped off that boat, I remained silent. Wouldn't you know, Harry noticed me then? He started doing so many thoughtful little things well before I handed the boat keys to the man holding out his hand back at the dock. Harry suddenly had so many nice things to say that the words kept getting caught in his mouth, so that they would all clamor out at once.

Isn't he clever? I thought. But I wasn't falling for it.

I vowed to never speak to Harry again. But on the very last night of my entire birthday package, in the plush 5-star hotel Harry reserved for us, he liquored me up real good and guided me to bed, one glass of champagne at a time. Still, I hadn't said one fucking word.

We somehow got back to life as usual. Harry still wore his anger and I wore mine. Only now we were back to having sex. We would bump angrily and continue on as if this were perfectly normal. When we were at home, we wouldn't look at each other or speak to each other for hours at a time. That was, until someone we knew came to visit. Then suddenly Harry would stand so very, very close to me, smiling and giving me that googly-eyed "I'm so in-love with you" look he gave to all his women. He would put his arm around me and stay real close the whole time. I'd escape his embrace and sneer at him.

Our friends would see this and think, *That one can be so mean and cold.* Of course they would think that because they didn't catch him seconds before they entered our domain—they didn't catch the distance between us that buzzed with anger, distrust and revenge. They also hadn't heard the words he silently spilled as we lay together the night before: words of how absolutely I am damaged goods, and, *"Why do I bother with you?"* and, *"Well, what do you expect, it's sex with you?"*

Really, he said much worse things that were too terrible to ever speak of, ever. They didn't live with this every single day, so they thought they were justified in telling me the truth.

"He's so in love with you. He speaks so kindly of you, and he says the sweetest things about you. He's never felt this way about anyone, he says. He never stops talking about you at work, that's all he does." And he must have rehearsed these lines because no matter who spoke them, they said exactly the same words.

I would get so angry I would tell them the real truth.

"Really? Because he only bothered to come stand near me when he heard you at the door. He rarely has a kind word to say to me, when no one is around. That's a real curious thing he does when he's around you because around me, when we're all alone, he's very, very different."

I saw how they looked at me, not believing a word I said, wondering why poor, poor, poor amazing Harry had ended up with such a mean, cold, bitch. After a while, Harry started agreeing with them all. He began talking with them, sometimes individually and sometimes in bigger groups, about what an awful cold-hearted bitch I was to poor, poor him.

One woman at his workplace got wind of all this, even though she never met me. It was curious how she and Harry started talking like old friends, except too many words that bespoke of crushes and desire had swirled and swirled. Then it was time for me to leave for my annual visit with my parents, who were now retired in Puerto Rico. My dad inherited his four acres from his family's land, and my parents had the most darling white house built atop a knoll that looked far out past the hills and valleys where secrets were still whispered, and still heard from miles away. And where the sea was the most amazing hiccup in the far horizon.

I sat on that most sparkling magical white veranda talking to Harry on my parents' house phone. I sat straight up with the phone barely up to my ear because of the heat it emitted, suddenly listening closely to what Harry was saying:

"...and she said the funniest thing, and I couldn't stop laughing. You'd love her, she reminds me so much of you. You two are so much alike."

"Wait. Are you talking about So and So?"

"Yeah, who did you think I was talking about? Were you even listening to me?"

"Yeah. So I'm curious, Harry, why after all this time I haven't met So and So, and why is it you always go out to dinner with her when I'm away?"

"What? I don't do that," he said, ignoring the first part of the question.

"Mm-hmm. So, here's the thing, Harry. I don't want you going out to dinner with her ever again, okay? You tell her to go find herself another man to befriend, one who's not married, okay? She probably doesn't want me coming to your work to make that clear to her, so you ought to make sure you take care of this, okay?"

"Oh my God! Are you jealous?"

"Let's just say that I don't care to share what's mine. So I plan on showing you how mine you are when I get back, which is in two days, you know."

I returned from my Puerto Rico visit two days later and showed Harry how mine he was, and things that night seemed to be back on the upswing. It was the morning after when I saw it. The entire thing was right there on the computer for anyone to read, so I read it. This So and So had written to Harry, thanking him for the lovely time she had "last night"—only, it was three nights before that they had that lovely dinner.

"I can't stop thinking about last night, and everything we talked about. It was perfect. Thank you again." I also read his reply to her email saying how it was perfect for him, too. And he meant what he said about having made a *"…mistake marrying Isabel, and I wish it was you I was married to instead of her."*

My heart plummeted. It was always interesting how I could be so shocked at Harry's consistent deceptions, especially when I mostly kept so much distance between us. Besides, how could I complain? I knew too well how, so many years before, I helped myself to what absolutely did not belong to me. I already expected to be tossed aside. I already knew I was destined for these emails. None of what I had just read should have shocked me.

And yet there was my vow, from only two days before, to make things work with Harry. I had been sitting thousands of miles away in Puerto Rico, on the widest coolest veranda, sucking on a juice-dripping cup of coconut Piragua, as the sweet promise of more good things to come put me in such a good mood.

I reread the emails, hers then his, and I decided to swallow the panic, the anger, and my renewed vow for revenge. Instead, I decided to carry on with my well laid-out plan to turn things around in our marriage, and to do the things that would make Harry love me again. I planned on doing a superb job, finally proving to the two-timing good-for-nothing cretin how I did love him. I was determined to lead him as high up as the sky would stretch—so I could finally fucking drop the cheating bastard.

Only these plans never seemed to stick with me for long. About two weeks after I read the lovebirds' emails, I couldn't seem to stop the anger from rising and taking complete control of the situation. That anger always drove me to ask the questions that got us rolling down that treacherous track toward total annihilation.

"So, what did you do last night while I went out with Addie?"

"I worked late."

"Oh? And did you come home straight from work?"

"Yeah, why?"

"Oh nothing. I thought maybe you had decided to go out to dinner again with So and So."

"No, I didn't. I worked late and came home."

"Oh yeah, that's right, I wasn't away on travel."

Sigh. *"Isabel, there's nothing going on with me and So and So."*

"Really? Because her email to you said otherwise."

"What? You read all my emails?"

"No, not 'all' your emails, just hers and yours that were there for anyone to read. I didn't have to do a thing other than sit in front of the computer and read them."

"Still, you read my emails. What is wrong with you? Wait. This is about the affair, isn't it? You're never going to forget it or trust me are you?"

"No, this has nothing to do with that. This is completely independent of that. This is you starting another relationship with another woman, again!"

"There's nothing going on between us, dammit! Nothing happened."

But I'd already figured out what those words really meant. I could easily read between that particular line. *"Nothing happened"* really meant there was no penetration, and because there was no penetration, then gosh, there was no sex, and well, there you have it: If there was no sex, nothing happened!

"Ahh, so something did happen. Maybe not intercourse, but something did happen, and really? 'What a perfect time you had? …You wished you were married to her instead of me?' And nothing fucking happened? You just happened to speak these words to each other and absolutely nothing happened? You really expect me to believe that?"

There we were again, with our nostrils flaring and wearing our angry suits that now resembled thick, shiny armor. Harry didn't bother continuing the argument. Instead, he got up from where he sat on our pink couch and left the house. I was uncontrollably mad. Inside our lovely picturesque home where we'd often watch the Sydney ferry come and go, and where lorikeets and kookaburras cried their desperate tunes right outside our glass doors, I paced and paced. I eventually decided that my good-for-nothing guy really needed to learn a lesson, and boy was I going to pay the bastard back this time.

Only, I never got around to meting out his first payback, nor his second, nor his third. Unless my purposely saying exactly the right things to match his words that always kept us too far apart could be considered a sort of payback. Or, keeping all to myself the many secrets that ensured no one would ever get close to me, not ever, ever, ever.

Then it happened again. Right in the midst of formulating my new master abomination plan, God in a long, white beard popped in my head, reminding me how far down Hell's path I already was. Besides the brilliant business ideas that assured my escape this was another thought frequenting my brain at that time—angry God. He looked angrier than ever as he shook his head. It hit me after I stopped pacing and nearing the final details of my payback plan. For as long as I could remember—probably starting when the unthinkable happened to a wisp of a girl so long ago that the memory became a swirl of air that vanished too quickly—demons in angry voices would speak words of retribution in my head. And after that time the Jesus had gotten into me, these same demons gyrated as they blared their warnings. Then after a few years more, those demons morphed into the white-bearded God who always looked down at me angrily. But lately, it seemed that all the demons I fought over the years to keep from destroying me had joined their forces with God to finally dispense my long-overdue punishment.

SEVENTEEN

Three years had passed when Harry's company moved his job from Sydney to Chicago, the company's headquarters. It was during our life in the quaint Chicago suburb when we both decided to end our marriage… the first time. The end happened because I became a student.

About one year into living in Sydney, I started receiving treatment with an integrative practitioner and felt well enough to function more productively. I decided to go back to school, this time to pursue something I always dreamed of: painting. I was forty years old when I was accepted to a prestigious art school in Sydney.

I loved being surrounded by like-minded people with more than half of the student body being over the age of thirty. It was divine! It was the perfect outlet to our dreadful marriage, even if it became our biggest thorn. Harry was not happy with his student wife and incessantly let me know what he thought—after his strong encouragement that helped me complete the application process. "Two-Mouth" showed up like never before.

I had stopped referring to Harry as "Mr.-Too-Good-To-Be-True" two months after arriving in Tokyo, precisely on the same day he admitted to his affair. Instead I began calling him "Bastard" and "Two-Mouth." He'd say things to get me drawn toward his bright words, and then turn around and fling at my face the complete opposite. "Two-Mouth" would enthusiastically agree to something, and say the things to get me even more excited about it. Then he would turn one hundred and eighty degrees and pressure the hell out of me for every interminable day after until I quit what we had agreed to in the first place. It was like living with a compressor attached to the top of my head, every day pressing more then a little, and then a bit more after that. Harry had been exerting these about-face moves almost from day one.

After I started at the art college, Harry would come home from work and say things like, *"It must be nice to not have to work and instead be able to play all day."*

"I wasn't playing, I was at school working eight hours straight."

"Well, if you can call that work."

"Wait, so you agreed to me going back to school before I applied, but you now badger me about it everyday? How is that okay?

"I'm just saying, it must be nice to be you. Instead of getting a job to help with the bills, as soon as you get better you go back to school."

"We had agreed that I'd go back to school so I could get a different kind of job. And the $450 a semester is hardly breaking our bank!"

"Listen, you could have gotten any kind of job. You could have found a part-time job at McDonald's, but noooo, you went back to school."

"You're kidding, right? You agreed to this before I even applied. You even encouraged me to apply. Do you even remember that? This is like when I first moved to Tokyo and you begged me to decorate the apartment because you had no clue how to do it, and

it was such a mess, and on and on you went about needing my help and as soon as I started decorating you gave me shit every single fucking day about taking over your space with "my" ideas and "my" touch, and you didn't feel like it was even your home any more. What the hell? What the fucking hell?"

When we first learned about Harry's job transfer to Chicago, we spent weeks planning how to proceed with my education. We finally decided I would stay in Sydney and finish the remaining two years of my BFA. I would fly to Chicago during breaks and Harry would visit me in Sydney during his vacations. We also decided that after I finished the BFA program in Sydney, I would get my teaching degree in Chicago and teach art there. But after finding an apartment in Sydney, and after buying me a brand new smaller car, "Two-Mouth" started up again. This he ramped up by too much for me to handle.

"*I guess now that you have this car and this apartment you won't have to feel so married anymore. It must be nice to be you.*"

"*'We' got this apartment, and 'we' bought this car. Remember? Remember how I couldn't make up my mind on the color of the car and you kept saying the red was more me? Do you even remember that?*"

"*Yeah, I do, but do you really think this is going to work with you all the way in Sydney and me all the way in Chicago? You know you'll never come home. What a convenient out for you. How lucky are you?*"

"*You insisted this was the best and quickest way for me to get my degree. And now after going through all the trouble and expense of securing an apartment, and buying a new car, you're going to give me shit about it as if it was only my decision? We talked about this for weeks!"*

"Yeah, but I think you wanting to stay in Sydney for the next two years is very telling about how uncommitted you really are to our marriage, and about how you really feel about me."

"So this was another one of your sick tests to see if I really do love you? What the hell? What the fucking HELL?"

After two more months of the heavy badgering and the unbearable compression, I sold the car, gave up the apartment, pulled out of art college, and got on a plane to Chicago. I transferred to SAIC the next semester and completed another year there, but barely survived Harry's incessant badgering.

"Wow, how lucky are you that you get to play like this all day while the rest of us adults have to work to make a living."

"Oh God! We had agreed for me to do this. We had agreed. PLEASE! Will you please, please, please, just leave me alone!"

Almost every day in that first year at SAIC, Harry found a reason to come into the fourth bedroom of our 4,500 square-foot house that I converted into a studio, searching for a "something," even though everything in there was art-related.

"Gosh, it must be nice to have your 'own' room in 'our' house. Isn't your life great."

"Fuck you, get out."

"How can I get out when this room is in my house?"

"Why do you do this? What the hell is wrong with you? I can't stand you! I can't stand living with you! Get the fuck out of this room!"

"Okay, I'm leaving 'your' room now."

One time he stepped on one of my paintings on his way out of my studio. *"Oops, sorry, it was in my way,"* he said, as he walked out of the room, smiling then snickering.

After two full semesters of this badgering, I closed the door to "my" studio and didn't open it again for many months. I applied for a leave of absence from SAIC and was granted one.

Now, you'd think after enough times being bludgeoned over the head, I'd wake up to the fact that the bastard was a bastard, and that any sweet words of love and encouragement oozing from the bastard's mouth should at all times be taken as a warning of imminent disaster. But no, I kept opening my path of destruction for a big dose of more destruction, and the bastard's sweet words were precisely the key that opened my internal door to hell.

I once again allowed myself to be led way up high to the brilliant limitless sky with enchanting words of how taking a couple of night classes at the community college could keep some momentum going with obtaining my BFA degree. The bastard was thrilled his student wife no longer attended a real college, but regardless of how happy he was, he simply could not help himself.

"So, I guess three classes doesn't feel to you like you're never home with me. Well, at least it's not breaking my bank like SAIC was. I guess that's some improvement."

"You insisted this was a good move. You insisted..." I said, feeling so incredibly exhausted. I started to cry. I couldn't stop crying for an entire day. I walked back into the studio, locked myself in, and didn't come out for two days. I'd had enough, again, after enduring five years of abuse. In my studio, crying and crying I kept thinking about how I was supposed to be the one paying the bastard back. How the heck was this anywhere

close to revenge? Five years after admitting to his affair, the man still had the upper hand. Oh God, he had the upper hand since day one.

I'd been so careful to try to keep the whole of our relationship pure, to keep my secrets locked and buried in my chamber's deepest bowels, even though the stench would often rise up to remind me of how unspeakably dirty I kept my life. I didn't stand a chance of surviving staying with this guy. I had to get the hell out of this place. So I wrote Harry a letter a "Dear John" letter.

Dear Harry,

I never in my wildest dreams thought that I could suffer more greatly than I had in my 37 years before moving to Tokyo, when I started my new life with you. But you have relentlessly demonstrated to me over the past five years how there truly isn't a limit to suffering. You win, and I quit. I cannot take another minute living the hell we've been living for these past five years. And it has been for me precisely as the saying goes, "a living hell!"

I'm leaving you. This is for the best. I'm sure you'll feel relief from my decision since I can't imagine that you've been happy with me, and knowing you as I do, making the first move would be too difficult for you. So I'm doing this for us, for our sanity, and for our health. I realize now that I can't improve my health by living with you, especially since I've grown more ill every day I've been with you. And you have aged ten years in our five years together. I think we both carry enough proof that we reached the end of our time together long ago.

I need some time to figure out what I'll do next, but my guess is I'll go back to Connecticut. Please give me a few more days to

figure things out, and then I'll pack up and go.
I wish you well.
With all my heart,
Isabel

This letter motivated Harry to sweet-talk his way back to me. He kept sending me emails telling me how much he loved me. How when he first heard our friend Dana mention my name how he couldn't imagine this Isabel. And what a lovely sight I was the first time he laid eyes on me, prettier than anything he'd ever imagined.

I deleted his emails, and I kept the door to the studio locked from the inside, never replying, never uttering a peep. So unlike that one time my high school shorthand teacher shouted at me, *"I don't want to hear another 'peep' from you, young lady!"* and I couldn't, just couldn't keep that damn word from shooting out from my mouth. There she stood, red-faced and miraculously twice as tall as her puny height, shouting, *"Get out! Get out! I don't want to see your face in this class again!"* And out I went. This time, though, not only did I not peep, but I didn't venture out once while Harry was home, not once.

Three days after I sent the "Dear John" letter I packed while Harry hovered nearby. He couldn't go into work that day and he couldn't think, and he couldn't sleep, and no way, no way could the man eat. And the weight of my biggest break-up sat heavy on my heart. I still hadn't bought plane tickets because I still hadn't told anyone back in Connecticut that I was moving back. I'd written the woman whom, years before, hired me as a consultant to run a satellite office for an agency she managed.

Chances were good, she thought, that I would have a job at the new agency she directed in Hartford, Connecticut. I started packing to get my clothes out of our bedroom and into the room that was my studio where I had been sleeping. I planned to have my bags ready for when it was time to escape.

But the idea of moving back to Connecticut, and dear God, to Hartford of all places, sat even heavier on my chest than our breakup did. It felt like I'd be regressing, even though I was already buried too deep after five years of marriage. I no longer feared what all the folks back home would think of me, with another divorce marked off. I no longer cared about the words that would surely flow from telephone to telephone. *"Oh, dear, I wonder what she did to mess things up this time?" "Hmm, she never can seem to hold onto a man, that one!"* And I definitely didn't care if my mother shook her head and tsked, tsked for the rest of her days. I had no doubt she would side with Harry, precisely like she had sided with Reza. I was the problem. I always had been.

That night, alone in my studio, I heard the ping of an email arrive on my computer. I checked the time on the clock on the night table and saw that it was 1:00 am. I'd been lying awake for hours, unable to sleep, worrying about my future after having decided to buy plane tickets to Hartford, Connecticut, the next day. Sigh. I got up and walked to the computer across the room. I sat on the chair and opened the email. It was from Harry.

My Dearest Isabel,
I can't find the words to express how saddened I feel. I'm most sad to finally be able to see (albeit too late!) that we are breaking

up without ever having given our marriage a real chance. I realize I am to blame for much of our troubles. We spent the past five years making each other miserable, and I recognize my part in all of this, only I now see it and it's too late.

Deep down, though, I know that we could have a different kind of marriage, one where love and trust could ignite much happiness for us both.

I understand and respect your decision to leave. This is your choice to make, of course. But I wanted to make one last plea to you, a proposal, if you will.

I propose we give our marriage one more chance. Only this time, we do all the things that we learned through therapy. I think we already know exactly what we need to do to make this marriage work. We've learned many tools to help us put our marriage on a solid track, but I know we have never applied any of them. We can turn our marriage around. I know we can do this. I just know we can. If after we give our marriage all our efforts to salvage it and we still can't make it work, I won't stand in your way. In fact, I promise to help you move on in whatever ways I can.

I also promise to you that I if you agree to stay, I will give 150% to make our marriage a happy and safe place for us both.

What do you say?
Your loving husband,
Harry

I read Harry's letter and knew I was being saved again. I felt the familiar warm sensation of relief spread through my entire body, and every time it felt exactly like years ago when I let the magic white powder seep into my bloodstream. Then I waited in anticipation for the most powerful rush of promise and valor to overtake my senses. The warm comforting glow I felt after reading Harry's letter was merely a new drug I became hopelessly addicted to on my unremitting path to destruction. There was no room for rationale, only the pure sensation of that perfect drug called relief. Oh, glory hallelujah! I sat there feeling my whole body being overtaken by relief's sweet grand nectar. I was being saved again… only a few short years before I became more than ready to die.

After I accepted Harry's proposal, we both vowed to work for one year at improving our marriage. If we were successful we would then try to bring children into our family. And if our efforts didn't turn things around, we would go our separate ways.

Harry and I spent the following year committed to saving our marriage. We worked through some pretty prickly issues, without any therapy. We grew close. We figured we deserved to have a family because of all the work we'd put into fixing our marriage. So we decided to adopt.

If I'd been able to speak the truth at the time—the truth that had been with me since the day I was born, even though I didn't have the words to speak them then—I would have written instead… *I never wanted to be a mother. I especially had no desire at age forty-two to get pregnant and I only arrived at adopting because yet again a damn ultimatum had been flung at me… and we had been moving along so nicely… fuck!*

When I announced to my family and friends that Harry and I were adopting, their eyes bulged, their mouths gaped open, then after a while they'd offer weak congratulations. But only after having asked, *"Really?"* or *"But, wait, I thought you never wanted children?"* or *"What, you're kidding, right?"* or *"So is Harry forcing you to do this?"*

I ignored their questions. Never once did I share the truth that an ultimatum had once again been tossed, and after life was finally turning toward the right direction. About six months into the year Harry and I were reconciling our marriage, he started bringing up the subject of children just about every day.

"But there's no way I would have dedicated all this energy and time into fixing our marriage if I knew there would be no children. There's no way I would have agreed to that," Harry kept insisting.

"I don't know about having children, Harry. I'm really afraid I won't have enough energy to take care of kids. I'm over forty, you know. I don't have as much energy as I used to. I'm only recently able to function somewhat normally. I don't want to get sick again."

"I want a family, Isabel. I'm not interested in a childless marriage. That's just not for me. You affirmed in your wedding vows that you wanted children. I've watched you with kids. You're a genius with them. You would be the best mom ever."

"I really don't think so. I really don't think I can do this." And I didn't assert myself. I didn't give Harry the whole truth, again.

"Then we can't stay together, even after all the work we've put into fixing our marriage. I want a family."

Harry and I had this exact discussion night after night. Then Harry finally said, *"I'm done waiting for you to decide, Isabel. You either do this or you don't. I need to know."*

He calmly walked out of the room. I already knew how this was Harry's clear signal that he was done talking about a subject. I found myself forced to face my future, once again with a looming ultimatum that threatened to sentence me to wretchedness. The next morning I sat in front of my computer, and no one was more surprised than me after I compiled the list of adoption agencies to call.

When I presented Harry with my list, he searched my face. Then he said, *"Wait, I thought you didn't want kids. Just yesterday you said you didn't want children. Are you sure you want to do this, Isabel? Because I don't want to force you into doing this."*

I reassured Harry that having children was what I really wanted. Then about a week after receiving Harry's ultimatum, as we ate breakfast, I said to him, *"I woke up this morning and realized that I'd regret not having kids."*

Those words were meant to stop Harry from searching my face every damn morning. Those words were the same ones I told everyone I saw, everywhere I went. I said them so often that even I started believing them.

It was Sarita who didn't bother with asking any questions because as always she could see what was hidden inside me. *"Listen, I don't know why you can never say no when you need to, but this is stupid. You never wanted to have children, and I can see you still don't. When are you going to stand up to that man?"* She said this with her fists on her hips, and she spoke to me in her I'm-fed-up-with-you voice.

"Sarita, this is different. I really want to have children. I'm not getting any younger. I'd regret not having children, I know that now."

"You're bullshitting me, Isabel. I can see the truth inside you, you know. Don't do this, please."

I quickly changed the subject because an ultimatum was threatening to disintegrate my life, and Sarita wasn't going to stop me. I continued with my story, the one I'd practiced again and again, while the truth got buried deeper and deeper—until that unfortunate day when the whole truth refused to stay buried.

EIGHTEEN

About one year into completing all the application steps with Chicago's premier adoption agency, Harry's company asked us to move back to Tokyo for a one-year assignment. While living in Tokyo a second time, after having completed our home study for adoption only the month before, we received the phone call that would change everything.

We were sound asleep when we heard the phone ring. Those days we kept the phone volume on high, just in case. And were we even asleep? It was the middle of the night so I assumed we were, but the one ring barely let out its trill before I grabbed the receiver in my hand and brought it up to my ear.

"Hello, Isabel?"

"Yes?"

"Hi, I hope I didn't wake you guys."

Really? It's 3:00am Sunday, how could you not have woken us? Or was I already awake?

"Yes you did, but that's fine. Why do I think you have good news for us?"

"Actually, I think I have great news for you." By this time Harry was hovering around me, trying to hear what was being said so I let him listen. *"There is a Puerto Rican family who gave birth to a baby boy four weeks ago. He's been in our nursery since after the birth. His birth parents have rejected all the dossiers we've presented to them because they insist on a family with*

Puerto Rican decent. We hadn't approached you earlier because you had said you needed time after the last rejection. But we also knew that you were keen on adopting a Puerto Rican baby, and well, here he is."

After we hung up with our social worker, we booked our flights to Chicago for the very next day. We were both so excited that we couldn't go back to sleep. We didn't even bother trying. Instead, we squealed and jumped, then ran into the room we designated for our baby. It was filled with seemingly random pieces that were carefully set down before we closed the door and waited. It was already five months into the overseas assignment in Tokyo and the room had stayed closed for all those months.

But now we unwrapped packages and tore open boxes and spilled contents onto the floor. It would have been clear to anyone who happened to peep in that we didn't know what the heck we were doing, or what we were getting ourselves into. But we kept going until the sweetest sight lay before us.

Our baby's crib was beautifully fitted with lace, silk and oodles of color and stuffed animals. A musical carousel mobile that we attached to one end arced over the mattress waiting to lull our baby to sleep. Every piece in that room oozed of sweet dreams and hope and we brought our morning coffee in there before we packed our bags. We ate our breakfast just inside the doorway and we reluctantly left that room four hours later to pick up our baby boy.

We were married seven years by now. While completing all the requirements for adoption, we talked for many hours about our preferences surrounding children and raising a family. You'd think this was something we would have taken care of before we got married, but with so much deceit and destruction to tend to, who had time to talk about a future? As it turned out, we shared very similar views and seemed well suited to parent together. We were quite surprised with this harmony, since no matter how small or large the issue was, a great gap separating us loomed. But to be honest here—because it must be said—I withheld my deepest fear throughout all this talk; I knew enough to mirror Harry's words. Never once did I discuss how my becoming a mother would surely cause our inevitable demise.

The day our baby came home, a throng of family and friends waited to greet him. He slept nestled in someone's arms from the time we walked through our front threshold with him, until finally it was time for everyone to leave or go up to their room.

We had a dilemma.

We received an email not even one month after uploading our profile onto the adoption agency's website. She was a twenty-two-year-old still in college, and she was only two weeks pregnant. When we received the phone call for our first baby, we'd been already communicating for a month with the twenty-two-year-old. Two days before we returned to Tokyo with our new son, she and her mom drove two hours to meet us. This visit went so well, Harry and I decided to move forward with adopting her baby as well—which meant that our babies would be merely seven and a half months apart. Like I said, back while we were assembling our son's new bedroom in Tokyo, we had no clue what we were getting ourselves into.

After living in Tokyo six more months, we moved back to our house in the quaint and seemingly idyllic Chicago suburb to prepare for our second son's arrival. But by that time, my insides had already started roiling again.

I was forty-five years old with a seven-month old baby, and anxiously waiting for a second baby whose birth was only two weeks away. Our demise was poised for its downward spiral.

My mom was right. She always warned us seven girls that raising children sucked the life out of you, and that, well, if we didn't get it out of the way early in life, we would undoubtedly find ourselves scrambling to find more life to offer this other being. Because life itself siphoned a bit more of the life inside people, and every year of mere living left one with a little less life. *"That's just how life is,"* she said, again and again. She explained how babies start out not having enough breath in them, and it was up to the mamas every day to breathe enough life in our babies so they could make it to the next day, and the next. Her warnings took a desperate turn when she noticed I was nearing forty, clearly the age when mamas began wringing their hands in the hope of a grandchild, and fretting about the implications the "holdup" presented. Time and time again, she said to me, *"You'll be sorry…"*

She was right, because I was back to feeling exhausted every day—after having improved my health enough to function at about eighty percent. Caring for one baby was surely sucking every breath of life out of me. Not that much life flourished in me at age forty.

One day, about one month after we returned from Tokyo to our grand, hundred-year-old dark, dark, dark house, our oldest napped upstairs. I sat quietly in our ornate living room that was adorned with the most stately-looking fireplace. I sat in that dark room, the darkest of all, with my dark thoughts that occupied more and more of my time. I was afraid to speak the words that would cause more destruction than the ones from too many years before, which waited in dormancy many layers below these. I gave my dark thoughts permission to roam a bit in my mind.

This was what I finally let loose up there: *I can't suppress any longer how I really feel since the words are fighting their way out of me.* Everyone else knew that something wasn't right. They had watched me repeatedly walk past our baby's crib, ignoring his cries. They had absorbed my words, threatening anyone who reached in to cuddle and comfort my baby. They had heard my ridiculous admonishments composed of too many useless words that were meant to clarify why this was better for him. I wasn't fooling anyone. They could all see how I wouldn't hold my baby any longer, and how precisely because of this, I wouldn't let anyone else try. In that most dreary room, I brought forth in my mind the stunned-looking faces desperately staring back at me as I relentlessly and feverishly explained that letting my newborn cry was my wise way of teaching him how to be on his own at seven months. They then watched me walk away, creating distance between me and my crying baby.

I fought for that distance every day, running out of the house or locking myself in the bathroom or hiring a nanny, then another, then another. Then my thoughts, of their own accord, moved on toward a truth I only sometimes let surface very briefly: *Parenting is not the most fun in the world.* This one time, sitting alone in the darkest room in the house, I moved even closer to the truth: *Parenting is not fun at all.* Then I allowed my thoughts to finally open wholly. And as the space in my mind expanded, I felt the tightness in the center of my chest constrict a bit more as the whole truth appeared: *Being a mom is the most unpleasant thing I've ever done, and is worse than getting through those first seven years married to Harry. I hate being a mom! I never wanted to be a mother. I never wanted to be a mother! I DON'T WANT TO BE A MOTHER!*

As my baby slept upstairs, those dark thoughts quickly began overtaking the normal functions of my body. My heart raced and an overwhelming tightness started seizing my body. When I heard my baby start fussing upstairs, I tried putting everything back in its place, but the truth refused to move back down. It stayed stuck in my chest, and I felt it threaten to come up and choke me. I sat in my quaint house, desperately trying to coax my damning thoughts right back into my secret chamber.

I tried taking deep breaths to help loosen the clump clogging my insides as my baby wailed upstairs. I paced and breathed, paced and breathed. I heard our nanny's careful steps approach me.

"The baby is awake now. Can I go get him?" she asked.

"No, he needs to learn to settle down on his own. I'll go up in a little while," I responded automatically, and not with the calmest tone. I heard the cry in my voice and I was sure she did as well, because she let her head drop.

At the drop of my nanny's head, my thoughts finally arrived at where they had been scrambling to get to: *I can't bring home a second baby. Dear God, we would all die if another baby sucked more life out of me.*

Weeks before, I started waking up every day with the

familiar low-grade anxiety that stayed buzzing all day. But all those previous days, I could keep the beast contained in my secret chamber. After my thoughts escaped, though, I no longer could control them. I was up and pacing that dark room, feeling like a caged wild animal as I desperately inhaled and exhaled, frantically trying to shrink the clump that seized my throat. Oh, how I dreaded having to walk up those stairs and enter the pretty room with the most precious pieces of furniture, adorned with mobiles and blankets and rattles and hopeful desperate cries—which every damn time forced me to pretend I was a happy, happy mommy!

That night after dinner, I finally told Harry I couldn't go through with the second adoption. I summoned enough nerves to speak the ugly truth, but only after the lovely bottle of chardonnay stood empty on the kitchen counter.

"What do you mean? We can't say "no" now, Isabel. It's too late. We have to do this. I will be here helping so don't worry. It'll be fine. It's going to be great," Harry assured me, and he smiled.

"I'm telling you, I can't do this. It's too much for me. I'm starting to struggle with our one baby. How am I supposed to handle two babies less than eight months apart?"

I knew he could see that I struggled with our one baby. But Harry had already started walking through me. It was clear that I was starting to vanish. I didn't dare explain how our oldest had sucked too much life out of me, and that I barely had enough life in me to give our one baby, and that for sure I would cease to exist with a second baby, which would surely kill that baby as well. I didn't dare warn him that more than one of us would be gone.

"Isabel, we can't say "no"," Harry said with utter finality. He calmly walked out of the room and I heard him walk up the stairs to our bedroom. He was done talking about it. At the sound of our bedroom door's click, I walked briskly to the refrigerator and pulled out another bottle of the lovely chardonnay.

Two weeks later, our youngest son was born. We brought him home to a welcome as ebullient as the first, with all the same family and friends passing him around, not putting him down for days and days. After about a week, our new baby boy started to cry, and he didn't stop crying for four months straight. He cried for twelve hours straight, and then he slept without stirring for twelve hours. During his waking hours I cried right along with him. And during his sleeping hours I drank and drank, and I never felt so completely exhausted. I had never been so completely strung out, not after all the drugs and partying, and not even after years of heart-wrenching deceit and destruction.

It was what I'd asked for. I knew better. I should have been willing to stick with "no." Again, I didn't heed all the warning signals that were precise this time. After all, in the middle of writing my personal profile to help birth parents get to know me better, I'd purposely left out my brain's forceful trumpeting how I never, ever wanted children. I'd been in denial since the very beginning—years before adopting—when I first penned and then declared the lie in my wedding vows. That lie caused my stomach to churn and my chest to constrict as I looked into Harry's eyes by the beach in front of one hundred and fifty guests. Or when I paced while my boys slept, dreading their waking hours as I quelled the panic that brewed and swirled upward, floating higher and higher. Or the fear that unexpectedly seeped out from deep inside me, with hissing whispers that intimated a mother who preferred her children invisible, and who could crush any sign of life.

In the months following the arrival of my second baby, I unraveled clumsily and too quickly for me to keep up with. I was back to bursting open with angry, hurtful words that scarred adults and two sweet precious babies. Day after day in the dark magnificent old dark house, I trudged through motherhood, growing weaker and more distant. And I found myself once again in a real pickle: I was now the "Two-Mouth."

Once my babies arrived, I could no longer match my actions to equal my words. Now it was I who turned one hundred and eighty degrees, this time on my family.

NINETEEN

It didn't take long after our second son arrived for my dark thoughts to play out in every day life. I was running away more and more each day. I woke up every morning and devised my escape plan for the day. Our nanny had her hands full!

Harry no longer searched my face. Every day he had enough proof unequivocally confirming that I did not want children. He didn't bother hiding his disgust, which was why we were back to destroying the heck out of each other—and which was why I was back in school, years after giving up on ever completing my BFA.

It was two years after our second baby arrived. I sat in the large industrial square room, excited to be there again. It was exactly the kind of outlet I needed to escape the claws of motherhood, even though I was old enough to be everyone else's mother. I was surrounded by kids who couldn't stop their zippy side-glances—nor could they keep their audible snickers—from reaching me.

I was back attending classes at the School of the Art Institute of Chicago (SAIC), after almost five years of being away. SAIC's recent letter warned me that I was approaching the five-year deadline that would wipe out the credits I'd earned. It was this letter that finally pushed me back onto my seat. After staying home with babies for two years, and not attending one class in almost four years, I was eager to draw and paint and write and study and learn and grow in the very few hours I dared escape misery. I fought my way back onto the stool I sat on in spite of the hurtful words that singed and scarred.

"How could you even think of abandoning your kids to just sit in a classroom? What kind of mother are you, anyhow?"

"We agreed to this. I wrote it into our adoption profile. I wrote I would continue with completing my BFA program, and I told you. I warned you that I couldn't stay home with kids full-time. I told you. I could never do that, I just can't."

"How you could so easily abandon them is what I don't understand."

With every fiery word, I moved further and further away, night after night, digging the distance that could relieve the suffocating heat. I was determined to not let any more words reach me.

Only one semester later, as soon as I turned forty-eight, I started a menstruation cycle that only took occasional breaks. By the time the bleeding started flowing right through me, I gave up on ever completing my BFA degree. I grew too weak to withstand the compression from Harry's old familiar badgering. I relinquished to the open air my deepest desire to paint, and instead, I willed myself to die. I accepted the ever-flowing blood as a sign that my plea was being granted. I waited for death to take me, but months later it still hadn't arrived. That particular winter in Chicago was in the height of its cycle with a never-ending snowfall, and I figured this was the sign: death would come in the spring. But it didn't come then either.

I spent the winter trapped in our house, where the only

sound I could not stop were cries that never ceased. I didn't care to step outdoors where the neighbors couldn't stop themselves from whispering to each other in hushed hurried voices. They hovered on the sidewalks, glancing this way, then that way, making sure the wrong ears weren't privy—exactly as their parents had done, and so on, and so on. This even though I stayed trapped in our massive house's basement with all the windows closed shut—never, ever escaping the two baby boys who cried and got wet again and again, and got hungry and got sick and cried some more, and, oh! There was always crying, somebody was always crying. The words that were whispered on those heavily stained sidewalks from the many generations of tittle-tattle always managed to float toward our house and penetrate the thick brick façade.

"She's depriving him of sex, what a miserable life for that poor, poor man."

"Oh dear, I don't know how that man takes it. He's a saint, I'll tell you that!"

When the healer arrived in that town, I made a fifth appointment with him. I decided if death wasn't going to take me, then I wanted to be healed of all my illnesses that had managed to return…tenfold. Every day I struggled to lift my head; I couldn't stop the bleeding that had started all on its own from somewhere so deep inside me, not even the many doctors could figure out how to turn off the valve. Rarely did this bleeding take a break, and oh, how unbearably exhausted my body felt after being emptied of so much blood. I couldn't, couldn't, no matter how hard I tried, get out of bed some of those dark wintery days. And who's the "Two-Mouth" now?

Who's the one going back on her words now?

"I can't, I tell you. It's too much. I don't have what it takes! I was never meant to be a mother. I only did it for you. I only did it for you. You gave me the fucking ultimatum again! I never wanted kids, and you knew that. You knew that!"

"I didn't force you to do this, Isabel. You did most of the work, and I'm so grateful you did but I didn't tell you to do it." Pause. *"You're going to leave us, aren't you? You're going to abandon our boys aren't you?"*

"No. I can't do that either."

"I think you are. I think you've already decided."

He was right. I had decided to abandon them, but not by walking out of that house. I had decided to end my life. But months later, death passed swiftly past me, leaving me in a heap of misery.

When I sat in front of this healer after having escaped that dark, cold, damp basement, it was this overwhelming need to exit life that I wanted him to heal most. I complained to him about the blood flow that was completely out of my control, and was meant to be the thing that would finally stop me from breathing for good. I complained about my exhaustion, and about two baby boys who day after day demanded more and more from me when I had nothing left to offer because the life in me had been completely drained by my oldest boy in his first year. I complained about how I was having these thoughts that were overtaking me. But never once did I say exactly what those thoughts were, because I was sure that releasing the words would break loose what little restraint I had on the beast. And never, never once did I mention how every night I lay too far from my husband, who was the gentlest, most wonderful father—and who was back to being a bastard.

But how could I blame him? I was the "Two-Mouth" now. I abandoned him and our sons, over and over again. I knew that if this healer didn't use his magic to expel all my illnesses it would only be a matter of time before I hadn't enough life left to abandon anyone.

When my session with the healer ended, I was shocked to hear the words that came barreling out of his mouth.

"There is something important I need to talk to you about," the healer said, using his stern voice—not the gentle one I heard the last time I saw him.

He looked down at me as I sat before him, feeling dazed after not having been healed at all. Already my brain reasoned that I was being granted death after all.

"Okay," I barely whispered.

"I understand you have two boys and it's been hard work for you, but you took this on and now these boys need you. They didn't ask for this, and now they need you. You have to stay with this and think of them and not yourself." The healer spoke with such remarkable force, his words were instantly repelled by my ears.

Again he stared down at me—not with the softest, kindest look that I expected from this healer, but a rather judgmental one. He didn't have a white beard, but still I waited for the demons that always followed the white-bearded force.

"Here's what I most need to say to you: You have an obligation to your husband. He is a man with certain needs and as his wife you must be willing to see to his needs. Do you understand what I mean?"

I couldn't speak. The demons weren't burning my insides like they normally did. They hovered directly above me, spewing droplets that singed my heart. I was shocked that the demons took on such an unlikely form. I stared in disbelief; words never once uttered by me were now being spattered on me with such smoldering force.

I nodded my head, I think.

"Good, now go home to your duties." He turned his back to me and went about preparing for his next visitor.

I went home. But I didn't walk back down the hard basement stairs. I fought to shut out the pleas calling out to me from that room below, the ones with wet tears, and the ones for my escape to the never life. I crept higher and higher, vowing to never again lay any closer to the one who marked already-stained sidewalks, whispering poison into ears that couldn't help themselves from frantically spreading damning news to more ears, and more ears. I inched all the way up the endless stairs that reached my new studio, our renovated attic. It was only half my studio, and half his. He couldn't see why I should have the whole attic as my studio when he absolutely needed an office in "his" house, even though every day he took the train to his real office with a real door with all the fixings one requires for conducting business.

I curled up in the corner on the floor of my new studio, where I rarely went to paint or draw because the open space included him talking on his phone too loudly and watching my every move. It was empty. I shut out the cries, the pleas, the words and surrendered to the burning, burning, burning.

One spring day while still waiting for death, I sat in a waiting room. I noticed two other women, who didn't appear to know each other, reading the same book. They looked enraptured. I dared to interrupt them and asked out loud what they read.

"*The Secret*," one said.

"*Is it good?*" I asked.

"*It is the most amazing book I've ever read,*" the other said.

"*What is it about?*" I asked.

"*How anything is possible,*" one said.

"*It's about living life with no fear,*" the other said.

Oh, I thought. Immediately after I left there, I drove to the local bookstore and bought the book that could save me.

The Secret completely changed my life. When I finally put the book down, I instantly had hope. I could see beyond the moment, and it all looked splendid. It was during that period of open optimism that leaving Chicago became possible. I practiced thinking and talking about a life where I flourished and I was drenched in sunshine. This meant California.

A year later, we escaped the quaint Chicago suburb and death and moved to California. As soon as my feet landed, I blossomed with life once again, even though I once again succumbed to my husband's maddening compression. In spite of the crying that evolved into hellacious angry words, in spite of the mornings I still struggled to pull myself from under those much finer softer sheets, and even as the bleeding no longer took a break, I found myself smiling and feeling alive those first months in sunshiny California.

Harry arrived in California loaded with fresh ammunition, our two toddlers with fear and excitement, and me with hope and an extra forty pounds. Before our move, I began a new health regimen recommended by a renowned endocrinologist, and by the third month, I'd gained fifteen pounds. Seven months later, as I joyfully said good-bye to my life in Chicago, I was forty pounds heavier.

But after those first months in California, my optimism started to wane, even after miracles had been sprinkled upon me. I was living in my dream house and I miraculously became a patient of the famous endocrinologist, who placed a name beside every demon she recognized, and who knew exactly how to exorcize them. However, neither miracles, nor sunshine, nor optimistically stifling desire and goals for the hideous body that only fitted in sizes that once were for those women, never for me, were any match for the compression that burned my skin, my brain, and my insides.

"It's all your fault that we're here in this awful house. I hate living here. I came to California because of you, you know. I hate being here. I only moved here for you," Harry complained every day.

"Harry, I warned you that if after we moved to California you started beating me up like you did in Sydney, I would leave you. Do you not remember me repeatedly asking you if you were sure you wanted to move to California? And that if you said yes and you agreed that I wouldn't accept you doing your fucking about-faced thing and badgering me for a year for your decision? I warned you that for sure if you did that I would leave you. Do you remember any of this, dammit?"

After we arrived in Sydney, Harry held me solely responsible for him quitting his job and starting a new one, in a new place, with new people. His words cut and bruised month after month, without letting up for an entire six months.

"I can't believe you made me do this. It's all your fault that I have to do this. I don't want to be here starting a new job, in a new place. How could you do this to me? It's your fault. This is all your fault!" He had complained day after day.

I refused to live through another round of that kind of verbal abuse in California. It was, once again, my insistence that drove us from Chicago. Eleven years before, I kept talking about how he was wasting his time working for a company that no longer appreciated his talents. Wouldn't it be grand if we didn't have to move to North Carolina where they intended to transfer us? Then again, in Chicago, Harry listened to my repeated desperate pleas to escape the long, harsh winters that always kept me trapped in the darkest house in that Chicago suburb.

What I never uttered, though, was how I desperately hoped to escape death, which surely would have arrived had I remained barricaded in that dark, old house. Nor did I ever mention how I decided to never allow tainted sidewalks to reach my home again.

After almost one year of the same old badgering that compressed, and compressed, further squeezing whatever little life had revived inside me—even after my repeated warnings—I'd had enough, again. By then, the distance between us was so great, we no longer occupied the same rooms in our beautiful new dream house. I took over the guest room. We exchanged so few words that even day-to-day life got confusing at times. And when words were spoken, it was to burn, and bruise, and keep the blood flowing.

"What the hell do you know about this? You don't even know what you're talking about, so you should just shut your damn mouth!" I screamed. I really could have thrown the steak knife at him that I clutched in my right hand.

"Ha! You're the one who doesn't know shit! You're an idiot!" Harry responded, and his face had definitely turned a deeper shade of red. His eyes bulged, and all I could think of in that moment was… *Let him die. Please, let him die!*

That sparkling Sunday afternoon, too many ugly words were hurled across the solid wood table that was set so meticulously with soft white linens and vibrantly colored fresh flowers and the fine delicate yellow dishes only sometimes brought down from the highest shelves. The cornucopia of gilded trays topped with grilled meats and vegetables, and sweet concoctions of rum and vodka kept arriving. Were those two bottles of wine empty now?

There beside us sat our two stunned friends who had arrived with so much hope and open laughter and easy conversations, like we used to share. Their two darling children were playing with ours in our perfectly manicured garden with its tall palm trees and plump hydrangeas and bright orange tiger lilies and the most perfect yellow and red and white rose bushes. Day by day, their supple leaves were turning brown from their very tips, but you had to look closely to see that.

So much vibrancy and beauty surrounded us. Yet there Harry and I sat, daring the other to make the first move over the brink. Later that night, after our friends left with the feeling that all was not well in that spectacular house, I couldn't stand another second of pretending. I jumped out of my bed in the guest room down and away from the rest of the house. I ran up the stairs that led to the room I no longer occupied. I opened the door to the room I'd walked out of months before.

I ran right up to Harry, who sat on the toilet reading, and I shouted, *"I want a divorce! I want a fucking divorce!"*

"Ha, you're fucked! How are you going to support yourself, you haven't worked in twelve years!" Then he went back to his reading.

"You better talk to a divorce attorney, because you're going to be shocked if you think that's how this is going to work out, you fucking idiot," I flung back as I made my way out of *his* bedroom.

After about twenty minutes, I heard Harry make his way down the stairs, through the open family room and to the room that was mine now. I heard his knock a moment before his knuckles tapped my door. He opened the door and he stood in the doorway looking sad and heartbroken. He said, *"I'm sorry things turned out this way. I gave this marriage everything I had. I never gave more to anything."*

With those ridiculous words, he stepped out of my room, softly closing the door behind him. I listened as he quietly walked back up the stairs to his room. I couldn't stop myself from sitting straight up on that bed as I heard the upstairs bedroom door close. Once again, I found myself amazed by Harry's ability to say the most absurd thing. I realized how absolute absurdity had flowed in and out of my brain ever since the day my naked body crossed the threshold to life.

He never gave anything more? God help the woman who got him when he wasn't trying! I thought. I let Harry's most outrageous words seep deeper into my cerebral cortex, causing my emotions to flare.

I was even angrier than before I raced upstairs. How could he possibly have missed his epic contribution to the divorce that was sure to come this time? Did he never hear his lips spew spite, or see the absolute wake of destruction his words caused, or feel his anger that lately was quelled only by tiny blue pills—which had turned his hair completely white and his face a permanent shade of red?

The next morning my anger was gone. During the darkest hour of the night, the fire that normally scalded my insides for hours and hours burned out. Now a depression that grew heavier with each illuminating hour took over. And like a couple of years before, I once again found myself overtaken by a mighty hope for a quick death. I never wished for death so clearly as that morning.

I forced myself from under the covers and walked to the table I'd set up with my computer and work things; I was working with an online company to start my own business. That was the very topic that started the fight at dinner the evening before in front of our shocked friends. It was the "final straw," or the "straw that broke the camel's back," or whatever other applicable idiom that damn "white" people used. Harry had provided that straw. The months leading up to the brink were filled with his relentless badgering that started with the move to California being all my fault, then to how the house we lived in was all my fault, and dear God! There was no way I could withstand another minute of the most recent one.

"What? You're in here working? My God, being in here is bad

enough, but what's going to happen when you have to leave the house at night to do this work? How do you expect to take care of our children then? How could you abandon your children this way? What kind of mother are you, anyway?"

I couldn't see a way out, not even with divorce. Not even The Secret could save me this time. I so naturally slipped into the kind of depression that year after year took hold of me, ever since memories became a blur so long ago when I was too young to no longer be innocent.

I picked up my laptop and walked back to my bed. I typed in, "how to commit suicide…"

Part Three

Her Divine Awakening

TWENTY

When I sat in my therapist's office that one time, speaking so clearly about how I intended to make divorce a breeze for millions of women, I could see that she wasn't buying it. Not because she believed I couldn't, but because she had heard the real story as it shed itself from me, bit by bit. She was the one who saved me from death itself. She had been there. She had witnessed the whole thing.

And that was the crux of it, wasn't it? I traveled so far out of Hell's path right before her eyes that the flames that shot up as I clawed my way out of Hell's clutch probably even scared her. She was my angel who saw my real path, even if I couldn't. For three straight years, I sat in her office every week and transformed in ways that got me thinking I was going to be fine, and I wouldn't have to die so soon after all.

The first time I sat on her couch, though, staring across at her in that small spirit-infused room, glassy-eyed and disoriented, I was still not divorced—only separated; we were still living in the same house. I was a mother of two, and I was still going to kill myself. That first time before the therapist even spoke her first word, I couldn't recall having called her, nor could I imagine why I sat across from her. I kept looking around, confused, straining my brain that had once more stopped working altogether. When precisely had I agreed to sit in that room? I felt there was a force outside of me driving my actions those days. I never looked closely at that force because it kept bumping up against my secret—the one about an ardent exit.

I was up to fifty-five pounds over my normal weight by the time I sat on that healing couch the very first time. My entire body was swollen and unkempt, and I reeked. When the therapist finally spoke, I only answered whatever questions I could manage to comprehend with heartless one-word responses. After I walked out of her office, I fought to remember where I parked my car. How did I get there in the first place, and where the hell was I?

The next day, that therapist called. I heard Harry pick up the phone before the second ring, *"Hello."*

I was in my room on my bed after having dropped the boys off at pre-school. I rarely ventured out of the house for anything any more, and I didn't let anyone see me during that month after I decided to die.

It reminded me of the time, two years before when I sequestered myself from the prying eyes of the chatty Chicago suburb, keeping that particular secret from being passed from house to house.

Our nanny had recognized the evidence the first second she saw me, but she couldn't believe her eyes. She walked around the house avoiding getting near me, shaking her head nonstop. I had it done because of that one dreadful incident in Whole Foods.

I was waiting in line to pay for my groceries, while my youngest sat in the child carriage portion of the cart. From the line to our right, a woman walked to my cart. She bent down to make all the cooing noises women make when they spot babies and toddlers. She said to my darling baby as if I were not standing right there: *"Oh, what a gorgeous boy you are. Are you being a good boy for your grandma? How proud she must feel to have such a darling grandson like you."*

After that woman's mindless proclamation, she walked back to her line and never once acknowledged me. I turned the cart away from the checkout line and I pushed it toward the exit door. When I got to the doors that automatically opened, I picked up my son and walked out the door, ignoring the groceries in the cart. As I walked toward my car, I vowed to never be referred to as either of my sons' grandmother, not ever again.

That was why, two months later, I went to see the doctor who could help me, and that was why in four more months I lay alone on a bed in the center of Chicago with bandages covering my entire face. For almost one week after the surgery, I didn't go to the mirror to see the debacle that was being covered up by red-stained pieces of gauze. I was flying high on the drugs to ease the pain that tranquilized me for one full week. I wouldn't allow Harry to see me, only the doctor and his assistant and the nurse who sat beside me the whole week. Harry's mom was helping with the boys while I supposedly was visiting my family in Connecticut. I waited for Harry's mother to leave before I picked up the single bag I had brought with me, walked out of that room and made the trip back home.

Our nanny and my two boys were in the kitchen, not expecting me. The taxi dropped me off in the alley that led to our yard. I wore a thick over-sized scarf around my head and I rushed through the yard and up the back porch stairs. I ran into the house and shocked our nanny. My boys were sitting on the kitchen floor and playing with kitchen things. They didn't recognize the creature in their mommy's scarf, until they heard my voice. I could see their confused faces, but still they cried, *"Mamamamamamamamamamamama!"*

I kept myself in that house and didn't leave for a full month. Harry dropped off our oldest at pre-school and our nanny walked the distance to pick him up. Finally, when I left the house, I noticed the one neighbor stare just a little too long at that one side where most of the cutting had been done. The phones started ringing after that; the thick snow-covered sidewalks from such a harsh winter were suddenly imprinted with filthy treaded boots, frantically huddling to talk more about this new development.

I heard footsteps approaching my room. Harry knocked twice, opened the door, walked to me as he scanned and assessed, and finally handed me the phone.

"Who is it?" I asked in a raspy broken voice, as he slowly walked back toward the door. He slowed down substantially at my worktable. I was sure I heard a snort. I was no longer working my business and cobwebs were creeping up the corners of that worktable, and I could hear Harry's sense of victory in his derisive sound. He liked that I'd stopped working, even though we were headed for divorce. No matter, because what he would soon learn was how he had inadvertently allowed death to come knocking on his front door.

"I don't know. It's for you," he said, not looking back as he walked out of the room quietly closing the door behind him.

After I was sure Harry was gone, I brought the phone to

my ear. *"Hello?"*

"Hi Isabel, It's Dr. So and So. I called because I can see that I have some openings and yesterday I agreed to let you know if I had any openings."

I couldn't imagine I'd agreed to such a thing. How did I end up on her sofa yesterday anyway or was it the day before? And how did she get my number? I blinked a couple of times and looked around the room I rarely left. I felt relieved my boys weren't home because I could feel my departure arriving. It felt so near.

"I've decided to not come any more. I'm okay now," I told her. The day before when I'd walked and walked around the first block, then the second and third, looking for my car, I vowed to not ever go back. I would stick with my original exit plan.

Silence. Pause. *"Um, I know I can help you, Isabel. I know I can help you back to feeling okay."* Was she even allowed to do this?

"I don't see how anyone can help me now. I don't want anyone to bother," I heard myself saying. I knew they were the wrong words. They definitely weren't the ones I planned on spilling from my brain. Where had those other words even come from? What was happening to me?

"You need help, Isabel. You have two precious little boys who want you back. I can really help you back to them. It feels unbearable now, but you'll soon see that you'll be back to them with a happier, healthier version of you. If you'll just give me a couple of sessions, I know you will be feeling very different than you do now. Please give me a chance to help you."

I couldn't stop the tears from spilling, and again this was

not what was in my brain. I cried and cried on the phone, and I let her mark her calendar with my next appointment for that afternoon. *"No, this afternoon is when I'd like to see you next, not next week. Now, would you be open to coming again tomorrow, and then the next day? Would that be okay? I have an opening all three days,"* she pleaded.

I said, *"We'll see."*

There I was, being saved again.

I was grateful for my angel's appearance. She stayed with me week, after week, month after month, year after year, until I could smile all on my own. But just when I turned away from death's door a second time, wouldn't you know death immediately came knocking on my door anyway?

TWENTY-ONE

I felt the lump again. There it was again. It had appeared several times before but I always was able to maneuver the thing until I could tuck it away where it couldn't bother me anymore. Now, as I prodded and pulled and pushed, it wouldn't go away this time. It stayed right there, prominently bulging in my view and for anyone to catch a glimpse if they were at all interested.

The next day I sat at the dermatologist's chair. As he took a closer look at my sunspots, he couldn't help but notice the thing. It really was easy to see. He touched it and he furrowed his brow. He looked at me and he asked me, *"Have you had this lump checked out yet?"*

"No. For several months now, the darn thing keeps going away and coming back. It's nothing, really." I said.

But then he got me thinking. The following week I was at my dentist's appointment. The dentist finally walked into the room where I sat, waiting for my cleaning on that overstuffed cold sticky vinyl chair with tools resting in pristine order on the tiny swivel platform closely in front of me. I told him about the lump that kept appearing and disappearing, but now was no longer wanting to disappear.

"I guess my locked jaw must have finally done some damage to the bone, huh?" I kidded.

He gave me that look that said he didn't think so, and he looked as if he didn't like the way that lump looked. He stared at it and he prodded and poked and pushed it, and he said, *"Humph"* and furrowed his brow.

Then he excused himself, carrying my file out with him. Five minutes later he walked back in, then straight over to the light box up on the wall across from where I was nearly falling asleep. He put up one of the x-rays that were taken almost a year earlier when I first became his patient. He asked me to come over to where he stood. He pointed to the jaw on my left side and said, *"This side of the jaw has a shadow across the whole bone here, see?"* He pinned up another x-ray beside the one I had been looking at. *"But this side does not. Do you see that?"*

"Yes," I said.

"Would you mind if we take a new set of x-rays of just your jaw bones, just to see what's there now?"

"Sure." My mouth had gone dry and my stomach flipped over and my chest got real tight. All these sensations felt exactly like when I sat on the examination table over thirteen years ago, and my gynecologist announced that the biopsy showed level 4 and 5 cells. I needed surgery right away; the good news was the cervix was so well contained, these cells don't usually venture out. The worst-case scenario most of the time meant a hysterectomy. She did have to cut and toss out quite a bit more than she had expected when she finally got in there, and she biopsied a bit and a little bit more, to be sure, and the news was good from those biopsies. But having babies probably was not going to be the best thing and getting pregnant would be even harder.

Why did I start thinking this new lump that now refused to go away might not be as easy for me? And why was this happening now when I no longer wanted to die?

The dentist's technician came in. I had sat back down, averting my eyes from the instruments in front of me, squirming in the chair that stuck to my legs. She told me she was ready for me. I followed her to the area where the x-ray machine stood. After both scans were completed, I walked back to the room where my teeth would be cleaned. I again sat in that ominous chair.

All this time I willed myself to not think, only feel the sensations that kept moving through me, and to only focus on the motions happening around me. I sat in that chair feeling how my bottom met the seat of the chair and the vinyl had felt cool at first but now it was warm and sticky. I stayed sensing and sensing, as I'd been practicing with my morning meditations.

My dentist walked back into the room where my teeth would at some point be cleaned, carrying the new x-rays. Again he walked over to the light box and pinned up the pictures. There before me was the dark mass on my left jaw that had been in the previous x-ray.

"It's still there, but the good news is it doesn't look as if it has spread any, but I can't be sure. I have a very good friend who is a surgeon and has over thirty years experience with this sort of thing."

Why can't anyone ever just say the word? I thought.

"I can call him and set up an appointment for you to see him if you'd like. I really think you should see him. I can make the appointment now, if you'd like." He was serious. His expression was so serious.

"Yes," was all I could manage to say.

"I am very sorry I hadn't caught this earlier. I guess I wasn't looking for it." He no longer smiled the way his eyes always did,

even when his mouth didn't. He handed me a stick-it note with his friend's name, address and the time for my appointment the next day.

I was leaving for Mexico in two days. I really didn't have time to sit in doctors' offices. I still needed to pack for my trip and I still hadn't fully unpacked in my new house where the boys and I had moved only the month before. This house had called to me in a swoosh of magical winds that drove my car directly to it. Everyone had marveled at the sheer magic of it all. Wasn't that the sign that all was finally well?

My teeth finally underwent the unpleasant cleaning that I had started out dreading. But now I welcomed it, allowing myself to feel every physical sensation from the tools scraping and scraping and tugging and tugging. Throughout the entire cleaning, I allowed myself to think only about my magic house, willing that one sign to reassure me that I would live. My new home was meant to finally offer me and my boys an endless reservoir of joy and laughter. That was the thought that became my lifeline.

After Harry and I separated and finally told everyone that we were divorcing, we decided to rent a one-bedroom apartment. Every other week, we alternated between living in the tiny apartment and the dream house so the boys wouldn't have to be permanently moved before we decided what to do with the house. Moving the parents around rather than moving the children I learned, was called "bird nesting." The "bird nesting" soon became an option Harry and I nixed, given that sharing the same living spaces, even while not simultaneously—still felt too invasive for all our raw emotions to settle. However, the switching every week on the same day became permanent. At least that one routine remained constant for our boys over the months when nothing else stayed constant.

One month after having started this new living arrangement, I was driving back to the house one morning after dropping the boys off at pre-school; it was my week with the boys in the house. I didn't pay attention to the route my car followed as I talked with my mother-in-law in the passenger seat. She was visiting from out of state and staying at the main house with us. Finally she said, *"Where are we?"* I suddenly hit the brake pad and the car stopped with enough force to jerk us forward.

I stared at the houses around me and didn't recognize them. I noticed that the street ended and we were up on a hill with very little room to turn the car around. *"Do you recognize this place?"* my mother-in-law asked.

For a split second I was overtaken by immense fear as a complete disorientation spread throughout my entire body. I couldn't imagine how I'd ended up at what felt like the end of the earth. I tried recalling if I'd even turned onto the main street that led to the neighborhood where the main house was, and I vaguely recalled taking the turn. I looked at the clock in the car and saw that it had only been twenty minutes since I dropped the boys off at pre-school. I couldn't possibly have arrived at the end of the earth in that time.

I slowly turned the car around, careful not to steer it over the ridge. I stared at the lonely-looking house at the very end, which appeared ready to take the plunge over the ridge beside it. I drove slowly away, staring at the house in my rearview mirror, taking care to pay attention to the route—so one day I could find my way back to the spot that felt like the most delicious escape from reality.

One week later, I announced to a local neighborhood Yahoo group that I was interested in securing a rental in the neighborhood of the main house. Only minutes after I hit the "send" button, I received a call from a nearby neighbor—one of the few neighbors I'd befriended.

"Isabel, I have the perfect house for you. I saw it last year. We needed a rental nearby while our house underwent renovations, but we weren't ready and now we won't be for another year or so. I'm pretty sure it's still available. I'll call the landlord and get back to you." We hung up and within five minutes she called me back.

"Okay, the landlord says it's still available and he'll meet you there tomorrow morning at 10am."

"Gosh, this is amazing! Thank you!" I said, not believing my luck as I wrote down the address.

I drove to the address as soon as we hung up. I found myself standing outside the house that stood at the edge of the earth—the exact same place.

That had been my sign that I was meant to live, and live big… really big after a horrific thirteen years. I still hadn't awakened to how I already was taking the first steps to healing the whole of my life, and that my thirteen-year marriage to Harry Fielding was only an extension and not the whole. My miracle house was the sign that motivated me to get out from under the covers early each morning and greet each day with hope and a smile.

This other *thing* that showed up on the x-ray wasn't supposed to happen right then. I had waited to die, and it never came while I waited for it. The timing was definitely all wrong! I hadn't even unpacked all the boxes in the new beautiful magical house. I could no longer sit still; I felt relieved when the hygienist finally finished her cleaning and I could get up and walk away from that awful chair.

The next morning at 10:00am, I sat in the waiting room of the surgeon's office perusing the magazines on the tables. I couldn't read; I couldn't really stay focused on any one thing. The old anxious buzz had increased its vibration, which made sitting still nearly impossible. Still, I focused on the sensations of the increased buzzing, like I'd been practicing. I breathed in and out as I pushed magazines aside. I didn't want to sit anymore so I stood and paced a little.

The doctor came into the waiting room and called me into the examination room. I sat in one of the two chairs across from his chair. I did have a thought right then that I should stay away from chairs, and then I breathed in and out to release that thought. The examination table was to the left and there was no way I was going to sit on that.

The surgeon only asked me a couple of questions. Then he got up from his chair and walked over to me. He bent down and looked at the lump. He pressed it and furrowed his brow. Then he grabbed hold of it, moving it this way and that way, like I had done twice before to tuck it away. Only now it couldn't be tucked away, and it really wasn't very movable anymore. He decided he needed to look at the x-rays that were emailed to him by my dentist. He walked out of the examination room, promising to come back soon. I stood up from the chair and paced and paced, noticing and waiting. I breathed in and out, again and again and again.

When the doctor walked back in ten minutes later, the calm I'd been struggling to keep collapsed. He no longer furrowed his brow. He looked downright scared. His eyes were wide and his lips formed a circle as if he were saying "oh"—but no words were said. He was breathing a little faster and louder and his words finally came out, and they were so clipped and hurried.

"You need to have the lump and your jaw biopsied right away. The lump is a lymph node and it appears to be draining," he said, as if I could possibly understand exactly what that meant. But I really didn't need a full explanation, did I? Because I knew exactly what the man was thinking, and I knew the fear he was feeling, because he passed the whole damn thing to me the second he walked into that room.

"I happen to know one of the top oncologists in this state. He's at Stanford, and I'd like to get you in to see him as soon as possible. He normally has a six-month waiting period but I'm sure if I call him I can get you in sooner."

"I leave for Mexico tomorrow and I'll be gone a week."

"Fine, I'll schedule it for when you get back." He left me in the examination room where the fear vibrated even after the very scared doctor walked out, and was that a pounding I was hearing? He returned with my appointment details written on another stick-it note. It seemed these scared doctors only knew to scribble on small pieces of paper, as if the shrunken piece could possibly transfer from their fear-pressured hearts the enormity of what they wrote.

"I've also called our image lab here in the building, and I've sent them an order for a Cat Scan. You need to have this done before you leave for Mexico so the oncologist can have it for your

Part Three: Her Divine Awakening

appointment next week."

"*Okay,*" I said. I walked out of his office and down the stairs to the image lab, and I endured the many minutes it took to complete the scan. I couldn't help where my thoughts kept going, and being inside that scanner made it impossible to escape those thoughts. After, I dressed and walked out of the building, already planning my funeral.

As I drove home, I cried and cried. I felt anguished like never before in my life. I kept thinking how I had crawled so far out of hell's hole only to be sent to die again. *How could that be? It just couldn't be,* I willed myself to say over and over! I could already feel the unbearable grief at having to say good-bye to my boys, who were still in a great deal of pain from their parents' recent separation and having to move out of our beautiful new house after it was sold. I didn't want them to experience loss again, not ever again. I had finally been enjoying them. My life was supposed to be grand now.

I arrived home and paced the miracle home that had found me. I paced and paced and the anguish grew with every step. I finally picked up my phone and dialed my sister Lourdes' telephone number.

"*Hi Lourdes, it's Isabel.*"

"*Hi Sweetie, what's going on?*" she asked.

I let go, crying hysterically, trying my best to say the words that could communicate clearly what happened. But she got it. I didn't need to say much to her.

"*I see. Here's the thing. You don't have to listen to anything that doctor said, Isabel. If you want, you can decide right in this moment that what he said is simply not true and reject all of it, including his fears. Who knows why the shadow appeared in the x-rays. Just because it appeared doesn't mean you have to own it."*

Years prior Lourdes had healed from breast cancer without the use of chemotherapy even after it had metastasized, which is why I called her. I absorbed her words like I had absorbed all those doctors' fears. I felt calm again and I could breathe normally again. After five minutes more, I hung up, looking at this whole thing a little differently.

Two hours later, I heard a knock on the side door that led to the carport and driveway. I walked to the door and saw a UPS truck drive away. I opened the door and picked up the package leaning against the door. I walked to the kitchen and pulled scissors from the top drawer and cut an opening across the top of the package bag. I pulled out a book I'd ordered the week before. It was the <u>Healing Codes</u> workbook. I'd forgotten I had ordered this manual. I felt a great relief zing through my body as I marveled at another sign.

I left for Mexico the next day, still carrying everything from those doctors' appointments, my sister's words, my new <u>Healing Codes</u> manual, and a bit of hope.

Over the next week, as I practiced the Healing Codes on myself every morning and night, I witnessed the shrinking of the lump. I befriended a local woman, Sarah, who was an energy healer herself. We did a "happy" dance each time the lump shrunk. By the time I got on the plane to return home, I felt no lump. I knew I was healed from whatever only a few days before had invaded my jaw.

At my appointment with the oncologist, two days after I arrived from Mexico, I waited two hours in the front room before he was ready to see me. After I'd waited another twenty minutes in the exam room, he briskly strode in. He even more briskly displayed all the images from the dentist's x-rays, the MRI, and the Cat Scan, for which I'd hurriedly returned to the image lab the day before. I could see the dark mass covering my left jaw in both of the dentist's x-rays. I could see something in that same area of my left jaw in the MRI. And I could see that the Cat Scan clearly showed a bone, along with a slue of other information. But in the Cat Scan, I couldn't see the dark mass visible on all the other scans. In that moment, my heart danced and danced.

Then the oncologist very abruptly and curtly announced, *"You don't have cancer! I don't know what this other stuff was, but it's not cancer and never was cancer."*

He made it clear that I was wasting his precious time; there were people with real cancer waiting to be treated. I simply smiled and smiled. Not for one second did I allow the oncologist's declaration to diminish my joy as if it were the "draining lymph node."

TWENTY-TWO

One spectacular sunny morning, months after separating from Harry and living in my new home, I woke up and there was nothing, absolutely nothing—not even the bleeding. And like so many mornings before, in that full state of nothingness, love sprouted from the deepest tendrils of my core and spread throughout my body. I luxuriated on my new extra plush bed in my light-filled bedroom feeling love's radiance inexplicably expand. I realized that it had been over four months since death knocked on my door. It had been over one year since I decided on a method to end my life that wouldn't leave my children poisoned with anger at their mother's suicide.

I had learned, as I read the many options for suicide, that decreasing my medications would worsen my symptoms, and that dehydration was a slow way to die. And so I'd decided I would use those methods as well as increase my intake of dry foods with little to no nutrition, for no death certificate would be indelibly imprinted with the word "SUICIDE" using these methods. I would eventually fall asleep, dreaming of a lifeless bloated body with eyes never opening, nose never breathing morning air, ears never hearing the familiar sounds of cries and destruction.

Divorce is rarely good for the children, no matter how easy it is for the parents. It never eases their pains or fears, even if their parents are the best of friends. I'd like to share one of the first things I learned and practiced to make divorce an okay next step in my life.

A couple of months before I screeched at Harry, I had already researched the subject some. I had been thinking about it for years, and I had already started talking to others about it…mostly to test how it sounded. Still, I resisted actual divorce for years because I didn't want to be labeled as "twice divorced." I researched divorce attorneys, I considered hiring one who would help me stand up to Harry's anger and knack for vengeance. I also researched the various methods to divorce. One was mediation. I'm not clear on why I continued researching this method since I still believed Harry was going to be an even more vicious adversary in divorce than in marriage. Still, I started reading and educating myself on everything about mediation.

I then decided to meet with an attorney who advocated mediation and friendly divorces. After that, I became convinced that this was the best approach for us.

That was before things blew up that night when I told Harry I was divorcing his ass, and he responded with the, *"Ha! You're fucked comment."* I thought a friendly divorce was going to be impossible. So once again I contemplated hiring the toughest divorce attorney. But in my search the same dubious words kept coming up: tough, aggressive, battle, relentless, etc. I decided I'd already experienced enough of these words in marriage, and that I wanted the opposite for my life after marriage.

In that moment of choosing a friendly divorce a second time, I realized how this decision required the kind of thinking that clicked into a permanent slot in my psyche.

So, one month after that night, I met with my first choice attorney again. By then, I'd been seeing my therapist for a month; I was starting to see a bit more clearly, and I'd been slowly softening my pursuit to commit suicide. She spent the entire hour expanding on the benefits of the kindly divorce versus the contentious kind most couples experienced.

"You can start this process by choosing to only use kind words when speaking to Harry," she said.

"But he's so angry with me. How do I get through that anger?"

"You start by taking a deep breath then sincerely wishing him well before you even start speaking, and then choose only words that will help him feel reassured."

The next day after we put the boys to bed, I walked back up the stairs to Harry's room. We were still living in the same house, not yet having told anyone about our separation. I knocked.

"Yeah?"

"Can I come in?"

"Sure."

This was how we had been communicating to each other—mostly one-word sentences and either a nod or a shake of the head.

"May I sit?" I asked him.

He nodded his head.

I sat on the chair…the very one that fourteen months earlier, I'd strategically placed by my side of the bed for those nights when I'd require more distance. Harry looked at me from his side of the bed, wary and untrusting.

I felt nervous, like in the moments right before speaking in front of an audience. I took a deep breath and in my mind said the words, *"I wish you happiness, only happiness."* Then I proceeded.

"I came here to ask you if we can make this divorce process as easy as possible for our boys. We never asked them if they wanted us to adopt them, we never asked them if they wanted to move to California, and we never asked them if it was okay that we divorce. I'm hoping we can find some way to get along for their sake."

"Yeah, we really need to think about them right now," Harry responded, which helped me relax and say what I had been rehearsing in my head.

"And there's something else I'd like to say. I'm not angry with you. I know we've said and done some awful things to each other in the past, but now I only wish for you to be happy. I want you to know that I'm not looking to take anything from you. I prefer being here for you. My greatest hope now is that we can both be open to helping and supporting each other in whatever ways we may need it."

He said, *"I really appreciate you saying this to me. I really want to make this easier for everyone. I think we're both ready for this and it doesn't make sense to make it hard."*

"Yeah, that's exactly how I feel. I've met with a divorce attorney, and she suggested you sit with one too, so we both can know what to expect."

Harry showed me the book he was reading, which was a comprehensive explanation on how to divorce in California without having to go to court. We stayed talking for another hour or so about our preferences and philosophies, and we planned the months to come.

For weeks I continued practicing using kind words whenever I spoke to Harry, even during the times I grew too angry or too afraid that standing on my own two feet felt completely wrong and dizzying. Time after time I resisted the urge to strike and hurt.

Before meeting with our mediator the first time, Harry and I had written lists of what we desired for ourselves and for each other. And wouldn't you know, we both discovered how much we genuinely hoped the other could finally enjoy real happiness? Of course, we had tweaked and tweaked our lists helping each other see for the first time what truly mattered, what we each most yearned for. These lists became the foundation for our Marriage Settlement Agreement.

We were once again in sync with another major family issue: divorce.

TWENTY-THREE

Slowly I began seeing how Harry wasn't a bad person. I could see his kindness and generosity. I have much proof that substantiates this about Harry today, and I guess it was always there. For example, he's the kind of father I'd never realized existed. The love he still drenches our boys with is unlike anything I've ever witnessed. Harry comes from the type of family whose men say things like, *"I love you"* without averting their eyes once. These men aren't afraid to hug their boys, even after they've grown. When others came to visit his family's home, both his parents had so proudly told, in baby-fine detail, sweet tales of their darling boy's remarkable developments. They would laugh about his idiosyncrasies. *How perfect is our little one,* they'd ask. They walked so near their growing baby boy that even his sneezes were tended to.

Then his parents divorced when he was still too young, and that was when the poison got into his heart. Divorce does that. It poisons the youngest souls. But divorce wasn't the curse that had poisoned me; not even being too invisible or the "ugliest" did that. I was gone when the innocence got drained from the baby girl. It's not safe to grow wise and broken before there exists enough words to explain the whole thing.

I had been married to Harry for too many years already when his mother pulled the truth from what I'd been saying.

"Well, Isabel, it's not normal to never have been hugged by

your parents. What do you mean they never told you they loved you? That's just not possible! That's just not possible! Don't you see how it just can't be?" she said, as if her repeated assertions alone could wipe out the truth of my past.

I could tell her heart was about to break, and that was when I felt it for the first time. I had been heartbroken my whole life and hadn't realized it once until that moment when Harry's mother pointed it out. Only then could I see how I had been empty of love long before I started messing with it. As I sat there feeling my heart grow more broken, I longed for love, even if I didn't know the first thing about it.

Like I said, Harry happened to step onto my perilous path all those years ago. He really didn't have a lick of a chance getting out of our marriage unscathed.

As I revisited this experience with my therapist, I realized how powerfully I had attracted into my life the hell that was my marriage to Harry. I don't think either one of us had planned to bring so much unhappiness to the other person. Deep down we both really did want to have a happy life, but neither one of us had a clue on how to go about doing that, with Harry's poison in his heart and mine empty of love.

It was when our glorious divorce happened that the space opened for love to fill my heart and the poison to get drained from Harry's. Now we're the best of friends, and we're both genuinely happy—the kind of happy where I squeal with joy for no apparent reason right in the middle of a store, or on a train among lots of people.

I can now see how it's easy for Harry and me to be friends because the angst that once filled our bellies and minds no longer resides in us. I could have stayed angry with Harry for all the suffering he caused me over those thirteen years, especially since that's how I had operated for most of my life. But divorce graced me with an awakening that miraculously filled my heart with insurmountable love and joy.

I recognize the moment I made the choice to step off my path of destruction, even though I willingly also recognize it took years to stop destroying altogether. It was the day I decided to keep my second appointment with my therapist.

The choice to wake up had always been there, and when the open door of joy called to me, I recognized its familiar sound. It felt ancient. For nearly fifty years I was in a dark slumber where, time and time again, a trance-like call seized my being and then led me toward destruction's fatal fire. The interesting thing about waking up was how much it felt like coming home. All my life I had felt bad, I realized, because the truth of me was being denied the path home.

When I finally woke up, I experienced viscerally how love blossomed from the depth of my soul to my lips. I could smile, and whenever I smile today, love grows some more, leaving me feeling the luscious fruit of sweet joy.

I also realized when I finally awakened that two precious and innocent boys were struggling with all the poison they'd been fed in their brief lives. I vowed to make my boys' happiness my priority, and this time, I have kept my vow. Now whenever my boys are home with me, I often carry their long lanky bodies that are really too large and heavy for me to be carrying. I can't seem to bring myself to put them down, as if I need to make up for the early years when I rarely held their soft vulnerable bodies, even when their cries grew louder and more desperate. I often put my nose on their heads and sniff and sniff, taking in their smells, and I can't stop my lips from kissing their plump cheeks. I want to touch them and hold them and never let them go. I often tell them how I feel like the luckiest mom in the whole world.

I no longer cry for so many wasted un-lived days and for all the hurt and poison I've dumped on them. Instead, I celebrate the two pure perfect teachers walking alongside me every day. I especially look forward to their eyes, heavy with sleep, as they come to greet me in my bed where we lay cuddling, just us three enjoying that early morning ritual.

TWENTY-FOUR

It became obvious to me in those first months apart from Harry that I'd started on a path toward something good—a new place that felt more promising than anything else I'd ever experienced in my life. How or why I was feeling so optimistic was a mystery to me. I had no solid reference point to rely on, no internal compass to direct my next move, even after the lump on my jaw disappeared. I was searching for answers.

But regardless, I decided to start trusting more in the mystery of hope and optimism. Miracles, like my magic home finding me, and the healing of so many illnesses like the incessant bleeding and the cancer made trusting in the mystery of the universe's machination easier to embark on. In those months, I still unconsciously carried around a big dose of skepticism. Trusting was still a very new practice for me, because the culprit of all my suffering had not yet been confronted.

At this point, I had been visiting my therapist on a weekly basis for about eight or nine months. I was learning how to recognize the bits of me that kept informing my destructive choices. She taught me practices that illuminated the contrasts in remaining "stuck," compared to allowing life to organically flow. My sessions were sixty whole minutes of soulful practices that infused me with hope. She guided me toward re-thinking, then *feeling* my way through healing—which was a deep contrast to the talking and talking about a past or a future as with previous therapists. For many years I had renounced therapy altogether because I'd sat through session after session with therapist after therapist that didn't help me one bit. The new practices I undertook with my new therapist were hard, and at times, quite painful. But I wouldn't trade that entire journey for anything.

After I graduated from being completely shattered to being able to get out of bed and function, my therapist began teaching me how to stay with what most scared me—which I kept resisting because, well, I was too scared to delve into such a big, fat, heavy load. In the early months of therapy, before the lump appeared, and before my magic house found me, I still felt profoundly challenged in the realm of emotional stability, and dear God! I was still desperately clinging onto my secrets. The idea of opening my chamber's heavy impenetrable door scared me more than anything. But I no longer was perishing in a horrific marriage, so I slowly began turning the dial of the combination that had kept my chamber locked all my life.

Still, my therapist had to guide me through the labyrinth of muck that was blocking my chamber's door. Completely unaware, I had devised internal "booby traps" that kept me, or anyone else, from entering my chamber. That meant I kept getting side-tracked throughout our therapy sessions, then side-tracked again and again in the mornings at home when I practiced what I had learned with my therapist.

It took many more months of practice to feel my way toward what turned out to be a treasure trove of fears buried so deep so long ago in the trenches of my being. By the time my therapist and I reached my chamber, I was already suspecting that I was closely aligned with fear…

It wasn't as clear in mind as, *"Oh, I see you fear, I've got your number now."* It definitely wasn't anything like that. When I finally discovered this deeply buried stash of varying fears within, I was shocked by its sheer weight. It actually felt heavy. This heaviness is probably the most difficult description to articulate, because it felt nothing like depression, nor like exhaustion, dejection or anguish, nor like any of the sensations I'd lived with for most of my life. I won't try to describe the weight of all the fears I had accumulated. Instead, I'd like to describe how *old* my treasure trove felt that very first instant I discovered its existence.

I recall that three-year old ugly, frail little girl already losing her way in life, so long before she began living, really. I can still feel her deep sense of dejection from repeatedly being discarded by the very people who were supposed to assure her and help her learn to feel and be safe. By the time that first early memory occurred, her dejection already had matured, ripened, almost like being past the expiration date. And she had felt immensely tired every day. That tiredness seemed to stem from lifetimes ago, when centuries of rejection instilled hopelessness, even before the first breath passed through her naked body at birth.

I realized then that this description sat far from the indoctrination I received in my early years as a practicing Catholic. It definitely was realms removed from when I was stricken by fundamentalist principles as a born-again Jesus follower. But for the first time in this lifetime, I openly began facing my fears.

When I began this work, I felt an inner sense of the possibility that the stockpile of fears I'd amassed lifetime after lifetime could offer the secret to finally being free. This single possibility gave me the greatest hope. With the guidance of my very wise therapist, I began practicing how to relate to my fears in a new way. Instead of running away from or burying them, I learned to turn around and face whatever fears arose in me. Every day I had a plethora of fears to work with, and quite often facing them became overwhelming. I didn't give up, however. I kept on practicing every single day.

One of the first practices my therapist taught me was to situate myself comfortably on my favorite chair, one that offered me great comfort and pleasure. It is today permanently indented. I propped up pillows and squirmed and shifted until sitting in that chair felt utterly scrumptious. The day before I began this practice, my therapist described it as, "*...seemingly floating on a cloud with your body feeling weightless yet lovingly and assuredly supported.*" I had never before experienced feeling supported like that. But when my seat reached its pinnacle of support, I instantly felt peace and quiet blanket my whole being. I sat for a while luxuriating in peace, and I could feel my entire body relax into my chair further and further.

When I felt thoroughly relaxed, I allowed a fear to arise that I had recently discovered. I allowed it to show itself to me without conditions or boundaries. I allowed the thoughts, emotions and physical sensations this one fear triggered in me to resurface. And since I could see it after recently discovering it, I felt able to face it. Then the most curious thing happened…the fear shrunk. This particular fear didn't physically shrink like the lymph node on my jaw. This sensation (because I did feel it) was quite different. It shrunk in veracity. I no longer saw it as the truth—or more accurately, I no longer saw that fear as my *whole* truth.

This was that first fear: Believing that I am worthy and loveable. These really are two separate truths, but during my whole life, I'd clumped the two together so that they coagulated and fed off each other. The crux, I realized, was risking allowing myself to feel worthy and to start seeing and accepting myself as a loveable being—only to be rejected again, which would then prove that this fear had real merit. It was interesting how a fear that created beliefs, and then cultivated actions that created my world, was originally founded on a lie that itself was founded on a fear of being vulnerable.

Vulnerability is the most naked state I've ever allowed myself to feel, and it's scary on every level. So in essence, I feared exposing the real me—so much so that I constructed a lifetime of defenses and protections through the beliefs I developed, the relationships I had, and the addictions I'd depended on for most of my life.

While working on the creation of my online center for women, so many have expressed this same fear of self-worth and self-love articulated through their unique life experience. The adornments encasing the fear deep within may sound different as these women describe them to me, but the culprit behind their great suffering is precisely the same apparatus.

For many months more, I moved from facing or leaning into this first fear I identified to a next and a next, and so on. I'm still discovering fears today. But now I simply practice leaning into them. Even if a particular fear or issue is tenacious in its hold on me, I stay looking straight at it until eventually it loses its grip.

There are many other practices I learned, and new ones I've discovered on my own, but there's one other piece to this sitting practice I wish to share with you. I mentioned earlier about relating to my fears in a new way that was critical in order for my fears to shrink, then dissipate. I learned to *treat* (relate to) my fear as a *friend*.

The first time my therapist introduced this concept, I laughed. It sounded ridiculous to me. But her loving kind heart just took hold of my heart and softened it enough to at least give it a try.

So not only was I allowing my fears to emerge, I was also inviting them up and out to sit and visit with me as I would a dear, close friend. Eventually, when I stopped telling myself that this was "stupid," I dared to offer this fear my kind words, and I extended it my love. The first time I sincerely carried out this second part of my sitting practice—and for the second time in my life—I experienced love so intense I was overcome by the most piercing joy. (The first time was the third day in Mexico while administering to myself the *Healing Codes*.)

I've heard stories of yogis who reached this pinnacle of love and immediately in that moment broke their practice to quell the intensity of the emotion. This sense of love and joy can be so powerful, it feels otherworldly, and moves from slightly to greatly overwhelming. But I didn't break from that experience that first time in Mexico, nor the second time while sitting with my greatest fear. Nor have I broken from it the other times joy visited me with almost too much force.

Here's the most remarkable discovery I've made with respect to my fears: treating a fear as my friend as opposed to foe magically illuminated its inherent blessed gift—a gem so bright that I was able to pick it off and don it.

Let me explain.

As I sat with my biggest and oldest fear, I purposefully began treating this fear as my "best" friend. I gave it as many human qualities I could conjure, assigning it ears and a heart and a conscience. I said to this fear these words, *"I see you and feel how vulnerable you are feeling in this moment, and it must be difficult for you to expose the real you. I am here for you in whatever way you need me. I am here for you, and I love you. I truly love you."*

As I floated on my most favorite comfortable chair, relating to my biggest fear and extending nothing but my sincere love, I began to feel it shrink further, because it had already shrunk in size when I dared face it. When I showered it with my reservoir of love that only recently presented itself to me, my greatest fear shrunk further and further until it no longer vibrated within me. As I sat celebrating the sensations of only love and joy in response to the fear's disappearance, the most brilliant truth emerged: I am love, and therefore worthy of anything I desire. I immediately donned this gift and showed it off to everyone.

To this day, I mostly feel this gem of truth. Sure, sometimes the old fear, that I'm unworthy of what life brings my way, pops up. I still find that sometimes I'm feeling down or I'm struggling. But the difference today is that I eventually find my way again to leaning into and staring directly at what's most troubling me, and then I choose to invite it into my heart space as I would a dear, dear friend. Then I shower it with my endless reservoir of pure love. And every single time, it lessens and often dissipates.

TWENTY-FIVE

Considering the long miserable journey to get here, my glorious life today is incredible. I wake up every day feeling great and I go to sleep at night feeling great. I get to do anything I desire, and no one is around to comment on how many Trader Joe's Nutty Bits I eat, or that I should be washing the pile of dishes spreading throughout my kitchen counters. I guess what I'm really saying is that after the mess that my life was, I'm finally free. I'm so free that I get to do what I want whenever I want, without guilt pounding on my chest like it did for almost fifty years. Above all else, my stepping into freedom and away from treachery has been the most delightful life expansion.

As I mentioned earlier, Harry and I are now friends, good friends. It didn't happen right away. It took two years of relentless work. I never wavered in my commitment to the morning practices. I also practiced forgiveness to help heal our post-marriage relationship. Certainly, in the first year we lacked enough trust to allow the other in, even after my heart was opened to love. Indeed, both of us kept saying or doing enough to let the other know that there still remained a deep moat separating us. (I was still learning to trust, and I find that still today it's the one challenge that keeps tripping me up.) But bit by bit, we drained that moat dry. Just as I had learned to treat my fears as a friend, I practiced relating to Harry's hurtful words as a way to heal our relationship. By this point, I had figured out that he obviously was hurting too, independent of me.

I eventually stopped blaming Harry for our failed marriage, or getting angry with him by putting more distance between us, like I used to while married. The guy was working with all he had; I eventually figured that out, and it is what I now believe and understand. This piece of wisdom came knocking a few times throughout our marriage, but I wasn't willing to allow that one in. It was so unlike that time when I eventually figured out that Denise unconsciously used her gang to threaten me as an outlet for her own personal venting. I'd allowed that wisdom to seep into my brain that one time, as I kept an open mind about her fanciful tirades.

What I didn't recognize for most of my life was how no one was to blame. I did eventually learn that placing blame on anyone, including myself, clogged up the space in which to be free and happy. I continue, to this day, catching myself use blame as a way to escape. I need to be hyper-diligent about looking at an issue plainly with no embellishments. After a lifetime of perfecting embellishing most everything with negative messages, this practice of opening my eyes fully is still the hardest work.

I can now see how each mishap in my life occurred because from day one on earth I had determinedly set myself on an eternal path of destruction. The universe could only oblige my pleas with more destruction. All those years ago, I had inadvertently magnetized into my perilous vortex the whole of my insufferable life, which explained why heeding warnings was not something I could manage. For most of my life, I thought that turning toward the brilliant ray of truth would blind me for good.

Part Three: Her Divine Awakening

It hit me one day, months after therapy, and months after Mexico, that I was one of those women I detested for withstanding spousal abuse. I used to swear that if it were me being beaten physically or emotionally or mentally, that I'd quickly get out. I could see in my mind how easy it should have been for women to just walk away; yet, I stayed in an abusive relationship year after year after year. Looking back, I realized I couldn't see the abuse, and definitely, I couldn't see my way out.

Today I understand that it was I who attracted Harry and the likes of him in all my ex-boyfriends and husbands. Each had precisely the same remarkable way of tossing me aside and treating me with utter disregard. They each managed to cheat on me and lie to me and talk unkindly to me and basically treat me as if I were truly an old dirty rag doll to trample on. Certainly, if the relationship lasted long enough, the dirty rag doll became just as invisible as the atoms in the air ceremoniously enveloping her. Then I watched the many men as they walked straight through me as if I were dirty polluted air, not a solid being made of bones and flesh. It was as if as soon as my adult life began, I picked up where I left off while living at home with my parents and siblings. I never once considered that the course of my life was meant to take new turns.

For sure, though, my marriage to Harry was the clincher! It was the turn on my road of destruction that finally got me to wake up to the implacable pattern that was sewn long before I formed a naked curse in my mother's belly. It took me quite a while to reassemble all the pieces of my marriage, as my therapist suggested—and what I ended up with was almost fifty years of fragments that utterly shocked me. The divorce came because of an entire lifetime of misguidedness. It was inevitable.

After I revisited the countless dreadful events of my unconscious life, I saw how far I have traveled to arrive at finally feeling whole and content today. I would love to tell you that the awfulness of my marriage to Harry was what truly led us to divorce, and that every bit of it was his fault, possibly to spark some camaraderie with you. But the truth is, the guy just happened to step onto my own personal path toward a total destruction, one that had started decades before he arrived at my proverbial doorstep. And when I really took the time to think things through, I saw how Harry didn't have a chance of escaping my vortex of 'crush, kill, destroy' antics.

TWENTY-SIX

Months after working on facing my fears, I discovered that, like all living things, there exists a light in me even within my deepest darkest shadows. It was on my way to dying that I made this discovery.

Well, I couldn't really know for sure that I would die from the quasi-prognosis I kept receiving in those doctors' offices. But I do know that it was in the midst of deep suffering after those visits, when I no longer desired death, that I discovered the light. That entire week in Mexico, I observed again and again how my internal light brightened ordinary moments. This light I speak of is not the literal illumination of the Einstein bulb, or anything else like that. It's more like a bright delight-filled essence that expands a vibrant space for understanding, and for a love so pure and whole to fill my entire being.

I had been walking toward this light ever since I was born. In Mexico, as every new day shined its bright essence on my being, I understood for the first time that it's impossible to escape this light, even before death. I recalled how the hospice worker who sat with our family the last weeks of Pedro's life had coached us to help him pass on. She taught us to encourage Pedro to *"see the light and to follow it."* In Mexico, I learned that one does not have to wait for death to see this light.

The first day I practiced the *Healing Codes,* I was desperate to live. I hadn't yet fully absorbed its power, but for the first time in my life I allowed myself to trust, honestly and sincerely, a practice I had never, ever engaged in. Not even The Secret's mighty impact, nor stumbling upon my miracle-house, nor being physically healed of over fifteen years of illness by the extraordinary endocrinologist, had awakened me to the power of my internal light. It was the act of forgiveness that opened the door to this light. I had never before practiced that one either.

At first I was reluctant to offer anyone forgiveness, especially on that first day in Mexico while feeling an anguish so deep that even walking hurt. I was still stuck on Harry being my ultimate cause for suffering, even after almost one year with my therapist. I wanted him to pay somehow, even when I had already started taking steps toward a post-divorce reconciliation. I realized then that I was holding onto an anger that sizzled beneath quite a few layers of miracles. *And how could that be?* I hadn't discovered my light just yet.

But I wanted to live, and the *Healing Codes* required the act of forgiveness to begin healing the 'issues of the heart', which were apparently what had caused my cancers and all my physical illnesses and suffering. I read about how any kind of stress, including emotional ones, damages our nervous systems, and invariably leads to an aftermath of symptoms. When I remained immersed in deep suffering, I was inadvertently subjecting every cell in my body to perform in disadvantageous ways; they could only sustain this kind of destruction for only so long. Of course, I'm grossly over-simplifying here the science supporting the *Healing Codes*.

Now, I can't omit how I had years before abandoned religion and spirituality in all its forms. I renounced God, even though the angry white-bearded guy and plenty of demons were still popping into my mind just about every day. After reading <u>The Secret</u> and feeling optimistic, I never once ventured toward spirituality; I instead held the principles I learned through <u>The Secret</u> as scientific woo-woo magic…whatever the heck that meant! But when life's stresses out-powered the optimism I had carried in those first months after reading <u>The Secret</u>, nothing I gained from the book remained. I was back to angry outbursts and feeling depressed all over again, and finally began trudging toward death.

I hadn't ever known that I carried every infraction I experienced as a plague that repelled love. From day one, I had been protecting myself in all my choices, including the ones that destroyed. Given enough time with this method, one might exit life before seeing the light that exists here today…now. There I stood in Mexico that first day, talking myself into applying the work outlined in the <u>Healing Codes</u> manual. Since the premise of the system is based on scientific principles, I finally allowed myself to try.

I started with the time Lupe called me a *"dog"* to the boys who taunted me, instead of sticking up for me. (I had believed this event was only a small infraction, but in the midst of this first practice I realized how deeply it had informed so many of my choices for self-destruction.) I closed my eyes and focused on my breathing for a few minutes. I then visualized Lupe standing before me and I thought I could simply forgive her—but in those first moments I could only see her guilt, and I could feel my anger grow. I realized this work wasn't going to be easy. I was more practiced at facing my fears; this whole forgiveness thing was something entirely different.

I continued breathing and allowing my emotions to sit on the surface of my consciousness, just feeling the jagged tall waves of anger oscillate. After a while, I stepped forward and extended my arms out to Lupe and in my mind I said to her, *"I forgive you, Lupe, for rejecting me in front of the boys who taunted me, and for causing me great pain, and for helping me see myself as ugly and defected, and..."* And it seemed I couldn't stop citing a hefty list of infractions caused by my sister.

When I finally finished my list, my face was drenched with tears and my head was pounding. It was then that my heart started to soften. I then held my hands in the healing positions I learned in the <u>Healing Codes</u> manual as I visualized my physical heart actually growing softer. I visualized my open physical arms receive and embrace Lupe, and she cried in my arms. In the next instant, I could feel her pain. I understood in that moment that Lupe had carried out all those hurtful infractions because she herself was suffering immensely. This realization opened my heart in a way I had never before experienced. I forgave for the first time in my life.

I moved on to another seemingly small infraction, then another, and it happened each time that all these bits were actually major infractions. There were no minor infractions, after all, because I had used every morsel of bad to fortify my hell.

By the third day in Mexico, I decided to forgive the monster who'd had such a hold on my heart for so many decades. It was remarkable and surprising to me that I could forgive this person that easily. It almost felt improbable which was why I kept revisiting forgiving the monster. Each time, I felt an open understanding of this person's suffering with no lingering bitterness or anger or fear.

This led me to see how perhaps I could be ready to forgive my mother, and this too was remarkable. Unconsciously, my mother's treatment of me had carved a deeper scar than molestation. During my adult-like thinking years, I didn't once consciously or vividly think about any of the awful things said and done to me by my mother. Unlike the horror of molestation that over most of my life kept sneaking out of my secret chamber and smacking me hard across my heart, keeping it bruised and strained. So I was stunned to be standing on the other side of forgiveness with the monster forgiven, and my mother not.

Practicing the same visualization process, I cited and cited and cited infractions until my throat hurt. I felt drained. But still I opened my heart to my mother's own suffering. And then my heart immediately expanded so immensely, I could barely contain the love emanating from it. By then the light that shone from my heart was already brightening most everything around me, but in that moment absolutely everything became blindingly bright. I basked in the brightness, feeling the highest magnitude of joy and love. Alone in that condo in Mexico, I held onto my mother and told her how beautiful and wonderful she truly was. I told her I forgave her, and I began releasing all the infractions I had held so firmly in my heart. I then explained to her how I now understood that she had done the best she could. Afterward, I could only see her light.

Almost one week after arriving in Mexico, the day before I was to return home, I opened my heart to forgiving Harry. By this point, the lump that had invaded my left jaw was down to the size of a budding pimple, and my heart space hummed with sweet joyous intensity. Everywhere I went, I felt such deep great love for everyone and everything. When I visualized Harry before me, I started crying even before I said any words. I could already feel how hard he had striven throughout our marriage, and throughout his life. And I could, for the first time, see his heart. It was on this day that I understood for the first time how it's virtually impossible for any human to cause another suffering without suffering first having a grip on one's heart. I could see how we all essentially are "good"—and this was a huge leap for me. I had believed, all those years married to Harry, that he was inherently bad, possibly evil.

But now, I couldn't feel anger toward him as I offered him words of forgiveness, and it was the first time I ever felt love for Harry. I could see myself carrying forward the work to reconcile our post-divorce relationship, which we had previously committed to doing only for our children's wellbeing.

By the end of that week in Mexico, forgiveness had healed my heart. I returned home with no lump and only feeling love in my heart. However, I still hadn't figured out that while there were others I still needed to forgive, there was also me. I still needed to forgive me.

In the following year, with my heart open and loving, and my body miraculously healed, I investigated other practices that could help me expand love. I also kept working with my therapist on visiting the many parts of my life that potentially held fear and unforgiveness. It was at the end of this year's journey when I arrived at forgiving me and discovering self-love as the sole source for infusing joy in all areas of my life.

I spent the next year exploring this light with my therapist and on my own. I began investigating all the suffering I had endured, starting with Harry. Then I moved on to my earlier years going further back until I arrived at my birth.

It turned out that my life had been poised for absolute brilliance starting from day one.

I saw my marriage to Harry as the final turn toward the life I enjoy today. I could clearly see how miracles had been sprinkled upon me starting from day one, and how my final deathblow offered the most powerful awakening to life.

TWENTY-SEVEN

When it became clear to me in Mexico that Harry had been hurting long before he stepped onto my destructive path, I began receiving his words with great empathy. This effort was in many ways an even heavier undertaking than facing my fears or forgiving. For most of our marriage, I'd cultivated some pretty ugly resentments toward Harry. At times, what I wanted most was to hurt him twice as much. At times, leaning into his words, and opening my heart and receiving them as a friend was excruciating work. But each time I worked through this practice, my heart would eventually soften, and I could find space in my heart and mind to forgive him. My innate deep reservoir of love would flow, and I would actually feel his raw pain.

This new way of relating to Harry allowed us to eventually grow close. Now, for the very first time since we had met, we conversed openly and honestly. Through our open dialogue, we learned to leave out conditions and expectations. We decided to let go of anger and bitterness. I realized one day, months after Harry and I were relating in a more friendly way, that I had inadvertently set forth an intention to have a loving friendship with him. I never really said those words to him, or even out loud to myself, but I carried them out as if we'd discussed them and proceeded to put them into practice.

Here's something else I learned through my new way of relating to Harry. When I treated his words as potential gifts, he inadvertently softened his tone, his words, and his anger. I realized that this new person talking more kindly to me was the real person, and not the bastard with whom I'd spent thirteen-plus years.

Today, Harry and I do things that some married couples no longer do, like laugh and laugh. We call each other every day, sharing so much life with each other. When the other is hurting, we stop our life to help. Whenever I talk about us to my family or friends, I always get a look that clearly says, *"Uh huh. So why don't you two stop messing around and just do it, just get back together!"*

But that's not how it is, at all. We are dear friends. I see how this is not what it's like for most divorced people, or even many married couples.

I often wonder: If all people were willing to receive words and actions seemingly directed at them *without* conditions, expectations, anger, hurt, fear or indifference, what the world would end up being like?

But then, I guess I can be forthcoming here and tell you that I myself so often don't accomplish this. Quite often, I still find myself wanting to hold onto anger. And too often, I let slip words that scar. In time I do find my way back—or as I now refer to this trek—my way home. It turns out that even after experiencing astounding highs, when it seems that life is permanently whole and well and perfect, contrasts still continue to weave their way in. It turns out that this is simply life, and I have to choose walking toward my own happiness again and again. And when I read that even our history's most benevolent and spiritual beings have also experienced these wide contrasts, I feel relieved.

TWENTY-EIGHT

After all the years of work and reconciliation and growth and settling into a delightful existence, I am still single. I have repeatedly kept my promise to stay single. I've stayed single! I've stayed so incredibly single that I've barely looked at a man in quite a few years.

Why would I want to do that? I get to dance around the house with no one to stop me or comment. I get to wear no make-up, and I don't bathe every day if I don't *feel* like it, and I don't wash dishes or pick up the phone. I sit and read for hours or talk on the phone if I *feel* like it, or I paint or write all day or I sit at the computer, designing my new business—creating, creating, creating for however long I damn-well please. Oh, my life is too perfect to even properly describe.

So many people ask me, *"Don't you want companionship?"* I say, *"I have my two remarkable boys. I've got all the companionship I need."* Then they ask, *"But don't you want to be touched?"* I tell them the truth, *"I get to kiss my gorgeous hunk of boys and love on them, and that's more than enough touching for me!"* I don't dare tell them that I've already been touched too many times, ever since I was too young to know better. Should I be touched ever again, it would most definitely leave horrid indelible burn marks on my skin. How would that look then?

One time, I gave my friend the most complete explanation I ever offered anyone on why I loved being single… because no matter how many times I assure family and friends that being single truly makes me happy, and that it's finally the most "right" choice I've made in my life, they continue probing to get to the bottom of what's really "wrong." I finished my long discourse on the brilliance and perfection of the single life for my good friend, and she sat there for a minute or two, looking at me with so much soul.

Then she said, *"I hear you, but I want the whole package. I want the relationship with the fireworks and I want to get swept away by my Prince Charming. I want to be truly happy. That's what I'm going for. If I could offer you one piece of advice, girlfriend, it's this: The love between a man and a woman is the core of life. So go for it! Don't waste any more time, and really go for it."*

With those words, I understood. I finally got what too many of the people in my life seemed to be stuck on: Most of my friends and family believe that one is only truly whole in life after they've secured a partner to share life with—even though most days they're miserable with these partners. It's as if life is composed of a distorted construction of panels that reflect back only disillusions; we live according to the falsehoods reflected back to us and we only stay feeling safe in them.

This belief that you need a partner to be truly complete explains why just about every person I've ever known is not okay with the idea of being on their own. Especially with many women I know. Most of them when they find themselves free from their partners or kids on a Saturday night will scramble to find someone available to fill the open space instead of seizing the treasure waiting to be explored in the vast openness of time spent alone. I've noticed how even before they've fully broken away from their husband or boyfriend or partner, they scheme and scramble toward that next relationship, never once pausing long enough to see what can be learned. I've repeatedly heard the belief that the highest affirmation for moving on from a broken relationship is to be on the arm of the next man. I remember telling another friend who actually said those words, *"Really? How about showing your ex that you've moved on by finally embracing the truth of who you really are, or what you most desire. You know, being and doing the things that bring you the most joy?"* And, no kidding, she responded with, *"But, being with this new guy is what brings me the most happiness."* Less than one year later, she broke off with what "most made her happy."

Some women I know express their desire for a life partner with an underlying tinge of desperation. It's impossible to overlook the smoky grey current swirling beneath their spoken words. I can see how the truth of what motivated so many women to settle and marry (oh, absolutely myself included!), or choose the same "wrong" man time and time again, or offer the side of herself who is more than *willing* in the desperate hope to snag the man or forego what she absolutely, positively, truly desires for herself in life. The truth beneath anyone of these and many others stays buried and festering.

I can also see how these women are unhappy with their choices but have learned to numb themselves in order to get by in life. And like I often did for years and years, they say the opposite of what they desire most so often—they grow to believe the falsehood themselves. But the current that vibrates beneath any falsehood remains hopeful, and waits patiently to be freed one day.

After that one friend shared her belief on the essence or truth about love, I finally understood what motivated me to enter all my hopeless romantic relationships. It was a deep fear of having to live life on my own, and an even greater fear of living fearlessly by honoring what I most desire to do and be. When I felt these realizations surface, I could actually see how the men in my life were faulty crutches that I had learned to use in order to get through my days. I understood why others kept conveying their hope that I would get back on track by getting a man in my life. I realized how my new choices feel too "scary" for so many because the open truth in my choices reminds them all too often that they are denying themselves that fearless life.

You may decide from all I've written here that my current belief is to forego life partners in order to be happy. That assumption would be as erroneous as the belief that a woman needs a partner to be complete. I know plenty of women who are fully appreciated and honored in their romantic relationships. Who knows if they started out this way? It really doesn't matter, because it's where they are today that I cherish. These women are genuinely happy and whole and I celebrate their happiness. I love knowing that these women have been gifted with great joy through the brilliance of their romantic relationship. It truly is a pleasure to be around them.

My hope is for others to be happy for my life choices today. Who knows what may come my way in one, five or ten years from now? It just might be the man who represents my life partner. I'm not against that at all. But, oh, how fully I'm enjoying the whole of today. And oh, how fun my life is today!

Here's something else I've realized since waking up: Everyone seems to think that I arrived where I am today not having had a hell of a life, and for sure I should be ready by now for real happiness. People keep asking me, *"So, are you done goofing off?"* and *"Are you done being unhappy and incomplete?"* and *"Are you finally ready to really live your life?"* Then finally, *"Hmm, if you don't want a man, then are you perhaps a lesbian?"* That particular rumor spread through the masses again and again!

"Well, this certainly explains why she's always so happy now. I wish she'd just admit it to us. You know, just get it out in the open. I only want her to be happy, even if it is with another woman!" And for months, it was all everyone could talk about.

When I think back to my friend declaring that the core of life dwells in a romantic relationship, I know I am absolutely in the right place, because I now know the core of my life is steeped in the absolute truth of my divine magnificence. I know that all of life grows from this perfect me that existed before I was born, and will continue well after my body ceases to be. I get to live life with the purest joy and the most delicious freedom every single day. In turn, I tell my friends to be wary of falling into a romantic relationship without having unraveled the most perfect You residing below the layers of falsehood, the You who still waits to be freed. Be careful to not burden your children with your poisons because you keep closed off the sacred swirl that is more real and true than all your lifetimes combined.

All these decades later, I get that the core of my life stems from this most holy source of love that is far greater and more powerful and true than any other, and that I can never run out of this stuff. I also get that this pure love is not a piece of a whole, but the whole. Oh glory hallelujah!

I finally can see how the pure love that resides at our very core fuels everything. Without allowing its brilliant magic to swirl upward and permeate all things, we flounder and struggle, then die.

TWENTY-NINE

It took the whole of my life to finally wake up. I hadn't realized that I was even in a slumber. From a very young age, I felt cursed and believed that my life was meant to be filled with hardship and pain. I learned to fear the "good" because inevitably the "bad" would follow. And the "bad" was always worse than I could ever imagine. And the "bad" always came.

At the lowest point in my life, when I designed my own death to escape the "bads" that had piled up so high, it became impossible to see anything. Good or bad, I genuinely wanted to die.

But just like I was cursed from day one, I got "saved," again and again. Just like the wrath of curses that became my permanent shadow, I couldn't escape "salvation." I was found and found again. I could not escape. I later realized that the whole cycle of being cursed then saved, or of moving from bad to good to bad, and so on, was a regurgitation of rot. There was no real salvation, not during my slumber. What I mistook for being saved was an addiction to the effects of being saved, which remarkably were quite similar to the effects from snorting cocaine. In a rather perverse endeavor, I inadvertently sought being dumped back down into hell's cesspool to then be saved, then dumped, then saved. And on and on this went.

True salvation only came the instant I woke up, and I really did finally wake up. It took falling to the bottommost pit of suffering (embodied by my marriage to Harry). Sure, my therapist guided me after I made the choice to be helped, but I now understand that quite often it takes that most drastic fall for true salvation to occur. The brilliance of my awakening was waiting all along for me to simply take one step out of the whirlpool I'd been stuck in my whole life. Today I can see how our most traumatic experiences offer the richest path for waking up to joy and freedom.

When I look back to the first time I met with my therapist, I couldn't recall what the woman looked like after I finally returned to my bed that afternoon. I only recalled how safe I'd felt in her therapy room. I left there fearing I would be "saved" again, and I didn't want to go through another cycle. I wanted all the cycles to end. I wanted to be finished with it all. But she was relentless and she fervently pursued me. She could see the dark swirl of death encircling me and she became determined. She practically held my hand every day for two weeks, which was when she first noticed death's smoky scent begin to dissipate. And that was when finally I could see what she looked like. She was composed of the most effervescent glow of brilliant sparkle. I still refer to her as my angel.

During those first months, when my angel taught me to lean into what I most feared, I mostly "feared." I feared waking up. I feared walking. I feared thinking. I feared even in the midst of what I believed to be salvation. I now could see how most of the choices I made in my life were to quell my fears—and of course, each time, they were the wrong choices.

I learned through many spiritual teachers how I lived inside my head. My thoughts ruled me. I was conditioned to live life through the fabrication of thoughts, as most people are. I could see how committed I was to my habit of thinking—thinking about what could or would happen next, or reliving a past event, like when molestation zapped innocence from me. I drew from that experience its inherent threat, and I fed off it for most of my life. I was stuck in the past and future, skipping the present altogether.

I cloaked myself with the fabric of false thoughts and went through life disillusioned by these materials I wore. Through life's complex journey, I only interacted with others dressed exactly like me. We were inexplicably drawn to each other. My false world with all its dangers and suffering was all I ever knew and it became comfortable.

But as I said before, the more I leaned into what I most feared and the smaller and more insignificant the fear grew, the more my capacity to face life fearlessly grew. When this occurred, a most holy love flourished within me. As love grew, my capacity to lean in *fearlessly* expanded, and as my capacity expanded, love soared. And when love soared, I became free.

It was through allowing love's power to expand in me that I was physically healed from all the illnesses I had acquired over the years of suffering. Love guided me through finally fixing my relationship with Harry. Love became the fruit I fed my precious baby boys. Love was the original source of energy that fueled my insight and profound wisdom at an early age, and only now do I heed its limitless power.

Every day, the moment I awake, I sit up and remain in silence, emptying any thoughts and emotions from my being. I observe as thoughts exit my mind, and invariably, love's pure holy essence flows up and out and around, shrouding me with its magnificent glory.

Through my healing work, I understood how I was born with love. It had been present all along—but I was born into a culture where, from the time that living beings roamed the earth, fear pervaded all thought and action; escaping the vortex of suffering was not an option. I am of the minority again, one of the few who can see the truth of love. It is not romantic. It is not maternal. It is not religious. It is not doled out to only a few worthy souls. It is the purest, most wholesome energy that does not weigh, judge, reject, condition or change. It is, and always has been.

I see so many people who stay drowning in hell's cesspool. And no matter how often I speak the truth, they jeer and laugh at my ridiculousness, at the absurdity of my assertions. I can't judge or blame them because I played in that same rotting pool of hell for too many decades. The false sense of reality that we learn to cloak ourselves in feels correct and safe, even though it is damning.

I'm no longer afraid. I wake up every day feeling like the luckiest gal. I have become so daring that I lean into the thrill of success and the divine glorious world of joy. I lean so far into audacity that I am free. I am free!

THIRTY

There were hundreds of fragments I gathered after my therapist suggested I take a closer look at the whole picture. Some fragments were from before my innocence was lost. I saw how each piece broadened fissures that started out faint and fragile at a naked birth, but became a schism in a shattered life. I wasn't surprised to learn that it took my entire life to cause my divorce. I can now celebrate the absolute thrill of who I have become, because I get to be the original me that was born but somehow got left in a hospital wing, waiting to be finally carried out. When I did reach my core, there I was! As pure as the day I was born, without all the false layers that for too many decades I'd worked relentlessly to tack onto myself, one layer at a time.

Reading <u>The Secret</u> three years before waking up was my first step on a journey configured by steep jagged summits and treacherous cliffs that dropped to hell's bottommost. It was during my first fall from optimism's platform that I noticed the stench buried deep in the bowels of my psyche. It took years to dig my way to the culprit of the unbearable stench. But when I found myself face to face with the ugliness, I no longer felt it inside me. I carefully scooped it up onto the palm of my hand and brought it up to eye level, and I stared and stared at its cunningness, its audacity. I took in a deep breath and blew it out. That's the thing about that particular culprit. It causes death to come early, it destroys entire nations, it inhibits the great, and it is the most inconsequential falsity in the universe. This was the truth I finally figured out about fear. It is nothing.

When I arrived at thinking that helping other divorcing women was what my divorce was all about, I didn't realize then that my divine glorious happy divorce was really about the precise moment I woke up to the real me. I didn't know then that my divorce was the final blow for opening my eyes. I was naked on that day, which was why I could finally, clearly see how for all those decades, every bit that had entered my life had so perfectly aligned with my awakening. I now feel a genuine appreciation for the abuse, the disregard, the beatings, the singeing, the deceit, the never-ending pain, and the destruction.

And because it has to be said, I feel the greatest appreciation of all for my marriage to Harry Fielding.

Author's Notes

Over ten years ago, I wrote a 3,000-word essay for my Creative Writing class. The assignment called for *serious* embellishment on a life event that actually happened to me.

Last year, I was about halfway into writing a workbook for the online business I had been developing for three years. Then a torrent of words spilled from my brain and onto the next page in the workbook. I had been writing about a specific topic related to a business process I developed, so as I typed these new words, I grew increasingly confused and, well, disoriented. It seemed I not only lost my place in my writing, but I felt strangely *displaced*.

That wasn't the first time I was struck by an inexplicable phenomenon, so I didn't freak out. I didn't rush to find a wooden cross and flail it about the apartment where I lived at the time in Helsinki, Finland. In fact, only one year before, an eerily similar mystifying phenomenon had occurred while I was contemplating the type of workbook I hoped to write for this same online business I was so diligently creating. I absolutely was "freaked out" that first time even after having experienced much healing in my life. And, no, I didn't flail a wooden cross about my apartment that first time either.

After this second phenomenon occurred, I opened the electronic file where I stored the essay I wrote for my Creative Writing class. It had remained a work in progress that over the years had somehow expanded from 3,000 words to over 7,000 words. I hadn't opened the file in over eighteen months, but I realized that the words that miraculously appeared in the workbook fit perfectly and precisely in this work in progress. I stared at the page feeling genuinely gobsmacked. I didn't move for quite some time, and I didn't dare move away from my laptop because I was sure I'd cut off whatever celestial stream of inspiration put those words onto the page in front of me.

After a few more minutes of wallowing in utter amazement, I decided to continue writing. I flexed my fingers, took a deep breath, and proceeded to write the next sentence. Nine days later, I finished writing over 70,000 words. And heck if I knew if any of it made sense, or if what I had just written had damned me to eternal hell. I hadn't read a single word as I wrote, and I felt anxious about having to read it.

After I finally read through those 70,000 words, I realized I had written a memoir that was mine—but not really. I once read that fiction is really the truth about the author, and that non-fiction is really the truth about someone else…or something like that. Well, this story is neither. I say it's loosely based on events from my life because many of the events turned out to be rather slanted versions of what really occurred. Additionally, there are quite a few bits in this book that never happened to me, or anyone else I know. And yet, there are other parts of my storytelling that did occur precisely as I've written them. I considered changing those bits to somehow protect myself, but I finally decided to keep them because it just seemed that the story flowed well with every piece in place. Really, I felt the story had miraculously come to me, and who was I to question a higher voice? I don't think it's important to distinguish which of the words had been penned for that Creative Writing class. But what strikes me now is that over ten years later, the rest of the current story flowed from those first words effortlessly, so completely seamlessly.

Finally, I've changed most of the characters' names from real life to protect them from my broad use of creative license.

I wish to thank you for choosing my book among so many great reads, and I hope the words that quite mysteriously made their way onto the pages will strike you as fully as they have me.

Acknowledgements

This debut book had been a dream for quite a few years, especially while in the thick of life. I kept thinking that my story was unique and, boy, wouldn't everyone like to read about it. Turns out, my story is not so new even if it is unique.

Many, many thanks to Andrea Cagan for helping me keep it going, and for the many hours spent fine-tuning the first, second, third, etc. drafts. You are truly a godsend! And thank you Acey for your final polishing!

I extend a special thank you to Joni McPherson for your brilliant artwork, and consistent, quick-turnarounds.

Thanks to the many women who read drafts and gave me their sincere and frank feedback: Rosita Torres, Michele Chadwick, Adelita Chirino, Diane Schwedner, Lisa St. Marie, Nicole at My Book Views, Evgenia Sofikitou, Kristen Snowden, Sheri at Shelted Fantasies, Sarah Goffman, Angela Nelson and Nikki Sasktel.

Thank you Chad for your continued, unflailing support. And finally, my deepest appreciation, once again, goes out to my boys. It is for you I create—and dream!

About The Author

Nelly is an artist, writer and entrepreneur. She first attended the National Art School of Sydney, Australia, and later transferred to the School at the Art Institute of Chicago in Chicago, Illinois, majoring both times in painting.

At the time of publishing this debut book, Nelly is launching Her LifeZest Institute, an online entrepreneurial center for women. Most days, though, Nelly can be found in her studio painting or writing creatively.

Nelly was born in Connecticut, lived in various cities around the world and U.S. before settling in Northern California, where she currently lives with her two sons.

Book Club Questions and Topics for Discussion

1. From the title *Her Turning Point: Her Divine, Glorious, Happy Divorce*, what immediate assumptions were arrived at, even before beginning reading? How were these early assumptions challenged throughout your reading, and how were they helpful or inhibiting?

2. Her Turning Point: alludes to a shift, in what ways did this create friction between you and the story? How was Isabel's turning point relevant to your personal life experiences with struggles and challenges? Was there more than one turning point for Isabel, and how did these impact her choices? What moral interpretations can one draw from the notion of turning points in one's life?

3. Isabel's mother, the family matriarch, set out to prepare her for the real world by indoctrinating her with unyielding patriarchal values such as—women equating wife and mother, and forgoing what a woman desires in order to take her proper place in the marriage and family. How were Isabel's choices impacted from adhering to these values? What consequences did Isabel experience from patriarchal values enforced by a matriarchal voice? How deeply are

these conventions still being followed today? And how do today's gender paradigms fail to or succeed in evolving gender inequities—to more fully meet society's sentiments, especially when considering how many more roles women must manage today. What other conventions struck you?

4. Isabel mentions wearing a pre-engagement ring during her first relationship, marking her spoken for, while Rafael roamed unspoken for. She resolved not doing that again with Reza, but still, she felt powerless until Reza proposal. What are the ramifications on marriage today from the tradition of the male proposing to female: who wields the power, and how does this power transpire in marriage? What are the impacts on marriage today from men and women continuing to honor traditions rooted in older eras and, therefore, potentially outdated value systems; like engagement rings, or women assuming the bulk of childcare (mother) and/or household (wife) responsibilities while still working full-time jobs?

5. Throughout her childhood, Isabel's family lost sight of her, and she disappeared from them time and time again. What do her disappearances encompass as well as symbolize? She was not a valued member of her family and was left to fend for herself with no real guidelines or know-hows to survival—in what she believed to be a treacherous world. She talks about being alone with *"no one around"* when the Monster molests her. She then devises a secret chamber for this secret and all the others that keep coming as the years progress. Was her practice of hoarding and fiercely

protecting her secrets warranted? If so, why or why not? How were her choices shaped and affected by her secret chamber? In what ways did her secret chamber help shape the events in her life? How did the experiences of her early years impact her choices throughout her life? What conclusions can be drawn from Isabel's marriage to Harry when measured by her childhood years, and the years preceding Harry?

6. Isabel was left voiceless time and time again during her childhood, then again as an adult. What most contributed to her silence? What voice did she give to marriage, motherhood and family?

7. For Isabel, wisdom appears many times as a possible influential component. How did she wield wisdom, or not? What can be extracted or understood from the notion that one can be wise from a very young age?

8. After she wakes up from her 50-year slumber, Isabel declares, *"But just like I was cursed from day one, I got 'saved' again and again..."* She explained that this cycle of being cursed then saved was a cycle she had unconsciously sought. How exactly did "being saved" emerge, and also evolve for her? What means did she employ for being cursed and saved? In what ways did family and the *world at large* foster her dance with the cycle of being cursed then saved, or just being saved? What are your thoughts on the possibility of one's choices being driven subconsciously?

9. In the Author's Notes, the author reveals that portions of

this story didn't happen to her or to anyone else she knows. How does this declaration affect your experience after reading the book? What thoughts immediately came to you? Which parts of the book do you most hope are true, or untrue?

10. The book ends with, *"And because it has to be said, I feel the greatest appreciation of all for my marriage to Harry Fielding."* What conclusions can be drawn from this ending comment? What were your reactions and thoughts immediately after reading this last sentence? What deeper commentaries was the author making? How fitting or unfitting was this comment? Why?

11. Racism is another recurrent theme. Throughout her early years, Isabel repeatedly dissociates from "white" people, stating clear distinctions between "them" and her. Then she is confronted with violence from "black" people at home and at school. How exactly are these races different from hers, and what values do they share? When did the racial barriers fade away for Isabel? How did barriers remain, even in her later years? Where do similar racial barriers exist throughout society—like in schools, the workplace, etc.? How have they changed?

12. Some of the characters in the story made significant impacts in Isabel's life. What two characters did you most resist and/or accept? How did you react to Isabel's own adherence or resistance to the two characters you selected? Can any of Isabel's resistances and/or adherences be considered outcomes of abuse? Can you identify with Isabel's stance

on any of her adherences or resistances? What larger statements can be made about how Isabel handled the impact other characters brought to her experience? Which character did you hope to learn more about? Why?

13. In Part 3, after waking up to *her truth*, Isabel realizes she had lived her life in a slumber-state. She chooses to live, and she chooses a path that is so different from all the indoctrination she had received early on. What were your immediate reactions to Isabel's work with healing, spirituality and forgiveness? How true does her transformation ring to you? Why? What learning can be disseminated from Part 3? What possibilities emerge for you? What would you say is the deepest truth Isabel revealed in the end?

CPSIA information can be obtained at www.ICGtesting.com
Printed in the USA
BVOW04s0109010414

349369BV00001B/1/P